Riding the Tiger

Short Stories

DAVID GARNER

2QT Publishing Services

First Edition published 2024 by

2QT Publishing Services
Stockport, UK

Copyright © David Garner
The right of David Garner to be identified as the author of this work has been asserted by him in accordance with the Copyright, Designs and Patents Act 1988

All rights reserved. This book is for personal use only: no part of this book is to be sold, reproduced, in any shape or form. Or by way of trade, stored in a retrieval system or transmitted in any form or by any means, electronic, mechanical, photocopying, recording, be lent, re-sold, hired out or otherwise circulated in any form of binding or cover without prior permission of the copyright holders.

Cover image: shutterstock.com
Printed in UK by IngramSparks

A CIP catalogue record for this book is available
from the British Library

ISBN 978-1-7385640-0-2

Other Books by David Garner

Non-Fiction: *Last Man in Paradise*
Casting at the Moon
Wild! The Misadventures of a Wildlife Gardener

Fiction: *Dancing with the Devil* (short stories)

More information at: www.davidgarner.net

Contents

Acknowledgements	7
Mrs Bridger's Ring	9
Bang on Time	23
Childhood's End	29
The Strange Case of the Dog that Disappeared in the Daytime	45
Mrs Contini's Daughter	53
Martin and Clare	71
Echoes of Empire	85
Mrs Kingsley's Salvation	95
Brief Encounter (in Garsdale)	129
Beyond a Joke	137
The Mrs Choudhury Affair	147
The Sergeant Major's Bull	177
Daughter of Darkness	187
The Majesty of the Law	225
Riding the Tiger	239

Acknowledgements

Once again, my profound thanks to Catherine Cousins and Hilary Pitt of 2QT Publishing for their unstinting help, advice and support. And to my wife, Christine, who is sometimes asked for an opinion, and bravely ventures one.

Mrs Bridger's Ring

LIKE SO MUCH else, the world of jewellery sales changed radically during the 1970s and '80s. The staid, pompous and forbidding jewellery shop, bedecked with mahogany counters, gleaming glass display cabinets and débutante assistants, was challenged by a new breed. Open doors, piped music and the glint of nine carat gold drew in a new generation of customers who would never have darkened the doors of traditional jewellers. Which was a pity for Feltham Bros, because they represented the very essence of the traditional.

The brothers, Charles and Ernest, had not established the business; they were the third generation. Nor had they inherited the entrepreneurial spirit of their grandfather, or even their father, who had managed to keep the business going even during the depressed 1930s and the difficult war years. Indeed, Charles and Ernest could summon only a marginal interest in the jewellery trade at all.

Charles was the elder, unmarried, although this was not due to lack of eligibility in his younger days. No, it was simply that he found moths much more interesting than girls, gold rings or pendants. The only exception was the day a customer brought in a brooch that resembled a moth – a narrow-bordered five-spot burnet, in his expert opinion. Then, for an all too brief moment, two vital interests in his life coincided. But, like Mars being in conjunction with Uranus, it was a very rare event, and never occurred again. At work, Charles preferred to dwell in the pokey office which he shared with his brother, although they had fallen in to a system by which often only one of them was present at the shop, thus avoiding any risk of overcrowding the office. Occasionally Charles would be required to leave this sanctuary to speak to an old-established customer, at which he would lay down his copy of *Lepidopterist Monthly* with all the reluctance of man being torn from the embrace of his loved ones. After a brief, polite conversation, he would hand the customer back to sales assistant Mrs Saxby and retire swiftly to the dingy office, like a disturbed nocturnal moth scuttling back into darkness.

Ernest was different. He was married, although in his thirties before finding a woman of similar age who had somehow been overlooked in the marital stakes. They had one child, a daughter, but the experience seemed to be more in the nature of an experiment than a desire for a family, and one they were never inclined to repeat. Apart from being burdened with a name that was old-fashioned even in the 1960s, Ernest had a visceral dislike of moths. Ever since they had ruined one of his better carpets at home, he had taken against moths in all their forms, however blameless in the ruination of his carpet. Instead, he was in thrall to stamps. His early interest in common or garden stamps soon refined into something much more esoteric: stamps of defunct countries. Thus a stamp of, say, Zimbabwe, would raise barely a flicker of interest, while that country's former colonial stamps, endorsed Rhodesia or, even better, Southern Rhodesia, would excite Ernest beyond measure, far more so than mere gold rings or pendants. *Philately Enthusiast* was his chosen journal, where current and past copies jostled for desk-space with *Lepidopterist Monthly*.

So there it was, a jewellery business tucked into a half-decent position on the high street but dependent on a partnership between two brothers whose principal initiative during their twenty-year joint ownership had been to change the name from Feltham & Son to Feltham Bros. And that had been in the first year. In fact, the business had only survived because of Mrs Saxby, who had been there as long as they could remember, certainly for the whole of their joint tenure. She dealt with the reps, ordered the stock and then sold it. She also cleaned, made the tea and tidied up the piles of magazines in the office, although she always felt uncomfortable venturing into the brothers' managerial domain. And now she was retiring.

It was shattering news, and the brothers immediately tried to dissuade her. They tried flattery, offered a promotion – to 'assistant manager' – and, finally, outright bribery, although their finances did not allow much scope for this approach. But to no avail: at age seventy-three Mrs Saxby thought she deserved a rest, a little peace and quiet away from the demands of looking after the brothers' interests. Since she was now a widow – the brothers struggled to remember if she'd mentioned the passing of her husband, or any husband at all – she was moving down to Worthing to see out her days with her sister. She would miss the daily routine, and even the brothers, but the time had come...

There was no escape. The brothers arranged an emergency meeting in their office, where an hour's desultory discussion, much punctuated by longing looks at the piles of magazines, finally produced a result. They would advertise for a sales assistant. The advertising rep of the local paper – a young girl on the Youth Opportunities Scheme – helped them with the ad's composition and, since she had been on several job interviews, she was also able to advise on the sort of questions they should ask.

There were four replies to the ad. One applicant worked in a shoe shop and saw it as a major advancement to move into jewellery. Another detailed her considerable experience of wearing jewellery, and enjoying it so much she thought it a natural career move, although omitting to mention any other experience whatsoever. The third applicant laid great stress on her impeccable, unremitting honesty, to such an extent that it planted vague, unsettling seeds of doubt in the brothers' minds. The fourth candidate's application was somewhat sketchy, as if written in a hurry between coming back from shopping and beginning hubby's tea, all while menaced by a pile of ironing. Despite this, her application bore a faintly imperial tone, somehow implying that the brothers would be mentally deficient if not appointing her.

Because all the applicants had clearly gone to some trouble merely in writing, the brothers thought it only fair to interview all four, in alphabetical order. Thus Mrs Bridger, she of the imperially sketchy application, was the first to be interviewed. Her arrival at the shop set a benchmark. Mrs Bridger was a large, middle-aged woman who wore her largeness well as she was also tall. She mitigated this largeness, although not her formidable bosom, by dressing skilfully in flowing, floral pattern dresses which, when coupled with her regal advance, gave the unforgettable impression of a galleon in full sail.

Mrs Bridger's interview proved unusual in that she asked most of the questions. The list of questions supplied by the Youth Opportunities advertising rep lay redundant on the brothers' crib sheets as they struggled to respond to Mrs Bridger's questions about the niche their jewellery shop occupied. Or their marketing plan. Or their perceived changes in jewellery fashion. What form of profit share was in operation? It descended into nightmare. The brothers could hardly wait for the interview to end but, like a relentless juggernaut, the unanswerable questions continued to come until, quite suddenly, Mrs Bridger stopped. Just as she had for the whole of the interview, she sat perfectly straight, not touching the back of the chair. Her grey, piercing eyes studied the brothers for a moment or two, before asking if there was anything else they needed to know. Stricken into silence, neither managed to answer. In that case, Mrs Bridger announced, she would see them next Monday morning at nine-o'-clock. She was looking forward to it, she added.

When she had gone, the brothers hardly dared look at each other. What had they done? Nothing, and that was the trouble. They could – should – have told Mrs Bridger that she was being a trifle premature; there were other candidates to be seen. But they had not, and now loomed the dreadful prospect of having this alarming woman permanently installed at their shop. It was too ghastly to contemplate. Not only that; they were going to have to sit through three more interviews – which might well identify the ideal candidate – in the knowledge they were utterly wasting everyone's time. Never were the two brothers more despondent.

As good as her word, Mrs Bridger appeared at the shop door the following Monday at exactly nine-o'-clock. The brothers were tempted to hide in the office until she went away, but their nerve failed them again. After a brief tour Mrs Bridger was ready to start. When, she wanted to know, did the cleaner arrive? Ernest explained tentatively that Mrs Saxby used to clean. Mrs Bridger pointed out in no uncertain terms that the advertisement detailed a sales assistant, not a cleaner. However, she knew of a reliable cleaning lady who would welcome a few extra hours. Leave it with her, and she would arrange it. Before either of the brothers could dispute this, Mrs Bridger had moved on; where were the suppliers' catalogues? New stock was needed, urgently.

And so it went on, interminably it seemed, although it was only ten fifteen when the brothers finally escaped back to their office. They had to make their own coffees and, later, also cover Mrs Bridger's lunch break, even though Mrs Saxby never took one, simply eating her sandwiches while discreetly shielded from customer view behind the ear-ring display cabinet. The reality of this new work regime was already proving even worse than they feared. There was just one flicker of consolation. At the end of the day there was a little more money in the till than usual for a Monday. But as to how they were going to pay for a cleaner ...

Even before the end of the week, Mrs Bridger's new stock began arriving. Not, in fairness, in a biblical deluge, just a few items here and there but, nonetheless, the brothers visualised the invoices rolling in at the end of the month with increasing trepidation. They could imagine the summons to the bank to explain the unexpected, and wholly unwarranted, additional demands on their overdraft.

It was on the Tuesday of Mrs Bridger's third week that Charles covered for her lunch-break. In her absence he conducted a now-familiar routine, checking to see what alterations or new stock had appeared since he last ventured on to the shop floor. It was when he peered into the window that he received a heart-stopping shock. There, plumb in prime position, was a beautiful diamond ring. Rather, it was a three-diamond ring, the magnificence of which was obvious at a glance even to Charles. A dull day could not inhibit its rare sparkle, which seemed to lift and illuminate the entire window display. 'Price on application' announced a small, beautifully hand-scripted card. After a moment's shock, Charles recoiled in horror, the inevitable cost in pounds sterling bearing down on him like lead. He rushed to convey the news to Ernest, who was, quite predictably, equally horrified. Bolstered by each other's alarm, they awaited the return of Mrs Bridger.

She listened in silence to their trembling objections about the cost. When they had finished, she studied them each in turn before deigning to speak. Then, drawing herself up to an even fuller height than usual, she pointed out that the ring had cost nothing. Nothing, queried the brothers querulously; how was that possible? It was perfectly possible. A lady had brought in the ring and wanted the shop to buy it. Mrs Bridger, assuming it was beyond the shop's resources, explained it was too much to take on after recent stock purchases, but what was the minimum the lady would accept for it? The answer was ten thousand pounds. Very well, said Mrs Bridger, if she cared to leave it with them, they would sell the ring for the best price above ten thousand pounds, give the customer her money and the shop would keep the difference, be it five pounds or five hundred That was the deal.

What could the brothers say? When Mrs Bridger sold the ring the following week for thirteen thousand pounds, the brothers were dumbstruck. The accumulating burden of invoices, the extra cost of the cleaner; suddenly the lowering storm clouds seemed to lighten, at least for the time being. But, at the end of the month, something else was noticeable. The sales ledger entries occupied noticeably more column space than usual. And Charles and Ernest felt it prudent to pay in the takings to the bank a little more frequently than their normal once a week. For Mrs Bridger was proving a formidable saleswoman. It was rare for any prospective customer to leave the shop empty-handed, an alternative purchase always being found if a problem arose, even if was not related to the original enquiry.

Other innovations followed. Mrs Bridger started a scheme whereby customers could pay in whatever they could afford and build up their savings until, at last, they had enough for their purchase. She always made this a moment of great import. One of the brothers would be drummed into making a presentation of the gift-wrapped item which, if expensive enough, would be accompanied by a congratulatory card and a bouquet of flowers.

A discreet notice appeared in the window: 'old jewellery purchased'. In the absence of a pawn shop in the town, this generated a steady trickle of enquiries, although the pieces presented were always sadly out of fashion according to Mrs Bridger. However, this major drawback rarely precluded a deal; it simply meant the vendor's financial hopes were never fully realised. Some of these purchases were sold on to a jewellery-making group to be recycled but Mrs Bridger kept the most saleable items on discreet display in the shop, not wanting their former owners to see them in the window priced at three times what they had received. She was a considerate woman in that way.

The weeks passed. Charles and Ernest, reeling under the unknown experience of a successful business, were forced to spend increasing time on the shop floor. *Lepidopterist Monthly* and *Philately Enthusiast* languished on their desks, at best merely scanned for any hot news about moths or stamps. In a reverse of the usual procedure, their bank manager called at the shop, tentatively at first, then with increasing enthusiasm when he came to believe their improving finances might be sustained. To the brothers' astonishment, he even offered to buy them lunch. The Chamber of Trade tried to recruit them. Inland Revenue sat up and took notice, or would do when the accounts were filed.

It was at this point, their brains perhaps dis-orientated by the rarefied atmosphere of success, that the brothers agreed to a suggestion of Mrs Bridger's. In view of the approaching season of goodwill – distant though it still was – she would like to buy in something special. She had never consulted them before, so a degree of prudence might have been exercised, such as asking what she had in mind. But, in the mad euphoria of the moment, they did not. So, when the ring arrived, they were, once again, reduced to silence.

It was magnificent, there was no doubt about that. It cast the three-diamond ring into the shade, making it look paltry. A dazzling single central diamond was surrounded by a cluster of lesser stones, although any of these would have been much admired had they featured individually. Charles and Ernest stared at the ring, all their old doubts suddenly returned like a persistent nightmare. What, they asked tentatively, had it cost? Nothing at the moment replied Mrs Bridger, but she could not deny the invoice would not be far behind. The brothers forced themselves to go on: and when it did arrive? Mrs Bridger smiled her most beatific smile: she had negotiated the dealer down to twenty thousand pounds.

The brothers were too stunned to respond. They retreated into their office, where each sat silent, contemplating a swift and humiliating return to the very worst of the bad old days. Eventually they did regain the power of speech, wondering whether they might return the ring to the dealer. But a special price had been negotiated; if they returned it now their reputation, never exactly high, would be trashed among the trade. The only option was to sell the ring, but was that even possible in their humdrum little town? And if 'yes', at what price? Their first thought was: any price that got rid of it, even at a loss. Its very presence unnerved them. What if it were lost? Or stolen? By armed robbers! Would their insurance cover it? They rummaged in the drawer, found the insurance policy and rapidly scanned the terms: maximum single claim, eight thousand pounds. It had never been updated during their entire management. They collapsed back into their respective chairs, wrung their hands and stared, unseeing, at the dust-covered piles of *Lepidopterist Monthly* and *Philately Enthusiast*.

Their gloom continued unabated for the next couple of days, utterly oppressed by the presence of the ring and its little accompanying sign, 'price on application'. And on arriving at the shop on Thursday morning, their mood was cast down even further. A brief, hand-written note had been pushed under the shop door. It was from Mrs Bridger, informing them that an urgent matter had arisen requiring her attention and that she was sorry her absence was at such short notice. Charles and Ernest looked at each other, their unspoken thoughts identical.

What chance now of selling the ring?

Fortunately, their recent attendance on the shop floor had at least taught them how to set up the shop for opening, and they did so now. Then they both loitered unhappily about the shop floor, managing to attend to the three customers who came in during the first hour without mishap. Then, as they argued about who should make the coffees, a man entered the shop. He was undistinguished, late middle-aged and not particularly well-dressed. The brothers stopped bickering, managed wan smiles of greeting and hoped it wasn't anything complicated that would delay taking their coffees. The man spoke up; he had seen the lady the day before and she had agreed to reserve the ring for him until he brought in a bankers' draft. He drew an envelope out of his inside jacket pocket and held it out. Ernest recovered quickest, taking the envelope and withdrawing the bankers' draft. The numbers reeled before his eyes: forty-nine thousand, five hundred pounds. If the brothers were dumbstruck, at least there was no doubt about which item the customer was buying. Charles had to take over from a motionless Ernest. Displaying previously unsuspected initiative, Charles congratulated the customer on his purchase, adding they would be delighted to make a special gift-wrapped delivery that very day as part of the service. It seemed he, at least, had learnt something from Mrs Bridger. Actually, he was concerned the bankers' draft might be a forgery. The customer thought a special delivery an excellent idea and the sale was rapidly concluded.

A decent interval after the customer had left – it was three minutes – Charles rushed to the bank, where the draft was pronounced genuine, largely because their own bank had issued it. Even the bank manager emerged from his office to admire it, and seemed anxious to treat the brothers to another lunch. On Charles's return, the ring was boxed and wrapped, one of Mrs Bridger's cards was written and an impressive bouquet of flowers bought. They closed the shop early to make the delivery, a taxi-ride into the country to a beautifully-restored old farmhouse.

The following week proved memorable for differing reasons. Mrs Bridger failed to reappear or even to contact them, but the brothers bore this with euphoric stoicism. They even failed to bicker about coffee-making. Then, on early-closing Wednesday, another undistinguished man entered the shop at five minutes to one. The brothers were not best pleased with this late-comer, but felt they could afford to put on a brave face. The man explained he was not a customer, instead wanting to talk to them about a business proposition. With the shop closed, they all three retired into the office, where Ernest had to stand because there were only two chairs. The visitor came straight to the point: he represented a major chain of jewellers and they wanted to buy Feltham Bros. They would offer a good price but, if not accepted, they would acquire a shop nearby, start from scratch and the brothers would feel the searing heat of real competition. But they would much prefer to do a deal.

Like any self-respecting agent, the man had done his homework. He knew the brothers owned the freehold of the shop, so the offer would include the property, business, good-will and stock at value. He named a figure, running comfortably into six numbers. The brothers were speechless, which worked to their advantage as the agent took their silence as a negotiating ploy and quickly added that the offer was not take-it or leave-it; there was scope for some flexibility in the value of good-will.

And so three generations of Feltham Bros came to an end. Charles was able to turn his attention entirely to moths, adding *Rare Moth Quarterly* to his regular *Lepidopterist Monthly* subscription and venturing out on night expeditions with other moth hunting enthusiasts. Ernest expanded his stamp collection of defunct states, becoming obsessed with Belgian Congo, later Congo, then Zaire and subsequently Democratic Republic of Congo: rich pickings indeed.

They heard once more from Mrs Bridger. A brief letter arrived ten days after her absence began, giving her notice 'due to unforeseen circumstances' and expressing her regret that she could not return. No explanation was offered. The brothers were strangely affected by her sudden departure, but consoled themselves that she would never have fitted in with the new owners. On the infrequent later occasions when they met, Charles and Ernest would fondly recall the extraordinary moment of their most famous sale, the magnificent gem forever known to them as Mrs Bridger's ring.

Bang on Time

NICK GLIMPSED THE house through the fog. A strange building; single storey and sited on a steep incline, it looked as if a giant hand had pushed the house back into the hillside. Although facing south, the panoramic windows were largely shuttered. Above the windows, an array of solar panels adorned much of the roof, with another cluster set on one side of a neglected garden. A hundred metres beyond, two modest wind-turbines rose above the surrounding forest to catch the prevailing winds. A short distance below the house, at the bottom of a cleared slope, a small, noisy river bubbled over its rocky bed.

Reaching the house, Nick climbed the steps and entered a small double-doored lobby reminiscent of a spacecraft airlock. Removing his mask and goggles, he brushed off the pervasive dust before removing his coat and repeating the exercise. Then he swept up the dust and tipped it into a bin with all the familiarity of standard routine. Passing through another door, he entered a dimly lit corridor leading to the subterranean back of the house where lay the living accommodation. As he passed an open doorway, a man's voice called out, 'You've been a hell of a long time. We were beginning to get concerned.'

'No need to worry, Phil. I just felt like a long walk.'

'Where did you get to?'

'I followed the river as far as the estuary, then climbed the big hill, got to the top and had a poke around on the way back.'

'Christ, that is a fair way. No wonder you're late.' Phil raised an eyebrow. 'Nothing in the fish traps, I suppose?'

'No.'

'Anything else to report? Could you see the sun?'

'Yes, but it's still just a faint disc. There's no perceptible warmth, although the temperature's risen by another half a degree.'

'Well, that's good,' responded Phil, both pleased and relieved. 'At least it's going in the right direction.'

Nick was not so sure. 'Maybe, but it needs to get a move on if we're not to run out of food. It's September now, and our supplies won't last much beyond spring unless we cut the rations. We need to be able to start growing our own food by then.'

'Why so pessimistic all of a sudden. You've been the great optimist up to now. Or are you still angry with Karen? And Jake, I suppose, since he must have had something to do with it.'

'We agreed, Phil. All six of us agreed; no kids until we could see a way through.'

'Yes, I know; they shouldn't have done it. But she's thirty-eight, Nick, thirty-nine by the time it's born. I imagine she was worried about her eggs, or something. Anyway, it's too late now. And don't start thinking we can do a Reynolds on them: they never fitted in and went of their own accord, even if we did nudge them towards the door. This is different; you would be completely out-voted.'

Nick stood and contemplated this remark, irksome as it was. 'They're only here because of me. I took the decision to include them, and this is how they repay me.'

'Steady on, Nick. We all appreciate what you've done for us, that initial inclusion. But let's remember you only knew about this place – and all its survivalist features – because you helped build it. Thank God the owners never turned up. What the hell would we have done then?'

'They were rich enough to have other options. I imagine they're getting by quite comfortably somewhere. They spent most of their time abroad anyway.'

'Well, they had the right instincts but it turned out to be for our benefit. They are forever in my grateful thoughts.' Phil gave a wry grin, wanting to change the subject. 'I had to smile to myself today, while I was chopping wood. It's a thought I sometimes have in quiet moments, despite our predicament. Want to hear it? It'll cheer you up.'

'Go on then; cheer away.'

'Right, get this. It's a typical day at the world-famous Yellowstone National Park and, as usual, thousands of tourists have paid their dollars to get some of the magic. Equally typically, they head for the geysers, where you can view all the spectacular action while handily placed for a Big Mac and fries. Best of all they've come to see Old Faithful, which blows every hour or so. You can hear the guide with his megaphone, "Any minute now, ladies and gentlemen, Old Faithful will deliver the thrill of a lifetime." And, sure enough, it does deliver, bang on time – after a six-hundred and fifty thousand year wait, the whole frigging Yellowstone caldera blows into the stratosphere, ending the world as we knew it. Wow, did those tourists get their money's worth!'

Nick nodded, a faint flicker of amusement playing on his face.

'Want to hear something else?' asked Phil, feeling he was on something of a roll. 'January will be the start of

2050, year zero for carbon emissions and the last chance to save the planet from irreversible global warming. Hell, you couldn't make it up.'

Childhood's End

FEW PASSENGERS REMAINED on the bus after it left the outskirts of the town. The upper deck accommodated only three adults; a youngish couple seated near the back and a middle-aged man wearing, for no obvious reason within the sheltered confines of the bus, a tweed cap. Near the front were four school-pupils, three boys and a girl seated a little further back in the opposite aisle. Two boys sitting together were baiting the boy sitting in front. He wore a different school uniform, grey to their green, which was partly the cause of the baiting, but also because he was reading a book. The words 'swot' and 'professor' were among the more repeatable of the language within the girl's hearing.

'Why don't you shut up and leave him alone.' She was a couple of years older and, although attending the same school as the two boys, was not swayed by any tribal loyalty. The two miscreants turned to view the source of this intervention, and might have had something to say except that the man in the cap was watching. So they did shut up, both leaving the bus a few minutes later along with Tweed Cap. When the bus moved off the girl rose from her seat and went and sat behind the boy with the book.

'You must learn to stick up for yourself, you know.

Otherwise you'll always be having a hard time.' This failing to elicit any response, she continued, 'I often see you sitting in the same place, reading. Although sometimes you do gaze out of the window, in a bit of a dream. I don't know what you see there; it's just fields. Anyway, what's your name?'

The boy twisted a little in his seat. 'Michael,' he volunteered, although so quietly it seemed as if he was a little unsure.

She leaned forward, resting both her arms on the back of his seat. 'Well, Michael, you don't have to thank me for helping you, but it would be the polite thing to do.'

'Thank you.' It was a whispered reply, without looking at her.

'That's all right, think nothing of it' She laughed, a tuneful, full-bodied laugh, the sort given by someone who enjoys laughter. 'My name's Julie. At school my friends call me Unruly Julie, ever since Mrs Hitchen told me off for being unruly, although it was lost on me because I had no idea what it meant.'

'I think it means untidy, or something.'

'Yes,' said Julie, 'actually, I was exaggerating a bit there, Michael. By the time Mrs Hitchen had finished, I had a pretty good idea what unruly meant, and it wasn't just untidy. Anyway, after a while my friends couldn't be bothered with the 'un' bit, so I became 'Ruly Julie, because it rhymes nicely and we hoped it meant the opposite of what she said. Like happy and unhappy, if you see what I mean. Sarah Elphick said there was no such a word as 'ruly', but we didn't care. It made us feel clever and that we'd got one over the old cow.'

'Yes,' muttered Michael, mindful of some of his own teachers' foibles.

'My boyfriend's name is Mickey,' continued Julie, 'but I suppose his proper name must be Michael, like yours. Except he'd die if you called him that, or else punch you up the throat. He's two years older than me, eighteen.' She paused for a moment, struck by a thought. 'How old are you, Michael?'

'Fourteen.'

'Really? Well, you're big for your age. Big enough to stand up to those boys, if you've a mind.' She paused again, digesting this information before continuing. 'Anyway, Mickey likes to say he's an apprentice engineer where he works at a garage, but I think he's really just a dogsbody. He's quite good fun but only interested in two things; motor-bikes and girls. Oh, and cars as well, I suppose.'

'That's three things,' came the helpful response.

'Yes, thanks for pointing that out, Michael. As it happens, I have managed to learn that two and one make three, even though maths is one of my worst subjects.' Not really put out, she smiled at him. 'I suppose you're top in maths, at that posh boys' school of yours.'

'No, I was only third.'

'Only third! That's terrible; you'll have to do better than that if you want to become a professor or whatever.' Julie couldn't see his face very well from her position, and wasn't sure how this was received. Being more sensitive than she cared to let on, she changed the subject. 'What are you reading?'

'It's about the universe,' replied Michael, suddenly more animated.

'God, what a subject. Is it really interesting?'

'Yes, they're going to land on the moon before long, one of the Apollo missions. That will be brilliant, travelling to other planets in the solar system, perhaps even beyond that, in time.'

'Is that what you'd like to be then, Michael; an astronaut?' asked Julie, conscious that she had no such soaring ambitions.

'Yes, although I don't suppose I ever will be, because there aren't very many of them and they are all American. Except for the Russians, that is, but they're not going to the moon.' For the first time, Michael swivelled in his seat sufficiently to look into Julie's face. He'd seen her on the bus before but never this close, which he found disconcerting. Natural politeness came to his rescue. 'What do you want to be?'

'What, when I grow up?' Double meanings came so naturally to Julie that she was hardly aware of them. It was probably lost on Michael, but she was more pleased that she had persuaded this shy boy into conversation. Julie thought for moment. 'Mmm, an air hostess probably. Flying around the world with lots of handsome pilots. Yes, that would suit me nicely, I think.'

'Well,' said Michael, 'you'd be a sort of explorer then, wouldn't you? Flying to lots of different countries and seeing strange new places. That would be really interesting.'

'Yes,' she mused, 'I suppose it would, although it wasn't quite what I had in mind.' Julie cocked her head and grinned at his guileless face. 'Where do you live, then?'

He named a small village, scarcely more than a hamlet, a mile or so beyond Julie's. 'God, there's not much there. Whatever do you do for fun?' Without waiting for a reply, she launched into another question. 'What do your mum and dad do?'

'My mum's a teacher at a primary school.'

'Ah, no wonder you're bright. What about your dad?'

'I don't know what he's doing. He doesn't live with us.'

'Why not?' Julie was an enthusiastic interrogator, if not always subtle.

'I don't really know. He went away saying he'd be back soon, but he never came back. That was years ago.'

'But don't you hear from him? Birthday cards, letters or anything?'

Michael's only response was a shake of the head. Even Julie the remorseless interrogator was rocked into silence by this revelation, although not for long. 'Well, if you want a new dad, you can have mine. We don't always get on.'

Without waiting to see if this offer was receiving serious consideration, Julie was away again. 'I get off here, Michael, but we can talk again another day. You can tell me all about the universe and being an astronaut. That is, unless you'd rather read your book?' Julie raised her eyebrows, a pastiche of the severe, questioning faces she not infrequently experienced from her teachers.

'No,' said Michael.

'Good. I'll see you tomorrow then.'

'No, not tomorrow; it's chess club.'

Julie choked back her amusement, her head shaking in disbelief. 'God, you're a one you are, Michael. All right then, the day after.'

And she was gone, leaving Michael bemused but not at all unhappy. He didn't see Julie as she left the bus. If he had, he would have seen another shake of her head and a rueful smile playing about her lips.

On Julie's part, despite her natural outgoing character, it was a cautious acquaintance for several weeks, although immediately settling into a slightly odd routine. More accurately, it was a ritual. She would get on the bus, climb the stairs to the top deck where Michael would be seated in his usual place. But she would not immediately join him, always taking her own place a little way behind Michael on the opposite aisle, just as on their first acquaintance. Julie would not acknowledge him even if he turned round, steadfastly looking elsewhere until any pupils from her school - usually the two boys - had left the top deck of the bus. Only then would she move forward and occupy the seat immediately behind Michael, rest her arms on the back, and friendship would be resumed. And it was only ever on the afternoon return journeys, never on the more crowded morning bus, even though they often saw each other.

Michael never asked about the meaning of this ritual. He sensed it was something important to Julie and assumed it was simply something an older pupil - particularly a girl - knew more about. Content to leave it at that, he almost never turned to see if those light footsteps ascending the stairs belonged to Julie. Besides, Michael usually knew who it was because he began looking out for her at the bus-stop.

They did not see each other every day. There was Michael's chess club, plus other activities such as drama and music which could have kept him late if he had been more theatrical or musical. He did sometimes stop to support the school's sports teams, but that was more out of a sense of collegiate obligation rather than a keen interest in the sport itself.

Julie, on the other hand, enjoyed sport, and was good at it. In fact, she was not a keen academic scholar, sport being the school activity key to her decision to stay on at sixth form. She was proficient at most of the sports practised at her school, the one exception being athletics, the necessary training proving too much like hard work, plus she didn't like the hanging about between events. Occasionally, though, she would be absent from the bus for disciplinary reasons. It being a progressive co-educational school, sixth-formers were spared detention but transgressors were required to stay behind 'voluntarily' to assist the teachers with blackboard cleaning and tidying up classrooms in preparation for the next school day.

The ritual became Michael and Julie's established meeting pattern during that first term, running up to Christmas. Then, soon after the start of the New Year, there was a sudden change. One day – it was a Wednesday, and Michael had skipped chess club – Julie climbed the stairs, walked down the aisle to Michael's seat, pitched his satchel onto the floor and sat down next to him. Michael was so taken aback, he didn't speak.

'Don't gawp at me like that, Michael; you look like a goldfish in a bowl. Anyway, why aren't you at chess club? It's Wednesday, and you're never here on Wednesdays. You quite threw me, seeing you here. Have you been banned because you win all the time?'

Michael rediscovered his voice. 'No, I just didn't fancy going, that's all. I play the same people every week, and it gets a bit boring sometimes.'

'Like I said; you must let someone else win occasionally; you'll be more popular that way. Not that you seem to worry about being popular.' She frowned, scrutinising his face closely. 'Look at me for a moment, will you?'

Michael complied, and Julie continued her examination for a several seconds. 'Good, at last I've seen the other side of you face properly. I got fed up with only ever seeing one side when I sit behind you. At least you're not hiding anything hideously ugly on that blind side, like warts or acne.'

'No,' was all Michael could manage in reply. There were times when he found Julie quite intimidating.

That day marked the end of the meeting ritual. From then on, regardless of the presence of any fellow pupils, Julie strode down the aisle and sat next to Michael as if asserting a right. And their friendship began to extend beyond school days. Julie invited Michael to visit her home during the Easter holiday. This involved a jokey subterfuge on Julie's part, with her promising he would see all the farm animals – her father was a farm bailiff – but, in the event, this livestock totalled just half a dozen chickens plus the family dog and a guinea-pig. After this necessarily brief tour, she had to explain that it was an arable farm, with not an animal on the place, except wild ones. She found this explanation decidedly funny and Michael, being in her company, was hardly disappointed.

The early April day proved overcast but mild, allowing Julie to lead them on a ramble around various of the farm's tracks and hedgerows during the morning. They stopped to examine a couple of derelict sheds and then to probe about in the margins of a neglected pond. It was Michael who spotted the tadpoles and a newt, Julie not being the keenest observer of wildlife. In the afternoon Julie relented in allowing her younger brother to join them, and led the way to the edge of the village where a makeshift swing had been constructed, simply a length of rope suspended from a tall ash tree. At the end of the rope was tied a tyre, the more adventurous straddling this in every imaginable configuration and not all secure, as occasional falls demonstrated. It swung out over a hollow and Julie was not entirely sure how Michael would take to this apparatus but, after a tentative start, he was soon swinging around with the best of them, which pleased her no end.

The visit seemed to go very satisfactorily to Julie. Her mother was cheerfully hospitable, feeding and watering the pair and, when Michael had left, praising his wonderful manners. Her brother had no particular opinion, but her father commented on Michael's youth and called her a 'cradle-snatcher'.

During the summer half-term Julie made a reciprocal visit to Michael's. Despite it being a lovely day, a good deal of the morning was spent indoors as Michael showed Julie his extensive collection of reference books, atlases, maps, a globe and a wall-chart of the night sky somehow pinned to the ceiling for added verisimilitude. This lengthy exposition took place in Michael's over-burdened bedroom and required a considerable amount of clambering over his bed, to the faint disquiet of his mother but to Julie's quiet amusement.

After lunch they played French cricket in the garden until Julie's enthusiasm got the better of her and she hit the ball so hard it flew over next door's and was lost for the rest of the afternoon. After which they sat in a couple of deckchairs, each with a drink of orange squash, while Michael expounded on various of his pet subjects, and Julie was content to listen.

Michael deemed this visit a great success, but Julie was not so sure. When school resumed, she mentioned that his mother had seemed a little doubtful about her. Michael vigorously disputed this, pointing out that his mother had said she thought Julie was 'quite advanced for her age,' which must mean she was impressed. Julie gave a rueful smile, said, 'that's all right, then', and allowed the subject to drop.

It was during the last week of the summer term that

Michael might have noticed a change in Julie's behaviour. With his exams over and done, he was destined for the fifth form at the start of the next school year and he was looking forward to it, perhaps enthusing a little too much for the more jaundiced Julie. But, as those last few days counted down to the start of the summer holiday, that was not the reason she became noticeably quieter. Her laughter, and even a smile, became increasingly rare on each succeeding day. Michael did become vaguely aware, although never sufficiently concerned to ask the cause, distracted as he was by his excited anticipation of the imminent first landing on the moon. Apollo eleven had just taken off and was on its way.

Although formerly infected by Michael's space exploration enthusiasm, on this particular Friday Julie did not give a damn about any moon, Saturn rocket or astronaut. She found his constant, and sometimes repeated, commentary increasingly jarring, for her mind was on other things. By the time the bus approached her stop, her mood had descended into a mixture of anxiety and unfathomable irritation. Michael was still speaking as the bus began to slow down, when Julie suddenly cut in. 'I want you to get off here with me, Michael,' she ordered. 'We must both get off, now.'

Bemused, Michael sat unmoving as Julie grabbed his satchel and then his arm with her free hand. 'Come on, we have to get off here. You can catch the next bus.' As the bus came to a halt both were making their way unsteadily along the aisle to the stairs, Michael too confused to do anything other than follow. They alighted from the bus with a couple of other passengers who immediately went their separate ways, leaving one agitated girl and an utterly baffled Michael standing by the bus stop.

Julie gathered herself. 'There's a seat over there by the war memorial. We'll be able to see the next bus if we sit there.' She led the way over the road and they both sat down, Michael still struck into silence by her behaviour. But it was also Julie's turn to be silent, hands gripping her knees as she stared at the ground in front. At last Michael mastered his confusion sufficiently to speak.

'What's the matter?' He sounded nervous, even a little frightened.

'There's something I've got to tell you.' Julie turned to look at him. 'I've been trying to tell you all week but you've been prattling on about that bloody Apollo thing. You were so excited I couldn't get a word in edgeways.'

Julie paused for a moment but Michael had nothing to say. So she continued, choosing her words with self-conscious care. 'I'm leaving school, Michael. Well, I've actually left now, today. This was my last day. I could have gone home at dinner-time but I waited to catch our usual bus because I had to tell you. I couldn't leave without saying anything.'

Michael stared at her, unspeaking, his face a picture of incomprehension.

'It's all happened in a bit of a rush, over this last two or three weeks. My dad said I was wasting my time staying on at school, and he's right. I wasn't really working at my lessons. The teachers pointed that out, but I already knew. And it's pointless going to school just to play netball and hockey. So I've left.'

'But... what will you do?'

Julie was on surer ground now. 'I've got a cousin in Northampton. She works in a department store and says there are jobs there if I want. She shares a flat with a friend and says I can live with them and help out with the rent.'

'Northampton? But that's miles away.'

'Yes, it is, Michael, but at least I'll be away from my dad and standing on my own two feet, which is what he's always on about. And it will be a lot more lively than living here, my cousin says, although that wouldn't be difficult. She's a bit older than me but quite a laugh. She's going to show me some nightlife around the pubs and clubs.'

Struggling to take it all in, Michael could only say, 'But what about Mickey? Will you still be able to see him?'

Julie managed a wan smile. 'You're a one, Michael. Is that all you're concerned about; me and Mickey? Look, he was just a boyfriend, very handy because he had a motorbike. I didn't want to be relying on buses late at night. Anyway, I've already told him I'm going. He didn't seem all that put out. He'll have forgotten me by the end of next week.'

Michael was nonplussed to hear this, as he had rather assumed they would eventually get married. Now it seemed a number of his assumptions concerning Julie might be wildly misplaced. He thought he ought to test another.

'Are you still going to be an air-hostess?'

Julie did not immediately reply, instead lifting both hands to her face, fingertips resting lightly on her lips, her gaze somewhere in the middle distance. Eventually she did speak.

'I talk a lot of rubbish, Michael.'

'But you seemed really keen on being an air hostess.'

'Yes, I know, but it's like you wanting to be an astronaut, although you might actually manage that. But I'm too young for a start, and there are loads of girls wanting to be air hostesses, plenty of them cleverer and better-looking than me...'

'No, they're not,' protested Michael, 'you're just as clever and pretty as they are.'

'Oh, Michael, you're such a dreamer.' Julie dropped her hands back into her lap. 'Look, I know I'm not a complete dummy: I've got five O-levels, even if my grades aren't great. If I'd worked harder I could have done better and might even have got another couple, so the teachers said. But I didn't, and now it's time to stop this school nonsense and get out into the real world, as my dad is always saying. I'm seventeen now, not a child any more, as you would know if you looked at me more closely, which you never seem to.'

This was not strictly true, and Julie knew it. Michael was briefly stunned into silence until another thought occurred to him. 'But we'll still see each other, won't we? When you come home to see your mum and dad?'

'It's possible, I suppose.' Julie hesitated, anxious to avoid this question. 'It's just that I can't see me coming home very often, Michael, not until I get on better with my dad. I shall miss my mum and brother, of course, but she always goes along with what my dad says, even if she doesn't agree with him.'

'Well, I could write to you, couldn't I?'

'I don't know the exact address yet; my cousin's meeting me at the bus station.'

'You could send it to me when you do know.'

Instead of answering, Julie resumed her study of the middle distance, and a long silence fell between them. After an indeterminate time, Julie turned to him and began to speak, very softly. 'You'll soon have better things to do than write to me, Michael. There's all your school work, exams, chess club, the moon landing; loads of things to keep you busy. You'll get lots of O and A-levels, because you're clever. Then you'll go to university and you're bound to meet a girl student – she won't be as pretty as me but she'll be able to talk to you about planets and space travel, and things like that, much better than me.' She stopped for a moment, uncertain whether to say any more. 'You're growing up, too, Michael; I can see the difference, even if you haven't noticed. You're not a child any more, either. It's time for both of us to grow up.'

This unanswerable point brought about another silence. They sat side by side, neither knowing what to say, each afraid to look at the other.

'Your bus is coming.' Julie picked up his satchel, stood up and held it out. Michael seemed reluctant to move.

'Come on. You'll miss your bus if you don't hurry, and I'll get the blame from your mother.'

'But I don't want you to go away.' His voice was barely more than a whisper. 'We were going to see each other during the holiday...'

'Shut up, Michael: don't say another word.' Julie dragged him to his feet and pushed the satchel into his hands. The bus was only yards away, but it was stopping to let passengers alight. When Michael had taken hold of the satchel, Julie placed her hands either side of his face and kissed him on the lips. Then she pushed him into the road. 'Go on, hurry. Don't you dare look back. Just get on that bus, quick, it's going to go.'

At the bus, Michael did look back.

'Go on!' Julie's cry was almost a scream.

Once on the bus, Michael declined to mount the stairs, taking a seat on the lower deck where he could look out of the window. As the bus pulled away, his last sight of Julie was of her standing beside the war memorial, head in hands, shoulders heaving.

The Strange Case of the Dog that Disappeared in the Daytime

AMANDA WOKE TO the dawn chorus at five in the morning. A skylark was singing, a joyous solo soon overlaid by the matchless liquid cadences of a blackbird. A wood pigeon began cooing outside the bedroom window, which prompted a collared dove to strike up in voluble competition. Unfortunately, the collared dove is one of the most discordant birds ever to emerge via natural selection, so it was little wonder that Amanda was dragged grumpily from her slumbers. In fact, years of exposure had led her to conclude that the whole dawn chorus thing was very much over-rated, three months of intrusive noise that she could well do without. She was always relieved when the avian breeding season petered out and she could get back to her full measure of beauty sleep. The only saving grace was that the birds temporarily ran out of puff soon after seven-o'-clock, when Amanda often went back to sleep and sometimes didn't wake until nearly ten! Working from home; brilliant! One of the Covid panic-demic's unexpected advantages, for which she was profoundly grateful!

While eating her muesli, Amanda glanced out of the window to a panoramic view that never failed to stir her heart: the wonderful Malvern landscape, epitomised by rolling hills dotted with woods, farmhouses and sheep. Far to the west, the Black Mountains were almost lost in a grey haze, a cloudless sky promising another glorious summer's day. Actually, as she looked more closely, Amanda did spot a single, white cumulus cloud. Small and fluffy, it seemed only to enhance the bucolic scene but, living so far west, she knew such clouds were often the harbingers of a weather front sweeping in from the Atlantic. That is why the locals so rarely saw the Black Mountains, obscured as they usually were behind an impenetrable curtain of mist and rain. Sometimes Amanda wished their regional precipitation (28.7" per year) was more like, say, Norfolk (25.1"), and she understood their property prices were cheaper, too. Still, you can't have everything in life.

Amanda just happened to be outside the house when she saw a woman approaching. She barely had time to categorize what class the woman was (it was middle) before the visitor launched into flurried speech. 'Thank goodness somebody is up and about in the village. I'm new to the area, you see, and don't like to go knocking on doors quite yet.'

This explained several factors, not least why Amanda wasn't acquainted with every facet of the stranger's life and family, as she certainly would have been had the woman lived in the village for more than a couple of months. But before Amanda could reply, the newcomer resumed speaking.

'It's an emergency, you see; my husband's dog is missing.'

Amanda knew instantly this was a Jane Tennison moment. Jane is the brilliant TV police detective Amanda always turns to in moments of crisis; 'What would Jane do?' But before Amanda could get a word in edgeways, the woman was off again.

'My name's Marge, by the way.'

Although humour isn't Jane's strong point, Amanda was tempted to ask if she could tell the difference between Marge and butter but, in view of their still uncertain acquaintance, refrained. Then, in what was becoming a tediously one-sided monologue, away went the woman again. 'Would you be willing to help find the dog? I'd be most grateful if you could, because my husband is so very fond of it.'

Of course, living in the same village, Amanda had no choice but to help - something all village folk learned long ago from listening to the Archers. Grateful simply for the chance to speak, Amanda said, 'Yes, of course; this is where we country dwellers differ so markedly from unfortunate townies. But, just to help, does the dog have any distinguishing features?'

'Yes', said Marge, 'it's deaf.'

'Right', replied Amanda, somewhat uncertainly. 'Not much point calling it, then. So, is there anything more... identifiable? Is it a dog or a bitch, for example?'

Marge considered this for a moment. 'D'you know, I'm not really sure. You see, I'm not keen on dogs, so I've never looked. And my husband is practically blind, so he's not always a reliable guide. Well, I say he's blind but I'm not sure how bad it is. It must be pretty severe though; he hasn't found me once in the last ten years and we sleep in the same bed. Mind you, it is super king size, so that might explain it.'

'Yes,' muttered Amanda uneasily. 'Well, if we're not sure whether it's a dog or a bitch, perhaps it's a hermaphrodite.' She always tried to lace her wit with a hint of erudition.

'No, it's a mongrel from the rescue centre.'

Some fall on stony ground thought Amanda, but felt obliged to persevere. 'Have you any idea where it might have gone? A favourite walk, perhaps?'

At this, Marge brightened a little, for she had become a little wistful when describing her husband's poor eyesight. 'Yes, Rover always takes Rex in the direction of Bluebell Wood.'

Amanda had to laugh at this slip of the tongue and couldn't resist remarking, 'So the dog takes your husband for a walk, eh?'

'What?' said Marge, apparently nonplussed. 'Oh, no, I should explain. My husband's name is Hugo but I call him Rover because he likes to lick his own...'

'Yes!' Amanda interjected hastily, 'Aren't we losing valuable time here? Rex could be wandering further away by the minute. We could go now, using my car.'

'Ah, that's my point', countered Marge, 'I can't come because I've got a hairdressing appointment.' She peered at Amanda. 'I could try and get you one, if you like. Spruce yourself up a bit after this wretched lockdown.'

Amanda was moved to think this remark would not have gone down well even in normal circumstances, but only a couple of days ago she'd spent two and a half hours and a small fortune at the hairdressers.

'Marge, I'd love to help – obviously - but I do actually have work to do, quite an urgent job in fact. Perhaps we could go later, when you're back from the hairdressers.'

'An urgent job, you say?' replied Marge sharply. 'Surely it can't be that urgent if you're wandering about outside in your housecoat at eleven in the morning.'

Amanda felt that the brilliant Jane Tennison let her down here; bereft of a suitable riposte she could see there was no escape. 'Well, maybe I could look until lunchtime.

Would that help?'

Marge's glowering face was instantly transformed. 'Oh, that's so sweet of you to offer. I'll pop in later to see if you've been successful. Byeee.'

And she was gone, just as swiftly as she had arrived.

The drive to Bluebell Wood is wonderfully scenic, rolling hills dotted with woods, farmhouses and sheep. And it was while absorbing this exquisite pastoral beauty that Amanda briefly ran off the road. There was a bit of a bump, but nothing she hadn't experienced plenty of times before. Unfortunately, a worrying sluggishness soon began to affect the steering, increasingly requiring Amanda to wrestle the car through every bend. When the car became dangerously close to taking control, she stopped. A quick walk round confirmed her worst fears: a puncture.

What would Jane do? Well, inspired by such a modern, competent woman, Amanda soon had the car jacked up, ready to change the wheel. But do you think those wheel nuts would come loose? Of course not; they were put on by a man. Worse than that, a man with a hydraulic wheel nut tightener. And as for the car manufacturer's wheel brace, it was pathetic, just a short L shape, totally inadequate to generate the sort of leverage required to shift those wretched nuts. You would think a company that makes millions of cars a year would understand what Archimedes worked out for himself two millennia ago. After all, he was the chap who offered - given a suitable fulcrum - to lever the earth back within the sun's habitable zone, should it ever go out of orbit.

Amanda was contemplating this conundrum when her eyes fell on a three-foot length of metal pipe lying in the grass. And its diameter allowed it to fit perfectly over the wheel brace, the sort of amazing coincidence that she thought only occurred in certain films and novels, particularly Pasternak's 'Doctor Zhivago', where the eponymous hero is forever bumping into Lara despite the fact that Russia is the largest country on earth and has eleven time zones. But never mind that; in very short order the wheel was changed and Amanda ready to resume her quest.

It is another strange fact of life that, when the tide of good fortune is running your way, it occasionally comes at a flood. Because – and, understandably, readers may find this hard to credit – as Amanda was about to get into the car, she glanced up and saw – a dog. It was sitting quietly, apparently mesmerised by the sight of a woman changing a wheel. She called to it but it took no notice, from which she deduced with Jane-like powers that it was almost certainly deaf. What a stroke of luck! Her quest was fulfilled, and it wasn't even lunchtime. The drive home, past rolling hills dotted with woods, farmhouses and sheep, was wonderful to behold, although she drove with a smidgeon more care.

It was half past eight that evening before Marge called, interrupting Amanda's evening tipple. She was not invited in. In fact, Amanda barely recognised her, such was the transformation wrought by the hairdresser. She thought Marge's new look completely over-the-top, but said nothing. Amanda didn't like to be bitchy but, really, no woman should ever have hair that colour at that age. If her husband's eyesight was poor before, he would surely be blinded now.

Marge took very little notice of the dog, seemingly happy just to have something canine to take home. Amanda could have mentioned one or two minor discrepancies - it was a bitch, for example – but for some reason, wasn't anxious to detain her. Demonstrating remarkable faith in Amanda's questing powers, Marge had brought a lead, although had to be shown how it fitted. As Marge departed, leading the dog down the garden path, Amanda had a flash of inspiration, the sort that often occurs after an alcoholic libation.

'Don't forget it's a bitch,' she called out, 'you'll have to call her Regina now.'

Wit laced with erudition, Amanda liked to believe, although Marge gave her the strangest of looks, leaving Amanda wondering whether she'd misheard. But, halfway through her third glass of Chardonnay, she really didn't care.

Mrs Contini's Daughter

CHANCE IS AN amazing thing, especially if you are a chancer. The truth of this was demonstrated to me once again when I was sitting, of all places, in a dentist's waiting room. Wondering whether the dentist might grant credit – he would have little choice - I took my mind off the subject by perusing the only reading matter, out-of-date magazines aimed at the high-end market. My random choice, a title and style long-since vanished, catered for women of a certain class, always a topic of interest to me. The personal advertisements perfectly reflected the 1950s, the country still recovering from that war-time austerity which had been such a bind for the well-to-do; the never-ending search for an experienced nanny or a well-bred girl willing to live-in and help with the horses. But the ad which caught my eye was different: a tutor wanted for a young girl, plus an ability to play tennis would be a definite advantage.

Now, among my various but not-obviously-useful talents is an ability with ball games. And not just ball games but anything to do with hand-eye coordination, deck-quoits, for example, or clay pigeon shooting. The tutoring element was more problematic, but the university of life had taught me a great deal about the merits of adaptability. I looked at the date of the magazine; more than two months old. Under other circumstances I would have regarded the opportunity long gone, but the tennis requirement maintained my interest. Of course, London might be alive with tennis-playing tutors but, somehow, I was inclined to think not.

You can imagine my letter, to a box number at the magazine, contained an impressive run-down of my academic and sporting achievements, particularly my time at South Africa's Durban University. This would certainly have resulted in a degree if only it had not been curtailed by National Service in Malaya during the Emergency. Now, in case this is not your area of expertise, you have to understand that the most plausible fabrications always contain a sound basis of truth. I did actually live in Durban for a few months, after I went absent from the troopship on the way to Malaya. I did go to Durban University, but it was to attend a dance with the woman who was sheltering me. But you can appreciate the neatness of this concoction: ask me about Durban and I can describe the town, its university, shops and parks. Ask me about Malaya and I can speak with absolute authority because, after I was detained in Durban and handed over to the British authorities, I ended up in Malaya anyway. Faced with the choice of military prison or immediate transfer to the infantry, I opted for the latter, where I served my sentence 'in the field'. Strangely, it was an experience I never regretted.

The reply to my application was surprising. Not only was the post 'unexpectedly still vacant' but Mrs Contini's letter bore a faint whiff of desperation. When a letter from a prospective employer asks how soon you can take up the post, a degree of optimism about the outcome seems fully justified. And I was asked to telephone to arrange an interview – in Hampstead – so that 'the process might be expedited'. I include the quotes to convey the sense of urgency.

I borrowed a friend's MG Magnette saloon rather than his sports car – I didn't want to appear too frivolous - to travel to Hampstead where, as expected, the house was impressive. I drove in through one of two gates and followed the semi-circular drive to find ample parking in front of the house. Quite modern, it conformed to no particular classical style but the two columns framing the large front door hinted at Palladian. It's always impressive to quote this sort of detail but do first ensure you're not talking to an architect.

Mrs Contini answered the door herself. I knew it was her simply because of the dress, perfectly moulded to every contour and obviously expensive. She was not as swarthily Italian as I expected but the Mediterranean was represented in dark brown hair cut short à la Sophia Loren at that time. She viewed me through elegant, bespoke spectacles which, I noticed, were jettisoned as soon as she had my measure. A middle-aged woman of some vanity, and I liked her for it.

She conducted the interview, if you could call it that, on her own and it was like batting against a slow spin bowler who cannot find any turn. The questions were few, more an invitation to talk about myself, to the extent that I sometimes asked if there weren't more details she needed to know, such as my educational qualifications. It all went smoothly enough, but I felt there was a certain nervousness on her part, as though our roles had been reversed. Eventually I had to ask what, precisely, my tutoring duties might entail. It turned out to be whatever I could manage, since Mrs Contini realised no one person could be expected to be an expert on everything. And the tennis? Yes, her daughter loved the game, was a promising player but wanted to become better.

All this was good news, but tactics have a part to play in job interviews. As we meandered towards a conclusion, I took the initiative, getting to my feet as if about to leave. Another interview, I explained, adding that I was sure she had other candidates to see. However, I would appreciate swift notification either way, as important decisions were in the offing. I think it's fair to say a look of some consternation suffused her charming face, and I was immediately assured the post was mine if I so desired. This, I said, placed me in rather a dilemma, since I had not attended the other interview. But if we could agree a suitable remuneration ...

It was soon settled to my satisfaction. To further a good impression, I asked if I could telephone my other appointment and tell them I would not be attending. Thus I was able to phone Mac the bookie and celebrate my good fortune with a pound on the favourite in the two-thirty at Kempton Park. On my return I asked if it was possible to meet the young lady concerned. Somewhat to my surprise, it was not, for Ginevra was apparently out for the day. So I left the Contini house buoyed by obtaining a job for which I was totally unqualified, impressed by my future workplace but without meeting the girl I was expected to tutor. Later I learnt the horse had come in second, taking the edge off the day but, even so, I thought fortune had favoured the bold.

Nine-thirty the following Monday saw me report for the first time. Mrs Contini introduced her daughter, a girl already taller than her mother, and more sturdily built, although both had admirable figures. It was her face that disappointed, youthfully pretty but spoiled by a sullen, downturned mouth. Or was that due to my imminent tutoring? After a few minutes Mrs Contini left us to it, Gina leading the way to the designated tutoring room where we set about getting to know each other. Now, I pride myself on my conversational skills but this was hard work. My easy-going questions elicited minimal replies and sometimes merely a mono-syllable. By ten-thirty I knew it was a contest of wills, so sacrificed a break-time to sap her resistance and underline my authority. When we broke for lunch it was still stalemate, although I had gleaned some very interesting information. For instance, she was 'suspended' from her private school, but we both understood she would not be returning. Hence the need for a short-term tutor until the new school year. I also learned that a tutor had been appointed previously and had soon left for reasons Gina chose not to divulge. He had my sympathy.

I escaped the house at lunch-time to clear my head and decide on tactics. A week would be a fair trial, I decided. If she was still difficult by Friday afternoon, I would have to admit defeat and leave, or there may well be a murder. It would be a pity, too, after all the effort and initiative invested.

On my return, and by way of relief, I suggested we play tennis. This met with unspoken approval on Gina's part, and she was suddenly a shade more amenable. It was my first sight of the asphalted court, immaculately maintained, as were the rest of the gardens. Having tightened the net, we began to knock up. It was immediately obvious the girl could play, strongest on her forehand but competent all round. I was rusty and fumbled some straightforward early shots, which caused the still-taciturn Gina to smile derisively. But I soon warmed up and had her scrambling around the court, although I deliberately kept the play even. When we finished it was easy to say she played well, and mean it. I refrained from saying she looked a lot more attractive in a skimpy tennis dress and when she smiled but, if I had, I would have meant that, too.

The following day began what became a pattern; laboured academic explorations on both our parts in the morning, followed by tennis in the afternoon. It soon became clear she knew more about maths, biology, chemistry and physics than I did, which wasn't difficult. We were on a par with religious knowledge but I held the whip hand in history, geography and English, although my Shakespeare is dodgy. Apart from the tennis, it was very hard work.

During a break in Friday afternoon's tennis, I judged it was time for make-or-break. As we took a breather on the court-side bench I told her I was a fraud, not a tutor or teacher at all, adding I was certain she had guessed that already. On the other hand, I knew a lot of interesting and life-enhancing oddities which I would gladly teach her. But this would require a Faustian pact between us, and I actually used that analogy. She would be complicit, carrying out a fruitful and undemanding charade of which not the slightest hint could be conveyed to her parents. If, I concluded, she felt unable to comply, I would leave that afternoon, never to return.

When I finished this short proposal there was silence. Indeed, Gina gazed into the middle distance for so long that I began to wonder whether I had made a serious misjudgment. Then, half-turning her head in my direction, she suddenly said, 'I'll do it.' I was surprised how relieved I felt.

So began a period of quite intense instruction. For what it was worth, we did peruse the various text books for a couple of hours each morning, as this was the price I demanded before she was rewarded with tuition in more interesting arts. Card games, and particularly tricks, have always fascinated me, and I was fortunate to be taught by a gifted friend before I had to do my National Service. I say fortunate, because cards and tricks kept me comfortably in funds during my eighteen months in uniform, even when we were 'up the jungle' in Malaya. So Gina, who was a virgin with cards except for Snap, began to learn the basics of pontoon, brag and poker. She was an apt pupil, soon learning the art of dealing a card from the bottom of the pack, but her favourite game was 'find the lady'. It fascinated her to see three cards so deliberately placed – the queen apparently obvious – only to find it wasn't there at all.

You might have thought our harmless conspiracy would have pushed us together, and it did to a certain extent. Gina seemed happy enough in my company but there was always a barrier of reserve. She had no great sense of humour, so my dubious wit was largely wasted. And then there was her mother. Delightful soul that she was, Mrs Contini was apt to drop in on our lessons at any time during the morning. Her excuses for doing so were quite transparent: she evidently did not trust us together. At first, I thought this just natural parental concern, but it soon became wearing.

It was Gina who eventually explained her mother's excessive caution. In a rare moment of confidence, she admitted being expelled from her fee-paying school because of a series of misdemeanours, culminating in being caught with a boy in her room. Well, however interesting this snippet of information, the consequences were making life difficult for both of us. There were one or two occasions when making the cards disappear was not so much a trick as a vital necessity. A remedy was needed.

I gave this imperative a great deal of thought, and a possible solution came in the form of a double bluff. Gina would tell her mother that I was dull and boring, although tolerable at tennis. Couldn't they find a tutor livelier and more interesting? I was confident this would go down like a lead balloon if Gina gave a convincing performance as a spoilt teenager, a role requiring little acting ability on her part. After all, the premise probably contained more than a grain of truth. I put this proposal to her, and she agreed with some alacrity. I sometimes suspected she did not always get on with her mother.

The stratagem was put into effect that evening. The following morning Gina briefed me on the outcome; her mother in consternation mode again. So when Mrs Contini peered round the door and asked if we could have a word, I can't say I was surprised. We went into the living room where I'd been interviewed. I noticed something I had not seen then, a photograph of Mrs Contini with a man, presumably her husband. I had begun to wonder whether Mr Contini actually existed, since I had not seen him in the four weeks I had been there. But Gina assured me he did exist, a director of a City bank with good connections to Italy and, something of a surprise, the Vatican. An unholy combination, I thought, God and mammon.

As expected, Mrs Contini was somewhat agitated. She beat around the bush for several minutes, asking whether everything was going smoothly, were there any particular problems or difficulties. My bland replies were not intended to quell her disquiet, so the same queries kept cropping up in different forms until I judged the moment right to ask if something was amiss. This was like uncorking a bottle, for she rattled off her concern that Gina wasn't happy. On the other hand, she, Mrs Contini, was perfectly satisfied with the arrangement, but worried that Gina was being 'awkward'. Was her daughter a difficult student? I rather laughed this off; no more than any other teenager I assured her. She preferred tennis to book-work; no surprise there, and not a problem as far as I was concerned.

At this, Mrs Contini's relief was obvious, but I needed to maintain the initiative. Gina sometimes became frustrated during static academic subjects, I said, but I had an unconventional solution if Mrs Contini was minded to hear it. Her guileless face lit up; unconventional sounded interesting, the very thing to combat dullness. I proposed obtaining a dartboard. Mrs Contini looked blank for a moment, as though dartboards were beyond her knowledge or comprehension. Yes, I explained, darts was an excellent antidote to boredom, a quick game of five-o-one revived the brain and sharpened one's mental arithmetic at the same time; a double benefit, if she would excuse the pun. Not being familiar with the rules of the game, this was lost on Mrs Contini, but she welcomed the proposal if I really thought it would do some good. I was sure it would. Another option, I suggested, might be card games, those requiring memory, judgment and decision-making. Useful social skills, too, I added.

So, at one masterful stroke, the problem of Mrs Contini's anxieties about her wayward daughter were laid to rest. Not only that, but cards were now a recognised part of the curriculum, as was darts. It really was a masterstroke, even Gina thought so. But life is full of strange twists.

The modified curriculum was a great success. The academic element was given even more superficial scrutiny, but Gina became skilled at memorising certain key words of particular subjects without having the faintest idea what they meant. But it sounded impressive, and she thought it was 'brilliant', to use her word. I thought it was brilliant, too, as long as she wasn't going to have to face an exam any time soon. In fact, her attitude towards me mellowed noticeably, although there remained a sense of reserve, as though she feared that one day my mask would slip and she would be accosted while defenceless in the stationery cupboard. Perhaps the age difference – thirteen years, a lifetime to a sixteen-year-old – was the cause, but it's just a guess. She was a strange girl in some ways.

One day Mrs Contini made one of her, now rare, interruptions. Very apologetically, she asked if I knew how to clear a blocked sink. Well, I said, it's not my speciality but I'd have a go. I had an audience of Mrs Pennington, the cleaner, and Mrs Contini while I struggled to remove the u-bend pipe. Success was much appreciated by both, although it was an unavoidably messy job for me. While Mrs Pennington resumed her cleaning, Mrs Contini insisted on mopping me down. For some inexplicable reason I chose this moment to say Gina and I were about to play a quick game of darts, and would Mrs Contini care to have a go herself. She seemed quite pleased to be asked.

I suggested she play Gina and I would assist if necessary. We played the shorter three-o-one, skipping the necessity of a double to get away, and I did have to help with her dart-hold. Accuracy was a problem at first, the wall suffering minor damage beyond the backing board, but Mrs Contini was not one whit put out. Of course, Gina romped home, so I insisted on another game, making

Gina work down from five-o-one, although she still won comfortably. But Mrs Contini clearly enjoyed herself, and expressed surprise at Gina's mental arithmetic skills. I regarded this little interlude quite favourably, believing it lent credence to my claims for the game. Gina was not so enthusiastic, grumbling a little about the interruption after her mother left.

I thought no more about it, so it was a genuine surprise when, the next day, Mrs Contini sought me out at lunchtime and asked if I would play her at darts. She had asked Gina but she was too busy resting. I gathered up my remaining sandwich, put down my book and off we went. Of necessity, it was a slow game but I really didn't mind. It was rewarding to watch a woman – whose life did not, perhaps, encompass much in the way of 'fun' - enjoying such a simple pleasure. And she quickly made it a regular lunchtime fixture. She was a bit erratic but made light of her deficiencies, seemingly pleased to do something frivolous. It was equally entertaining for me, never one to avoid charming female company.

When Mrs Contini asked if she might extend her sporting apprenticeship to tennis, it took me completely by surprise. It had been a revelation to see this dignified, even regal, woman standing at the oche lobbing darts at the board and giggling when it all went wrong. Now tennis: where would it all end? Unfortunately, a snag soon materialised; Gina. She took a dim view of the prospect of her mother joining us on the court, and I had to agree that three was an awkward number. It meant one person always had to sit out a game, unless we played two versus one. This didn't appeal to Gina, nor did my suggestion that I coach her mother separately for half an hour after we had finished, although I could not think why.

Mrs Contini joined us a day or two later having acquired suitable attire. It was a tennis dress equally as skimpy as Gina's, and equally as well filled. She had to wear her glasses to see the ball but the sight of her limpid brown eyes looking expectantly at me for instruction failed to detract from her appeal. Her coordination was poor at first, which required a good deal of close-proximity help from me, while Gina muttered and grumped from the other end of the court. But within a few days she was returning a ball well enough to sustain a few rallies, even though Gina smashed some simple returns back with unnecessary venom. But her mother displayed a degree of competitiveness, and even some agility, which I had not expected, making the sessions more enjoyable. And it is a coach's duty to say so, which seemed to please her considerably.

Now here's a curious thing. Very soon after Mrs Contini joined us for tennis, Gina's attitude changed. She not only became a little more accepting of her mother's presence on the court but was suddenly more willing to seek my help with aspects of her game, not a trait she had displayed much before. My time became more equally divided between helping mother and daughter, sometimes requiring me to shuttle from one end of the court to the other with almost as much frequency as the ball. It was tiring, but it had its compensations.

Even more surprising, this change carried over into our house-bound activities. I won't say Gina buckled down to serious study – that was never likely - but she became less moody and, whisper it quietly, more pleasant company. Smiling, not one of her favourite occupations in the past, was suddenly more in evidence. There was something else, too, another change in Gina's behaviour, initially so subtle that it defied definition, annoying for a man who flatters himself attuned to women. The answer evaded me for days.

When it struck, it was like a revelation on the road to Damascus: the girl was being coy, a euphemism for flirtatious in my experience. I could only guess Gina had entered into an imagined competition with her mother out of some misconceived idea of jealousy. It was a shock, and not a welcome one. Being closeted with an attractive young girl for three hours every morning was bad enough, but with added flirting, well, as someone once said, I can resist anything but temptation. I tried to put her off as subtly as possible, keeping at least an arm's length between us, but this only made her less subtle each succeeding day until her antics became practically brazen. She knew I was interested, that was the trouble. She was well aware I'd made a thorough, approving appraisal, and now the goods were evidently on offer. Or were they? What if it was a horrible trap dreamed up in a fevered teenage mind? It was a dilemma requiring one of my more inspired solutions, and the sooner the better.

The next morning I alighted from the bus and began the five-minute walk to the house. No solution had sprung to mind overnight, and I wasn't much looking forward to the day. With a mind preoccupied with the Gina problem I approached the corner to the Contini's road. Suddenly I became aware of Mrs Contini standing beneath a lilac bush which overhung the pavement. As ever, she looked charming, although her expression was serious behind her bespoke glasses. We have to talk, she said.

I joined her under the lilac bush where she explained, with extraordinary coolness, that Gina had told her father everything. Mr Contini knew all about the faux lessons, the card games, the darts and, most wounding of all, a supposed affair between her mother and me. It was absolutely damning and a severe test of my philosophy that all good things come to an end sooner or later. I was certainly willing to hold up my hands about the supposed tutoring, but poor Mrs Contini was blameless. Mrs Contini, I began, at which she held up her hand and said that if I didn't call her Isabella, she would scream. This took me aback somewhat, but I managed to say I would do anything to help her, including facing her husband.

Isabella was adamant this drastic step should be avoided, as her husband was very angry. She had slipped out to prevent this very thing from happening. Who knew what would result? But the false accusation had made me, if not angry, then determined, and I said so. We argued to and fro under the lilac bush until, at last, I prevailed. I gave Isabella five minutes' start, and then followed.

Mr Contini opened the door. About fifty, of average height and a shade portly, he hardly fitted the part of a Mafia killer. But he did look like a prosperous banker stirred to cold anger, which was hardly less reassuring. Without a word he led the way to his study, a generously proportioned room previously unseen by me. Once inside, he shut the door and faced me, still without speaking. I presumed I was to do the talking. I said I was sorry to meet under such circumstances, and that some of what Gina had told him was true, but exaggerated. I was gambling here, that Gina would have lied during the course of her school expulsion and been found out, thereby reducing her credibility. Regarding the allegation about Mrs Contini and me, it was a shocking lie which surely his wife refuted. I said he could do what he liked about the tutoring, but

Mrs Contini was entirely innocent, which was why I had come to see him.

He must have been a handsome man in his younger days I thought, studying his still-silent face. But now there was a heavy jowl and an incipient double chin, although perhaps these are mandatory for important bankers. I waited for a response but he seemed locked in some parallel world, one consisting largely of torment judging by his expression. At last I felt obliged to ask if he accepted that at least Mrs Contini was blameless. After further pause, and without looking at me, there came the faintest inclination of his head. It was the signal for me to leave, without hearing him speak a single word, rather different to one or two other confrontations I had experienced.

I headed straight for the front door, but Mrs Contini, or Isabella as she had inexplicably become, was hovering anxiously in the living-room doorway. I was beyond wanting to talk, so gave a thumbs-up instead, at which she looked less relieved than satisfied. There was no sign of Gina. I opened the front door, glad to escape and prepare for another of Life's great adventures.

A couple of days later, while I was still recuperating, the postman delivered a short, handwritten note, signed Isabella. She wanted to meet to explain about Gina and apologise for her behaviour. A *bijou* private hotel was named, along with a day and a time. There was no need to confirm; she would understand if I did not attend. It was a surprise, that was for sure, but how could I not go?

We met in the hotel lounge, and she looked wonderful. Gone was the diffident, anxious Mrs Contini; here was a new, more confident Isabella, graciously asking if I'd had a good journey. Over lunch she offered several explanations.

First, between our meeting under the lilac bush and my arrival at the house, she had told her husband that she was aware of his affair with his secretary, and had known for some time. Secondly, playing darts and tennis had reminded her of her younger days, and a realisation that she was still capable of frivolous enjoyment, something no longer experienced with her husband, and she had told him that, too. Mr Contini's tortured silence was accounted for.

Finally, she said she and Gina were temperamentally different and often struggled with their relationship. Isabella was sure, however, that things would improve as Gina matured. In the meantime she, Isabella, was going to join a tennis club and, perhaps, a swimming club, too, since it was another abandoned interest.

After lunch she expressed an interest in learning some of my card tricks. I procured a pack from the barman and we adjourned to her room where we amused ourselves until it was time for dinner. And we continued to amuse ourselves through the evening and the next day, also taking in a show, visiting a museum or two and walking in a nearby park. On the third day, we rose very late and skipped breakfast, preferring to take a bath together. We enjoyed a leisurely lunch, during which I delicately hinted that it might be fun to repeat the exercise. But I was not in the least surprised when this received no response, and we said our fond farewells on the steps of the hotel. My last sight of Isabella was of her waving to me from a taxi. Chance is an amazing thing, especially if you are a chancer.

Martin and Clare

THE DULL DECEMBER daylight was slipping away. A never-ending stream of dark, swollen clouds hurried past on a tearing south-westerly, hastening the dusk as if anxious to end such a dismal day. Exposed rock glistened wetly, caught in the thin drizzle carried on the wind in the lulls between driving rain. The Lake District mountains in winter are not for the faint-hearted but, to Martin, this was an added attraction. The solitude, the primeval sense of being alone in a raw landscape, made him perfectly content to keep company with the wind, the rain and the hills.

His solitary hike on the mountain was his own decision, undertaken even though official advice warned against such excursions in these conditions, particularly at his age. Most walkers had heeded that advice, and the few that had ventured out were long since returned to more hospitable surroundings. That being so, Martin, carefully descending the rocky path, was surprised to glimpse a figure in the distance. The poor light allowed no detail, merely the dark outline of a solitary figure, perfectly still, facing the wind and apparently mesmerised by the fast-fading view over the valley below.

Martin continued his steady descent, carefully picking his way along the rough track. But he also glanced frequently at his fellow walker who, it became clear, had deviated from the trail. That was surprising this late in the day. Reaching the point that brought him closest to the still-stationary figure, he stopped. Detail was still sketchy but the build was slight enough to suggest it was a woman. Martin watched the unmoving silhouette for perhaps a minute. Then he left the track and began a slow approach across the rough, tufted grass. A dozen yards from the figure, still unseen and unsuspected, he stopped.

'Excuse me,' he began, quite loudly, fighting the wind. The figure turned, and it was a woman. 'I'm sorry to trouble you but I've had a fall and I'm still a bit shaky. I wondered if you'd be willing to see I get down all right. I'm so sorry to interrupt your day.'

She was a young woman, perhaps just in her thirties, although it was difficult to tell in the bad light, face half-hidden between a buttoned-up jacket collar and a bobble-hat pulled down to her eyebrows. Despite this, Martin noticed she was not well dressed against the weather. Yes, her lightweight jacket might be rain-proof, but hardly proof against a wind-driven Lake District deluge. The same with her shoes; fine for a country stroll, but not mountain-walking. It was a second or two before she replied.

'Yes; yes, of course.' She took a few tentative steps. 'Are you all right, I mean, able to walk? Should we call the emergency services, to be on the safe side?'

'No, it's nothing that bad, I assure you. Nothing's broken or sprained. It just knocked the breath out of me, that's all.'

'Shouldn't you phone ahead; warn somebody you're coming down and might need help?'

'No, really, it's nothing to warrant that sort of fuss.' Martin shook his head and grinned. 'Falls are an occupational hazard up here. Most of us go over at some time or other.' He omitted to say he that never brought his phone on to the hills, holding out his hand instead. 'I'm Martin, by the way.'

There was the faintest hesitation before she walked forward and took the proffered hand, as though she had some doubt about making a new acquaintance. But shake hands she did, if a little self-consciously. 'I'm Clare.'

'Well, I'm pleased to meet you, Clare. Something of a providence really, under the circumstances. There weren't many of us out today, and most of them cleared off long ago, sensible people.'

'Yes, I hadn't realised quite how late it is.' She glanced around, as if to confirm her observation. 'We'd better get going, hadn't we, if you're up to it?'

They returned to the path together and continued their descent. There was not much opportunity for conversation as they picked their way down in increasing darkness, their attention focussed on the uneven track, slippery in places. Martin did discover that Clare was staying at his hotel, which was not surprising, being a hotel situated in splendid isolation – a unique selling point according to its advertising. One other factor also became apparent; Clare was not an experienced hill walker. Rather than helping Martin, it was she that had to be assisted over a couple of rougher sections, although these petered out as they reached the gentler slopes leading down to the hotel.

It was virtually dark when the white, stuccoed walls of the hotel became visible. They climbed the style over a dry-stone wall and walked across the gravelled yard at the back of the building. Lights were on in the kitchen and there were faint sounds of activity from within.

'Well, we've made it, Clare. I can't thank you enough for staying with me; it was very reassuring.'

'Not at all, although I did nothing.' A wry expression crossed her face. 'In fact, you were more help to me than vice versa. But it's good your fall doesn't seem to have done too much harm.'

'No, I'm as right as ninepence now. Like those dolls. You know, the ones that you push over and they stand back up on their own. That's me, except my old bones creak a bit more nowadays.' Martin studied what he could see of her face. 'I hope you don't mind me asking, but are you here on your own?'

Another hesitation before she answered. 'Yes, I am.'

'Then may I thank you by treating you to dinner? I feel I've intruded on your day and I'd like to make up for it – except I might be intruding on your evening as well. That would be unforgivable! Even so, it would be a pleasure to have your company.' Martin kept his gaze on her face. 'I'm a hundred and seven years old, Clare, so you'll be perfectly safe.' A grin accompanied this remark, and Clare managed a faint smile in return.

'I'm sure you're not a hundred and seven, Martin.'

'No, but I soon will be. But I don't want to embarrass you, Clare, seen dining with some old ancient, if that isn't tautologous. It would be wonderful to have some company, but I'll understand if you decline.'

'It's not that, Martin; not at all.' She struggled to find the right words. 'It's that I really wouldn't be very good company. You would certainly regret it.'

'Well, we won't know that until we've tried, will we?' Martin kept his eyes on hers. 'It's a risk I'm willing to take, if you will do the same. And you've got to eat sometime.'

They had reached the hotel lobby, where both now stood, Martin waiting for an answer, aware his persistence was almost certainly unwelcome. Clare, the visible part of her face taut with damp and cold, was in no hurry to reply. She studied the carpeted floor for a moment, but it failed to inspire a suitably polite excuse. Perhaps it was equally tired.

'It's very kind of you, Martin.'

Taking this as an acceptance, Martin was quick to follow up. 'You've made an elderly man very happy, and we haven't even ordered yet.' He became more serious. 'However, I'm quite old fashioned about these things; if you would give me your room number, I will come and escort you to the dining room. But don't feel the need for a little black dress, jeans will be fine by me.'

Clare's collapse was total. 'It's room number twenty-three. On the second floor,' she added, in case Martin might be unfamiliar with hotel room numbering.

'Excellent. Shall I call for you at seven?'

'Yes, that will be fine.' Then, quite spontaneously, she added, 'And it may have to be jeans, because I haven't brought much else.'

On her way up the stairs, Clare was suddenly struck by a thought; the jeans remark was her first attempt at banter, however feeble, since... when. She really could not remember.

Martin was as good as his word. At precisely seven-o'-clock, he knocked on the door of room twenty-three and it was answered promptly enough. Clare was not in jeans but dark cotton trousers, coupled with a thick woollen sweater that Martin thought might be Arran pattern. But he was not an expert in these matters. He was more expert in reading peoples' faces. Clare's was fine-boned, shaped like a plover's egg, although Martin was immediately aware how few people nowadays would have the faintest idea what that meant. But her fine features were marred by a pale tiredness, faint bags visible under her eyes. She wore no make-up but had tidied her short, bobbed hair.

She managed a smile of greeting, although Martin was certain she viewed this dinner date as something of a trial, to be endured and then ended as soon as decently possible. Understanding this, he kept the conversation light as they made their way to the dining room, making asides about the hotel décor, the service, other guests; studiously avoiding any personal questions. He was good at this, putting people at their ease, particularly if they were as reticent as Clare.

Out of season, the dining room was not busy. A young waitress led them to a table and took their drinks order while they consulted the menu. Having ordered, Martin kept up a flow of inconsequential chatter, at various times volunteering that he had been married to Jean for forty-eight years, had a married son and family living in Australia and a married daughter living near Edinburgh, among other things. This information was delivered in penny packets rather than a life history. This was quite deliberate, because Martin was more interested in Clare, gradually inserting questions about her childhood, upbringing and education. As he guessed, these had been happy periods in Clare's life, and she began to respond with more feeling. It would be too much to say she became animated, but she did become perceptibly more relaxed.

As they drank their coffees at the end of the meal, Clare began to wonder how she might make her excuses and leave. Not that she was unappreciative of Martin's company. On the contrary, despite her initial reservations, it had proved an interesting experience. Under other circumstances, it would have been enjoyable. Martin had proved a good conversationalist, with wide-ranging topics and a nice line in self-deprecating humour, for which Clare was grateful. But she was also very tired. She was about to speak when Martin, sensing the moment, cut across her.

'I'd like to tell you something, Clare; something I've never told to another living soul.'

She was a little taken aback, before hoping it would be nothing embarrassing. Martin's expression had changed, she realised, suddenly more serious. He seemed to leave Clare's company briefly, his attention somewhere in the middle distance while he searched for the right words. Then his eyes switched back to Clare's.

'Nowadays,' he began, 'when I go out on the hills, like today, I am never quite sure whether I shall return. Not an accident, you understand, but a deliberate act. It's something I began to consider a year or two ago, a desire to die at a time and place of my own choosing. I loathe hospitals: I'd rather die in a ditch, or anywhere else, as long as I'm under an open sky. I've taken to carrying a bottle of barbiturate tablets on these hikes, so that when the moment arrives – and I will know - it will help me take my leave. You look a little shocked, Clare, but please bear with me.' Martin gave a smile of reassurance. 'It's nothing at all alarming. It's just that I've reached the point when I'm tiring of an aging body, sometimes even of life itself. And it becomes more sharply defined with every passing year. Perhaps it's because I have no sympathy or understanding with much of modern life; it's obsessions with screens, pseudo-experiences and other trivialities. I don't understand many current attitudes, such as the damnation of our history. I shouldn't take such things too seriously at my age, but it seems I can't help it.'

Martin leaned back in his chair and gave a rueful smile. 'There, I've just managed to ruin our evening.'

Clare stared at him, frowning. 'But you're not ill or anything, are you? I mean, you look perfectly fit and well. You were much more sure-footed than me.'

'No, it's nothing like that. I'm healthy enough, except for my blood-pressure pills. But my body is wearing out. I'm like a marathon runner, trying to gauge what I've got left but not knowing where the finishing line is. I'll know when I reach it, though, because it will be self-determined. And that's when I will end my life, where and when I choose.'

Clare did not reply immediately, her brow furrowed in shock and perplexity. When she did speak, it was a whispered question. 'Why are you telling me this, Martin?'

'Perhaps it takes one to know one, Clare. Call it intuition. I saw you near the crag edge and guessed what you might be thinking: a couple of quick steps and, a second or two later, it would all be over. Am I right?'

For an indeterminate time, there was no reply, Clare's attention riveted on an empty coffee cup. Then she looked up, her expression one of bewildered frustration. 'My life is a complete and utter mess, Martin. You're right; I did think about it, but I couldn't find the courage to do it. Another failure, to add to all the others.'

Martin projected a sympathetic smile. 'Well, it seems we have at least one shared interest, Clare; always helpful at the start of a friendship. I hadn't fallen over, by the way, out on the hill; it was just an excuse to speak to you, I was that concerned.' He leaned forward and put his arms on the table. 'We may share a common interest but you surely realise we are at opposite ends of the spectrum. I'm seventy-eight – yes, you can look surprised; quite a few people are – and closing in on a certainty. Only the date and place are uncertain. You, however, must have at least fifty years ahead of you, fifty years of Kipling's triumphs and, yes, almost certainly a few more disasters. But that's just life, isn't it?'

There was no response from Clare, still locked in her own private hell, so Martin continued. 'I've told you something of my background, that I'm married, have a family, some of my interests. What I haven't told you is that my wife died six years ago; she was only seventy-one. Or that my son lives in Australia and I only see my two grandchildren via a screen. Or that my daughter lives in Scotland with a husband who is an ardent Scot-Nat. I don't like him much, and certainly not his politics. And so it goes on, Clare: I lost a close, lifelong friend last year, plus a few others along the way. It happens at my age. But your situation, although you think it disastrous, is completely different. You have ample time to change it. All it needs is your courage and determination.'

'I don't think I have those qualities, Martin.'

'And I'm sure you do. I can't believe you're naturally depressive.'

'Not always, no; only recently, since the disasters.'

'Then you certainly have the resilience to overcome your problems. I don't want to sound like some penny-dreadful agony uncle – there, you see how I'm trapped in the past? How many of your generation have any idea what a penny dreadful is?' Martin gave a resigned grimace before continuing. 'Look, you may take the view that your problems are nothing to do with me, Clare, and you're absolutely right in the narrowest sense. But I tell you now, if you were to take your own life, I would be devastated – the utter waste of it. And there must be many others – family, friends, work colleagues - who would feel far, far worse. In your heart, you surely know that is true.'

Clare had resumed her study of the coffee cup, lips tightly compressed. No reply appeared to be forthcoming, so Martin pressed the point.

'Well, am I right? Whatever has been said or done, deep in your heart you know it's true.'

At last she raised her head a little, eyes now focussed somewhere on Martin's chest. Her voice was hardly more than a whisper. 'Yes, I suppose so'

Martin clasped his hands in relief. 'Well done, Clare. You've just taken the first step to sorting out your life.' He leaned back in his seat. 'I think we both deserve another drink, don't you?'

Clare lifted her eyes, met his gaze and gave a wan smile. 'Yes,' she nodded.

Before the waitress reappeared to take their order, Martin was already back to his chatty self. 'I'm thinking of going to Carlisle tomorrow. Never been there before but it's a place with bags of history. A castle, a museum and, I'm told, a very good bookshop within sight of the cathedral. Should be really interesting. Why don't you come, too?'

Clare had just finished loading the dishwasher when her phone buzzed. She did not recognise the number. 'Hello.'

'Oh, hello. Are you Clare Rawnsley?' A man's voice, with a distinct Scottish burr.

'Yes, I am.'

'Ah, good. I was afraid your number might have changed. My name is Jamie McNeil; you don't know me, but I believe you knew my father-in-law, Martin Flitcroft?'

Clare felt a sudden constriction in her throat, and it was a moment before she could answer, 'Yes, I know Martin.'

'Well, I'm sorry to tell you Martin passed away recently.

He left various instructions, including a note that you should be informed, and that's why I'm calling.'

'I see.' This must be the Scottish son-in-law that Martin didn't like, and it was a dislike Clare was already beginning to share, however irrationally. She searched for some suitable words. 'Well, thank you for letting me know - and my condolences to you and your family.'

This was acknowledged with a subdued 'Thank you', and there followed an awkward silence before Clare could ask, 'You say Martin died recently' – she baulked at his euphemism, knowing it would have annoyed Martin – 'but I wasn't aware he had been ill. Could you tell me a little more?'

There was another delay, as if Jamie was reluctant to go into detail. 'Yes, he was hiking in the Lake District and died on one of the hills. The weather was bad, but he always insisted on going anyway, regardless. He was somewhat eccentric that way; despite his age, he wasn't keen on taking advice about the dangers of hill-walking alone in winter.'

'No, he was very independent,' was Clare's considered response. Among her mixed emotions a voice was whispering, 'You found the finishing line, then, Martin'. She felt moved to add, 'He loved the outdoors, so it was probably how he would have wanted to go.'

'Maybe, although it put a number of people to a lot of trouble, what with the mountain rescue team, a helicopter, the police, among others. And there will have to be an inquest because of the circumstances, to establish the cause of death. Not really what anyone wants in the run-up to Christmas.'

She could hear the resentment in his voice, and it gave her a frisson of satisfaction. Good on you, Martin; your instincts on this man were sound. 'Perhaps, but he was a wonderful friend to me; kind, thoughtful, always good company. We didn't live in each other's pockets – you must know how he loathed social media – but when we spoke or emailed there was always an immediate rapport, as though we'd been in touch only the day before.'

Jamie made no response and Clare felt the constriction return in her throat. She had to wait for it to clear before continuing, 'I doubt I shall be able to attend the funeral but I would appreciate knowing the date, when it's finally arranged. If you would give me the funeral director's contact details, I'll ask them to let me know. I expect you have more than enough to do.'

The details provided, Clare felt no desire to prolong a conversation with a man so clearly carrying out an unwanted task. He had nothing to add so, after repeating her thanks and condolences, the call ended. She put down her phone, walked through to the living room and sat down, seeming to contemplate the Christmas decorations, although they did not register at all.

A little later, with her baby on her lap sucking at his bottle, Clare spoke to him. 'Well, Joel Martin Rawnsley, now you'll never have the chance to meet the man you're named after, which is a great shame. But I'll tell you about him, when you ask. And on his funeral day, I shall leave you with your daddy, if you don't mind, while I go out for a walk on my own. We don't have mountains here but I hope it's cold and raining and blowing a gale, so that I can say goodbye to my friend Martin in just the way he would have wished.'

Echoes of Empire

AT ITS HEIGHT, the magnificent British empire spawned so many inspiring examples of human endeavour that other nations were cast deep into the empire's metaphorical shadow. Across every continent, intrepid British explorers climbed mountains, penetrated jungles, journeyed up rivers and crossed deserts, simply because they were there. Like tentacles, they spread around the globe with their Union Jacks and derring-do, until no tribe, however elusive or misanthropic, was safe from discovery. The rest of humankind stood still, reduced to silent awe at the extraordinary achievements of this island race.

If these endeavours sprang from the playing fields of Eton, many other public schools also contributed to this brilliant cohort of explorers and warriors. One such was St Swindells, a red-brick former mansion nestling in countryside so preternaturally English it was rumoured Constable had set out to paint it. Sadly, it was so hidden away, he failed in his quest and went home to paint a cart stuck in the middle of a river. Meanwhile, the last of the Swindell family died of a rare form of luxurious penury, unique in being suffered only by indebted landed gentry. There being no traceable offspring, the property was put up for sale and purchased by a Dr Kray, an apothecary with a side-line in converting base metals into gold. But, with modern medicine usurping the apothecary trade – he was believed to be the last British practitioner – and dwindling numbers of new investors in his base-metal-to-gold experiments, Dr Kray was eventually forced to consider his future. In an unusual moment of lucidity, he remembered the saying 'those who can, do: those who can't, teach'. That was it! He would establish a school for the sons of simple gentlefolk.

That is how St Swindells school came into being. It did not prove academically outstanding, rather the opposite; the school taking the radical view that success in exams could render pupils excessively elitist. Nor did it dominate in sport, having sold most of its grounds at an advantageous price to an experimental explosives company. But, in one respect, St Swindells was unchallenged: its pupils had the highest percentage of double-barrelled names of any British public school. Parents of prospective pupils with only a single surname were immediately advised to adopt another to have any hope of admission. In fact, in an ambitious bid to maintain the school's surname superiority, it ran a brilliant publicity campaign targeted at triple-barrelled names, a limited market but which resulted in the arrival of the boy, Bluffley-Twisleton-ffrench, a major coup for St Swindells.

Which brings us to two of the school's more modest pupils, Crudgington Minor and Stewkley-Fothersgill. Normally, they would have been quite undistinguished boys, particularly Crudgington, who bore the heavy handicap of just a single surname. But his parents were nothing if not resourceful, pointing out to Dr Kray that they had an elder son currently searching for lost tribes up the Limpopo river. True, he had not been heard of for seven years, a sad addition to the crowded pantheon of lost British explorers. But the possibility of his continued existence, however remote, meant that their second son - albeit of uncertain hereditary status – could be known as Crudgington Minor. Thus did Dr Kray relent and the boy gain admission to St Swindells.

Stewkley-Fothersgill was different. He was descended from a line of aristocracy so tortuously illegitimate that Debrett's Peerage refused to include the entry for fear of undermining public morals. It did not help that his paternal grandfather's sole lifetime achievement was third place in a village idiot competition, although this did not seem to impair his ability to father children. Indeed, he was hard at work on the thirteenth when, at the climactic moment, he carelessly catapulted out of the hayloft. An unlucky thirteenth it turned out, though the mishap might not have been fatal but he landed on a bull which, enraged at the interruption of its own nuptials, immediately gored him to death. At least, such was related in the proud oral history of the Stewkley-Fothersgills.

Now, it so happened that Crudgington Minor and Stewkley-Fothersgill both suffered a similar physical handicap – one leg shorter than the other, and it was this phenomenon that first brought the boys together. Crudgington Minor had a shorter right leg and Stewkley-Fothersgill the left. When walking, this caused each boy to lurch in the direction of his shorter leg, and it was to counter this tendency that the two boys were first paired together. Thus, with Crudgington Minor walking on the left and Stewkley-Fothersgill on the right, any lurching tendency was effectively negated. That is how the boys became inseparable friends.

It proved a fruitful association. Not only was their joint walking speed now considerably enhanced but, on sports day, they romped away in the three-legged race. Buoyed by this success, they attended the local village fête and cruised to another three-legged victory, winning a five-shilling postal order in the process. Utilising Crudgington Minor's financial acumen, they were soon entering three-legged races throughout the district and were even excused school for this specific purpose, Dr Kray merely exacting a twenty percent levy on their winnings. In the bigger villages, prizes could be as much as seven-and-six or even ten shillings, but the boys' fame began to spread and they had to resort to ever-heavier disguise to obtain admission. Inevitably, the tax authorities also became aware but the fête season was drawing to a close and so a scandal was avoided.

As well as education, St Swindells believed in developing character, over the years achieving a fearsome reputation for its school expeditions. In the proud tradition of empire, no destination was deemed too far or too dangerous, nor was any boy spared. If a more ambitious expedition set off with a dozen boys and returned with just ten, this was deemed a great success. Indeed, some families deliberately chose to send their surplus sons to St Swindells in the fond hope that they might never return from their expedition, thus saving much time and expense in trying to place them in a career.

It was in the fourth form that Crudgington Minor and Stewkley-Fothersgill went on their first expedition. It was a modest affair, as they were included in a group comprising various disabilities ranging from myopia to plain simple-mindedness. Wales was the approximate destination, somewhere in the Brecon Beacons or Black Mountains it was rumoured. To foster a greater sense of mystery and adventure, no-one was told exactly where.

They alighted from the train at a tiny, isolated station with an unpronounceable name and immediately set off up the nearest mountain. It was then that our two heroes discovered a disagreeable truth; three-legged walking up a mountainside did not work well. They found it impossible to achieve the rhythm vital for successful three-legged perambulation. It was a ghastly discovery. They soon fell behind, cries of 'Oh, hurry up Crudgers' and 'do stop dawdling, Stewkers' growing ever fainter in the distance. At last, when the main group had long disappeared from sight and earshot, the two boys stopped. They were a little downhearted but not surprised at the disappearance of their fellows, being only too aware of one of the school's principal mottoes – 'St Swindells boys never turn back'.

It was while pondering their options that Crudgington Minor – temporarily separated from his companion – made a startling discovery. Walking a few yards to ease a touch of cramp, he found walking quite comfortable, even normal. Quickly utilising his sketchy knowledge of geometry, he realised the angle of the mountain's incline perfectly compensated for the shortness of his leg, provided he kept to a lateral line. As soon as he attempted to climb or descend, the old lurching problem recurred. In excited tones he relayed this information to Stewkley-Fothersgill, who immediately launched an experimental walk of his own. To his unmitigated joy, it worked for him, too. There was just one problem: their shorter legs being on opposite sides, for each to benefit, they would be obliged to walk in opposite directions.

This was a serious blow to the inseparable friends. Although thrilled at the prospect of walking solo, it would be an enormous wrench not to enjoy the literal support of his chum. They discussed this dilemma at some length until Crudgington Minor, in a blinding flash of geometrical logic, declared that he had the solution. If each set off in opposite directions around the mountain, they were bound to meet at the point of half-circle. Here they would enjoy a moment of companionship, catch up on any interesting happenings that had occurred on their respective journeys and, more importantly, what the weather had been like. Stewkley-Fothersgill, always impressed by his friend's superior intellect, was enthusiastic, and could hardly wait to start.

That is how the boys solved a seemingly intractable problem. Unable to ascend and unwilling to dishonour St Swindells by returning from their expedition as failures, they decided to settle on the mountain and enjoy their new-found mobility. They built a shelter of rocks, slept soundly on beds of moss and lived on the kindness of strangers such as ramblers, met on their daily perambulations. They settled into a contented daily routine, each walking a solitary path until their happy half-way reunion, then continuing on their way to meet again at their camp. Here they would pass the evenings discussing their solitary, somewhat repetitious, adventures.

This idyllic existence continued until the autumn sheep round-up, when the boys were discovered coercing sheep into their hovel and sleeping under them to ward off the colder nights. The removal of the sheep prompted a rapid reappraisal of their situation. A kindly farmer acted as an intermediary, eventually negotiating their return to St Swindells. A disciplinary panel deemed the months spent on the mountain just sufficient to obviate a punishment, although Dr Kray, having engaged a signwriter at some cost, was irritated at having to remove the boys' names from the plaque commemorating those lost on the school's expeditions.

And so the boys returned to continue their education. Those halcyon days of solitary mobility began to fade into memory, although this was offset by renewed earnings from three-legged racing. However, the cost of ever-more complex disguises and travel to ever-more distant venues proved burdensome. And, since both boys had progressed to the sixth form, disparities in stature with eight-year-olds became ever more difficult to overcome. Their futures looked bleak.

But the world was about to change. Unknown and unknowable, the British Empire had reached its zenith. The glorious summer of the Edwardian era had passed and, although the sun still blazed down upon Britain and St Swindells, new and dangerous rivalries were abroad. Deeply enmeshed in another three-legged race season, war came as a shock to Crudgington Minor and Stewkley-Fothersgill, as to many others, not least the belligerents. Too young to volunteer, they nevertheless donned their best disguises, joined the queue at the recruitment office and succeeded in passing the initial screening. It was only when ordered to march to the barracks that their scheme failed. They had hardly set off before Crudgington Minor began to veer to the right and Stewkley-Fothersgill to the left. A closer examination by the medical staff soon revealed the cause and the distraught boys sent back to continue their education.

But it was not the end of their military careers. By the time they left St Swindells in the summer of 1916, Kitchener's New Army had been in action on the Somme. Casualties had been such that, to obtain sufficient replacements, physical specifications were considerably reduced, at last providing the opportunity our chums craved. Aware of the formation of many Pals battalions including a battalion for artists and even a Bantam battalion for those more vertically challenged, they began to lobby for a Minor Disabilities battalion. They badgered their respective MPs, questions were asked in Parliament and, eventually, the authorities were forced to relent. For some inexplicable reason, the authorities baulked at naming it the Disabled Pals battalion, preferring Special Services instead. Joyfully, second lieutenants Crudgington Minor and Stewkley-Fothersgill, newly commissioned as was their privately educated right, joined the training camp.

There, an astute lance-corporal, observing the pals' lurching tendencies, suggested attaching a wooden block to the shorter-leg to compensate. And it worked! Lurching became a thing of the past, although this prompted unrest among those soldiers who had no solution to their particular disability. For the sake of morale, both Crudgington Minor and Stewkley-Fothersgill voluntarily reduced the depth of their blocks by a quarter of an inch, sufficient to induce a noticeable limp and thus quell any incipient mutiny.

The battalion moved to the Flanders front in September 1917. Heavy rain was blighting the British offensive, casualties were heavy, progress slow. Another effort was ordered but, advancing in the mist and rain, our heroes eventually found themselves alone in a shell-hole. Amid the exploding landscape, their eyes met, silently acknowledging their desperate situation. It was Crudgington Minor who spoke first. 'We can't turn back; what would St Swindells say!'

'No,' agreed Stewkley-Fothersgill, 'it's unthinkable.'

The two youths looked at each other and then, without

a word, set about removing their respective boot-blocks. Using their puttees, they bound their two shorter legs together, relishing that oh-so-familiar feeling. Then, with bayonets fixed, they went over the top, surging towards the enemy lines with all the facility of their triumphant three-legged races. For a moment, enemy fire fell away to nothing, no doubt daunted by the extraordinary sight of Crudgington Minor and Stewkley-Fothersgill bearing down upon them. Then a swirling mist enveloped the two figures, and they were never seen again.

Back at St Swindells, the names Crudgington Minor and Stewkley-Fothersgill were added to the plaque commemorating the school's fallen, this time for good. A disillusioned Dr Kray handed the school to a charitable trust, retiring to resume his study of converting base metals into gold. But, mirroring the Empire, St Swindells fell into decline, the Great War having grievously thinned the ranks of double-barrelled surnames. At its closure, the school's commemorative plaques were placed somewhere for safe keeping but, like Crudgington Minor and Stewkley-Fothersgill – indeed, the Empire itself - they are now lost to posterity.

Mrs Kingsley's Salvation

ON WAKING AT her usual hour, Isobel Kingsley quickly realised something was wrong. The house was silent. The usual muted domestic sounds generated by the servants were entirely absent. Puzzled, she listened with concentrated care but was not mistaken; silence reigned. Where was everyone, by which she meant the native staff? Her husband was staying at the plantation and both children sent away to school, but where were the staff, so numerous and diversely employed that she did not know all their names? Her tentative exploration of the house revealed not a single servant. Nor, once she had washed and dressed, did a visit to the separate servants' quarters. She would not enter the building, sensing it was empty, as if abandoned.

It was while she was outside that Mrs Kingsley first noticed the smoke, rising in dark, unhurried columns above the town. Puzzlement gave way to anxiety, and she quickly made her way to a first-floor balcony. This offered panoramic views across the distant river, but that was not the attraction now. She looked towards the town, a view partially obscured by the garden's numerous trees. Even as she watched, two fresh columns of smoke appeared, rising lazily into an otherwise cloudless sky. Listening with acute attention, she thought she detected a faint, irregular murmur which swelled and fell as borne upon a fickle breeze. The knowledge that she had few European neighbours, and that most were away at their own plantations, fuelled her anxiety. While some wives chose to accompany their husbands and others retired to the social pleasures of the state capital, Mrs Kingsley did not. For reasons known only to herself, she had declined these options, now resulting in her unusual isolation.

Soon after nine-o'-clock she made her third visit to the balcony, each more fraught than the last. The formerly isolated columns of smoke had largely merged into one billowing cloud spread, as far as she could tell, right across the town. The murmur was now an amorphous hubbub which was, almost imperceptibly, growing louder, and closer. Mrs Kingsley's anxiety began to slip into a nameless dread. As she stared with growing alarm towards the burning town, a nearer movement caught her eye. For a moment, with nothing obvious visible, she thought she was mistaken. Then, from between a fine display of bougainvilleas lining the drive, a figure emerged, walking towards the house. Mrs Kingsley felt a surge of relief, for she recognised him.

'Mr Rawlins, Mr Rawlins, wait! I'm coming down.'

Rawlins did wait, to see Mrs Kingsley emerge from the house, half-running in her flustered rush to reach him. 'Mr Rawlins, what a providence you're here. What on earth is happening? Where is everyone? Why is the town on fire?'

Rawlins, a youngish man of unremarkable appearance except for a mop of undisciplined blonde hair, was a journalist on the local English language paper. 'I'm here for a story but, more to the point, Mrs Kingsley, why are you still here when the town is in the grip of insurrection?'

'An insurrection?' She looked and sounded incredulous.

'What do you mean? Have they taken over the town? But what about the police? Can't they restore order?'

'Those that have stayed are besieged in the police station. They won't move until the Army arrives, which may be a few days if the trouble is widespread. Meanwhile, I'm afraid the mob is in charge and looting already well under way. And it won't be long before they reach here. They've crossed the bridge already, the shrewd ones who know where the best pickings are to be had. It's one of the problems of living in a wealthy enclave.'

'Oh my God!' Mrs Kingsley clutched her throat. 'Aren't we in danger, if they're coming this way?'

'Well, you certainly are, a white woman on her own.' said Rawlins quite matter-of-factly, hardly sparing the woman's feelings.

'My God!' repeated Mrs Kingsley, 'what can we do?'

Rawlins frowned, considering his answer. 'Well, I'm supposed to be covering the story, but I suppose your predicament must take priority.' His frown suddenly deepened, and he swivelled to peer in the direction of the distant neighbouring house. 'Did you hear that? I'm not sure they haven't reached next door already. Best get inside for a moment while I think what to do.'

Mrs Kingsley did not need to be told twice, hurrying back through the front door with Rawlins at her heels. 'Surely we can't stay here, can we?' she asked in voice strained with anxiety.

'No, we can't,' decided Rawlins, 'we must get away from here. We should take some food and water, or anything else to drink; I've no idea how long this will last. Not too much, mind you, we don't want to be too weighed down. Quick as you can, while I keep watch. How do I get to that balcony?'

Rawlins disappeared up the staircase while Mrs Kingsley began collecting essentials. Despite her fear, she remained remarkably focussed, choosing a capacious shoulder bag before gathering a selection of tinned foods. Nor did she forget a tin-opener. Bottled lemonade was the only available drink, but the bottles were heavy and she had to abandon some tins to save weight. After taking a light cotton coat from the rack, she called up the stairs to Rawlins, who joined her. The looters were getting closer, he announced, it was time to leave.

They left by the rear of the house, making their way through the gardens to the boundary fence. There was no gate, and Rawlins had difficulty levering some boards off the rails to make a gap. Beyond the garden was the outer edge of a park, fringed with trees which afforded some cover to the fleeing pair, if only anyone had been present to see them. Rawlins led the way, weaving between the trees and seeming little concerned whether Mrs Kingsley was following, for he hardly looked back. The edge of the park was not delineated, merely becoming thicker as it merged with the bushy scrub, and their progress slowed accordingly.

When they were a short distance into the scrub cover Rawlins halted in an open patch, put aside the heavy bag and sat down. He was breathing audibly, sweat glistening on his face, a few strands of damp blond hair clinging to his forehead. Mrs Kingsley rapidly followed his example, for she was a decade older and certainly in no better condition.

'This will do,' muttered Rawlins, 'at least for a while. I could do with a drink, too.' He rummaged in the bag, giving a wry laugh when he saw the contents of the bottle. 'Is this the best you could do?'

'My husband only drinks spirits, I'm afraid.' She, too, managed a grimace of a smile before adding, 'Do you intend to stop here?'

Rawlins reflected for a moment. 'No, but it will serve my purpose. There is something you must understand before we go on.'

'Oh,' said Mrs Kingsley, still breathing hard, 'and what might that be?'

'It concerns my role in your escape; the nature of my reward.'

Mrs Kingsley's expression registered momentary disbelief before locking into shocked disdain. 'I see. Well, I'm sure my husband will see you financially rewarded, if you feel entitled.'

A shadow of a smile flickered across Rawlins's sweating face. 'No, Mrs Kingsley, you don't understand. I am not remotely interested in your husband's money. It is you that commands my attention.'

For some moments Mrs Kingsley sat silent, staring at Rawlins as if to determine whether he was serious, or simply making an appallingly ill-conceived joke. But she already knew the answer. 'Is it your intention to take advantage of me?'

'Yes,' replied Rawlins, quiet and calm.

'That is unspeakable. Shame on you.' She was equally quiet, but furious. 'It is absolutely unthinkable.'

'Of course, I knew that's what you would say, and you therefore have a choice. You can come with me and survive with some little discomfort – for I know a way – or you can take your chance on your own.' Rawlins leaned forward. 'Just remember though, without me, you would still be in the house, a sitting target for ghastly rape and murder. I've brought you to temporary safety, done my white man's duty as you would see it, but now it is for you to decide how you want to proceed.'

Mrs Kingsley glared at him, not speaking, which prompted Rawlins to a make a more conciliatory opening. 'Do you remember that day when we spoke in the church?'

'No, I do not.'

'I'm sure you do. It was only just over a year ago.' When she did not reply he continued, 'You seemed in very low spirits and I asked if you were quite well. Then you began to talk, hesitantly at first, I remember, but then you opened up and we actually conversed. No-one else was there, we just sat in the pews and you talked about your two children going off to school and how you missed them. Then you spoke of your own childhood, growing up in England and how you missed that, too. It was a charming interlude, and I was smitten, Mrs Kingsley, completely smitten.'

'I wasn't well, and now you are trying to take advantage.' Her fury was righteous, but a shade defensive. She did remember, after all.

'You said you had not a single true friend within your circle, so I suggested we might bump into each other again at the church, and you smiled. Then, at the garden fête, you cut me dead. Do you remember that?'

'Don't you see?' Mrs Kingsley's face flushed afresh. 'Don't you understand I can't be seen talking to you. We are from different social circles. It is not my wish, but it's how things are. This wretched place lives on gossip, most of it untrue. And you are a journalist, peddling stories that make it worse. That's why you are so disliked among the white community.' She turned away and studied the ground. 'You were kind to me in the church, I don't deny it, but you can't hold a momentary aberration against me.'

'I hold nothing against you, but it seems to me there

are two Mrs Kingsley's; one hopelessly borne down by a stultifying social straitjacket, and the other who knows there is so much more to life but doesn't know how to find it.' Rawlins paused, studying her downcast face, unusually beautiful even in her anguish. 'Enough said; we both know where we stand. I'm going off to find some higher ground with a view of the town, to try and understand what's happening there. I'll be away a while, perhaps half an hour or more. If you're gone when I return, I'll quite understand. You know the way back but don't go to the town for at least two days. And take the bag; you'll need some provisions.'

Mrs Kingsley made no answer, nor did she look up to see him depart.

Rawlins took great care to mark his trail, breaking obvious branches or twisting the lank, tall grass into a loose knot. He walked up the gentle incline for some way, but no view offered itself. Eventually he climbed one of the taller trees and managed, with some difficulty and by breaking numerous branches, to obtain a leafy view towards the town. A pall of smoke was still the dominant feature, no better or worse than when they had set off. In truth, he expected nothing less, and it was not the main reason for his journey. The woman needed some time on her own, he had decided, and it wouldn't do him any harm, either.

An unfamiliar call, loud and harsh as a peacock, caught his attention. While he wondered at its identity, a second call came from a different direction, to be answered by the first. Rawlins halted his descent from the tree and waited, motionless. Circumstances had made him exceptionally wary, even suspicious. What if they had been seen in the park? Was it possible they were being followed and this was their way of keeping in touch? Rawlins was not a natural jungle man; it was not his friend or ally, nor sporting arena, unlike some of his acquaintance. Another call, closer this time, caused him to climb back to the leafier part of the canopy, where he waited and watched. Half a dozen small, brightly coloured birds joined him briefly in the branches, before taking wing again. Rawlins wished he had that facility. A movement in the undergrowth caught his eye, not thirty yards away. Nothing more for a few seconds, then a small deer emerged into view. With unhurried, dainty steps, it passed almost directly under his tree before being swiftly lost to sight.

When Rawlins returned to the glade, there was no sign of Mrs Kingsley, nor the bag. He did not trouble to conduct any sort of search, merely casting a swift glance around the surrounding undergrowth. If he was disappointed, it did not show on his face. He intended to strike for the river, and had taken a few paces when he heard her voice.

'You said you had a plan. What is it?' She had moved to some thicker cover and was hardly visible.

'Well, that would be telling, wouldn't it?' replied Rawlins, who had immediately stopped, her reappearance prompting a faint, sardonic smile. 'But I can tell you it will give us a fair chance of getting us out of this spot of bother. And the best part is, you will emerge a heroine, with a reputation to match. Because, despite what you might think, I am mindful of your reputation.'

'How is that possible, with what you are proposing?' She had emerged from her hiding place and now stood a few yards from him, sceptical yet determined.

'Right, let us each be perfectly clear. If you will agree to my proposal, and give me your word upon it, I will trust you to keep it. I will then tell all based on your word.'

'But surely you can give me some idea?' She wrung her

hands in exasperation.

Rawlins considered for a moment, mindful of her obvious distress. 'Very well; I can say you will be under cover and tolerably comfortable in a proper bed. And safe. That is all, until you choose to give your word.'

She stood for a long time, studying Rawlins as if for some sort of sign. But he gave no sign, his face expressionless as he waited for her decision

'What choice do I have?' she said at last. 'Very well, you have my word.'

'Thank you.' His expression barely altered except, perhaps, for something akin to relief. 'Now I can explain. You may be aware this area, the reed marshes, is a haven for wildfowl, offering the best duck shooting in the state. A number of the great and the good make use of this bounty including, on occasions, even your husband. To minimise any hardship in that pursuit, they obtained a former barge and had it converted to a floating hostel and gunroom, so that they could stay out for two or three days without interruption. Does this sound at all familiar?'

Mrs Kingsley was suddenly curious. 'Go on.'

'The barge is very basic by your standards, but it will suit us. It's stocked with some provisions, and at least we have a tin-opener.' If this was meant as a joke, it failed to register with Mrs Kingsley, so Rawlins continued, 'There's a maintenance man who cleans up before and after each shooting party. They've provided a skiff for him to get out there, and it's moored at the edge of the marsh. The path he uses is close by; that's why I stopped here.'

Her brow furrowed. 'How do you know all this? I can't believe you have ever been invited to join a shooting party.'

'That will be the day!' Rawlins gave an ironic laugh before adding, 'How do you think I get my stories? Because

I learnt to speak the language of the servants, the clerks and even the occasional policeman. They know everything, and are perfectly willing to share it with a sympathetic journalist, often for free. The maintenance man took me out to the barge for a private viewing; that's how I know. It enables me to write with inside knowledge. And now we can turn it to our advantage.'

She stared at him but made no further comment, so Rawlins took the bag from her, swung it over his shoulder and set off to find the track. After a moment's hesitation, Mrs Kingsley followed.

The path was hardly used, overgrown and difficult walking in places, but it took less than an hour to reach the edge of the marsh. Here the undergrowth thinned, giving a view across endless acres of reeds, apparently bereft of any open water. Rawlins pushed on, hoping his recall of the route was accurate, although he voiced no doubts to Mrs Kingsley. Close to the edge of the marsh, quite suddenly, a strip of open water barred his way. A tiny geological fault had left a narrow channel through the marsh, too deep for the reeds to grow. And, just as Rawlins remembered, a small rowing boat lay at the end of the channel, half-hidden beneath some over-hanging branches. He breathed a muted sigh of relief.

The skiff, tied between two posts, sat low in the water because, as Rawlins immediately discovered, it was half-flooded with rainwater. Since he was already hot and muddy to his knees, it was of little consequence to wade in to the thigh-deep water, untie the boat and tip it over on to the bank, a heavy job needing all his strength. Righted and re-launched, it was left in the sun to dry out before boarding took place. Mrs Kingsley, who had not spoken during the journey except to ask that he slow down, clambered aboard unaided and sat silent in the stern. Rawlins followed and set about testing the oars, crudely carved and rather too short for the boat. Nor were there proper rowlocks fitted, each oar merely wedged between two stout wooden pegs. Their progress was erratic at first, requiring constant adjustment on one oar or the other, but the channel was a quarter of a mile long, giving Rawlins sufficient time to master the oars and directing the boat.

The channel eventually opened out into an extensive lagoon, where the barge lay moored at the edge of the reeds. Pulling alongside, Rawlins tied the skiff to a cleat beside a short boarding ladder and clambered aboard. There was a cramped deck at what had been the stern of the barge, with steps down a companionway to a locked door. But Rawlins went to the far side of the barge where it pressed against the reeds, bent down and searched for a key he remembered hung from a string beside a fender. It was not there.

'They've moved the key,' announced Rawlins in frustration, only half to Mrs Kingsley. She did not reply, waiting in the skiff as he worked his way along the barge side until, with a low exclamation of success, he retrieved a key. Returning to the companionway, he unlocked and opened the door before turning back to retrieve Mrs Kingsley. Perhaps glad to escape the skiff, she needed little assistance to climb onto the barge.

They explored the interior together, although Mrs Kingsley's survey was far more cursory. It was surprisingly square and spacious, a reflection of the barge's original purpose, even Rawlins having sufficient headroom. Being adapted by men of means used to comfort, it was hardly surprising that it had been well fitted out. The galley contained a small, oil-fuelled stove and a search of the fitted cupboards revealed a limited selection of food, both tins and packets, plus various utensils. A substantial table and six chairs abutted the galley, with more comfy bench seats fitted against the barge sides. A washroom and separate toilet lay beyond the living area, while the sleeping quarters were in the bow section, four bunks divided off by wooden panels. A large, triangular-shaped bed had been built right into the prow.

His exploration concluded, Rawlins offered his opinion. 'I think this should serve our purpose well.'

Mrs Kingsley was less impressed. 'How long will we be here?'

Rawlins considered for a moment. 'I don't know, but I can't see it being less than two or three days, perhaps more. At some stage I'll take the skiff to the main river and see whether any traffic has resumed. That will be our most reliable guide.' One glance at her face was enough. 'Look, I know it's not what you're used to but at least we are under cover, have food and drink, washing and toilet facilities, and running water, even if it is pumped up from the lagoon. And we are safe. Try and be grateful for small mercies.'

Ignoring this entreaty, she changed the subject. 'When are we going to eat? I'm hungry, thirsty, dirty and tired.'

'Quite so,' agreed Rawlins, suppressing a flicker of annoyance. 'Why don't you have a wash and brush up while I prepare something to eat? It will be cold, I'm afraid, although we may be able to boil water over a lamp to make tea. I don't want to use the stove until after dark; the smoke will give us away.'

Mrs Kingsley took up his offer, returning some time later noticeably refreshed but no more communicative.

After a makeshift meal, Rawlins suggested they both rest, she in the spacious prow bed, he in one of the bunks, a suggestion she immediately adopted. And so they established a form of domestic routine, even if relations remained strained on her part.

Despite his exertions, Rawlins could not sleep. He lay awake on the bunk for a while, then, finding inactivity uncongenial, went up onto the cramped deck where he tried to settle. But the sun was still hot, so he undressed, climbed down to the water and, with the exception of his jacket, rinsed out his clothes. Having laid them out in the sun to dry, he returned to the water and embarked on a leisurely exploratory swim. The water was not deep; close to the reeds shallow enough to make swimming difficult. He swam further out where it proved deeper, although he could still touch the muddy bottom in places. Tiring of swimming, Rawlins tried floating but this was not a skill he had ever mastered, and failed again now. Adopting an economical life-saving stroke, he drifted around the lagoon long enough that he hoped his clothes had dried. Striking out for the barge, he was half way back when he noticed Mrs Kingsley watching him from one of the portholes.

Mrs Kingsley had woken, made her way to the galley for a drink, and found herself alone. Where was he? Curiosity sent her to check on the skiff, when she found his clothes laid out around the deck. Looking across the lagoon, it was a moment or two before she picked out his nearly-submerged figure in the distant rippled surface. She watched for a while, then returned below, not wanting to be seen taking an interest. What was she to make of this man? He was not a brute, yet she was subject to coercion. He was sometimes considerate, but occasionally harsh.

He was her saviour, yet demanded an intolerable reward. It was a perfect conundrum.

She saw he was drawing back towards the barge, unhurried strokes that made little disturbance in the water. Turning away from the porthole, she thought she would try and make them both a cup of tea, having watched how Rawlins had done so earlier. It seemed a reasonable gesture under the circumstances, without implying any form of acceptance. There seemed little point in making both their lives even more miserable.

His clothes were not quite dry, but they would have to do. He dressed and, on going below, found Mrs Kingsley had made some tea. This surprised and pleased Rawlins, resigned as he had become to her taciturnity. Not that she spoke now, but at least they sat together at the table, although she avoided his eye. He tried to prompt a conversation but without success. She projected a studied neutrality, although Rawlins regarded this as something of a step forward, certainly better than outright hostility. And so it remained for the rest of the afternoon. The barge housed a selection of a dozen novels and Rawlins suggested they read, but either the book was dull or she could not concentrate, for it, too, proved a failure. She preferred to sit silent, engrossed in her own thoughts.

As the light faded into dusk, Rawlins began preparing a meal. This was not a demanding task, merely selecting which packets and tins should be opened and heated. He asked if she had any preference and if she would prefer to do the cooking honours, but these offers were declined with a shake of her head. Nor did Mrs Kingsley eat well, picking at the food in a desultory manner until abandoning it for good.

'You must eat, you have to keep your strength up.'

'I'm not hungry.'

Rawlins pondered this reply, although it took no great leap of imagination to guess the reason for her lack of appetite. He was at a loss what to say, but settled for directness. 'I understand you are apprehensive, but I would like to reassure you...'

'You cannot reassure me,' she interrupted, 'I have known no man other than my husband. Nothing you can say will give me the slightest reassurance.'

'Perhaps not, but I'm going to tell you anyway.' Rawlins, whose will had been wavering, suddenly found his determination renewed. 'Look, it will be dark, you can remain clothed and I promise you there will be no pain, rather the opposite. It will be far from a fate worse than death. No-one will ever know and your reputation will remain unblemished.'

Mrs Kingsley made no reply. In truth, she had come to the conclusion that the uncertainty of waiting was as bad or worse than the imagined event. She made herself look him in the face. 'I want to get it over with,' she announced, hearing the words with a sense of being spoken by someone else.

Rawlins met her look, and held it for some moments. 'Very well. Take a lamp, do whatever you feel you have to do, then extinguish the lamp when you are ready. I will take that as your signal.'

Rawlins kept his word. Mindful of her apprehension, he was slow and gentle in foreplay, displaying a range of techniques taught him by the best of the town's ladies of pleasure. He had been an adept student, always willing to fulfil his partner's desires. Certainly, Mrs Kingsley had never experienced anything like it before. And if she had wished it soon over, she was mistaken, for Rawlins would not finish until he felt her begin to move involuntarily. Neither spoke when he left soon afterwards.

The next morning Rawlins waited until Mrs Kingsley appeared before preparing tea and a makeshift breakfast. She remained quiet, only responding to his greeting and enquiries about food and drink, although that may have been instinctive politeness. After they had eaten, she a little more wholeheartedly, Rawlins went aloft, climbed onto the barge roof and looked towards the town. A pall of smoke was still the dominant feature but, although the conflagration seemed widespread, it seemed reduced in volume from yesterday. He reported as much to Mrs Kingsley, who made no comment.

There being little prospect of conversation, Rawlins fetched a notebook and pencil from his jacket pocket. Opening the notebook, he laid it on the table and began writing. When it went beyond one page, then a second and on to a third, Mrs Kingsley found her curiosity piqued.

'What are you writing?'

'This is my version of your great adventure: how you escaped the mob and survived to tell the tale.' Rawlins gave a sardonic smile. 'Don't look so aghast. It will appear the day after your return and will be so absurdly exaggerated that no-one will give it the slightest credence. It will be a perfect example of a story entirely concocted from rumours and half-truths, for which I am so well known. You will be famous, at least for a few days.'

'I don't want to be famous. I want to forget this whole sordid business as soon as possible.'

'You don't have any choice,' responded Rawlins, his voice suddenly urgent. 'Don't you see? Whatever the explanation for your survival, it's going to be a big story among your people, even country-wide I wouldn't be surprised. I can see the headline now: "Plucky Englishwoman survives Insurrection". You cannot avoid that sort of exposure, and you must be ready for it.'

Her mood switched from anger to anxiety. 'But how will I know what to say, to make them believe me.'

'You stick as closely as possible to the truth.' He was quite confident now, projecting certainty. 'You leave the house when you hear the looters coming, but have the presence of mind to take food and drink. You go into the scrub to hide but come across a track, which you follow. You find the skiff and bail it out with your bare hands, because your husband has told you about the floating shooting lodge somewhere out in the marsh. You row out, find it – you can hardly miss it, really – struggle to find a key but succeed in the end. Everything else falls into place from there, working out how to use the stove, the lamps etcetera. In other words, it is exactly what you have experienced bar any mention of Rawlins the journalist.'

Mrs Kingsley raised her hands to her face. 'Who will believe I was capable of all that?'

'Everyone,' said Rawlins, with conviction. 'They will be only too pleased to have a good news story after the shambles of the riot. You will be a heroine, whether you like it or not. If you want to avoid reporters, be taken to the hospital to recover from your ordeal.'

She shook her head, struggling to believe. 'You make it sound so easy.'

'I don't say it's easy, Isobel; but I do say it's straightforward.' It was the first time he had used her first name. 'Listen to me; you are a capable, competent woman. Why do you think I admire you so? You just have to believe in yourself and you will be fine.'

Isobel Kingsley studied his confident face, wanting to believe. In addition, she was disquieted by an awareness that her feelings toward him had become more ambivalent. Shrugging this aside, she asked, 'When will we leave here?'

'When I judge it's safe. The smoke is fair indicator, and it seems to be diminishing. Perhaps tomorrow I'll row to the river and see if there is any traffic.' He smiled at her, a charming, gentle smile which took her by surprise. Even more surprising, he added, 'Don't worry, your ordeal will soon be over,' before resuming his writing.

After lunch, his article largely finished, Rawlins was ready for another swim. Mrs Kingsley being still reticent, he asked whether she would care to join him, although this was more in hope than expectation. She did not immediately answer, which prompted him to add she would feel all the better for it. To his great surprise she agreed, although with conditions. Rawlins was to go in first and swim well away from the barge. She would follow, rinse out some of her clothes as Rawlins had done, and lay them out to dry. As for swimming, she would but intended to remain close to the barge, being not such a good swimmer. Or out of modesty, Rawlins thought.

She was as good as her word, keeping close to the barge, although for so long that Rawlins began to tire of circling around aimlessly at a distance and eventually began to draw in. Very quickly she was back on the barge. On coming aboard, he found her wrapped in a blanket, beginning to make tea. They sat at the table to drink it, she shrouded from head to toe in the blanket, although Rawlins noticed she seemed more relaxed. It had an unsettling effect on him which, after a while, he found difficult to bear.

'Talk to me, Isobel, or I shall go mad.'

'What about?' Her expression gave nothing away.

'Tell me about your childhood, like you did in the church.'

'Why would you want to hear that again? You've heard it once, it's nothing out of the ordinary.' She seemed genuinely puzzled.

'I just want to hear your voice, transporting us to a different world. Where there are no problems or difficulties, or dangers, come to that. It would make me happy, just as I was in the church.'

'Hmm, it's not quite same, is it, under these circumstances.' For the first time since Rawlins had found her at the house, she managed a ghostly smile, devoid of amusement. 'But since you ask, I will talk to you. I can tell of my life here, the crushing, stifling boredom of being a planter's wife. Nothing to do, thanks to servants, no expectation to do even a simple manual task like making a cup of tea – you can't imagine what relief I've gained just from making tea here. My children were brought up by another woman, and now even they have gone. I shouldn't have let it happen but, somehow...' Isobel Kingsley shrugged her blanket-draped shoulders. 'It was so easy to fall into those habits, guided by the behaviour of others, and judged by them. For years I've watched myself slowly become idle, dispirited and ill-tempered; an ugly person, whom I despise.'

Startled, and a little dismayed, at this sudden litany of despair, Rawlins was uncertain how to respond. 'Surely it would be better to talk about happier times, your upbringing in Hampshire, for example?'

She looked at him, curious at his interest. 'Yes, it was a happy childhood, adolescence not so much, early adulthood even less. I was the fourth of four girls, the last before my one brother appeared, the longed-for heir to the farm, a spoilt favourite. We girls were expected to marry, the sooner the better, but I once overheard my mother say I was the plainest of four and could be difficult to match.'

'Your mother had no eye for beauty, that's for sure,' muttered Rawlins, scowling.

'No, she was right – you are the one with a strange conception of beauty - but I wish I had not heard that truth.' She paused for a moment, wondering whether she should be so frank, but already feeling better for it. 'So, you can see what incentive there was when Mr Kingsley was introduced. I was nineteen, he a few years older but the third boy of another farming family. We were each a liability: he, the heir to nothing, me, the cost of a dowry. His father advised seeking a fortune abroad, and encouraged it with some money. And, credit to my husband, he has been shrewd in business, remarkably successful. But such application comes at a cost, not least in the common humanities.'

Rawlins felt impelled to ask, 'But you must have made some friends here over time, someone to share confidences with?'

'Yes, Charlotte Hungerford was a particular friend, but they left two years ago and no-one has taken her place. Perhaps that was the start of my troubles.'

This dour note ended their conversation, she suddenly subdued and preferring to read. Rawlins went up on deck, rearranged her still-damp clothes to catch the dipping sun, and then settled to watch nothing in particular except a distant raft of waterfowl. He thought about the unhappy Isobel Kingsley, and that the smoke over the town had reduced almost to nothing.

Rawlins went to her again that night. She could have objected, arguing that her word had been kept and that she was now exempt, and he might well have been persuaded. But she did not object, and could not explain why, even to herself.

The next morning there was no smoke visible over the town. After breakfast, Rawlins took the skiff and rowed beyond the lagoon along a broad channel which opened out to the river. He was increasingly cautious as he neared the open water, tucking in among the thin marginal reeds and punting the skiff along like a gondola. When he had an adequate view across the broad, sluggish waterway, he pushed in among the thicker reeds, squatted down in the skiff, and waited. More than an hour passed before anything appeared, a native fishing boat with two occupants and a net draped across the stern. Another half hour elapsed before he saw another. When that moved out of view, Rawlins returned to the barge.

He secured the skiff and climbed aboard, where he found Mrs Kingsley looking at him questioningly. 'Two fishing boats, so it's possible things might be stabilising.' She nodded in acknowledgment, looking thoughtful. Rawlins wondered if she would insist on their immediate return, but no such request materialised. At least, not yet.

Mrs Kingsley prepared their basic lunch, after which they swam again, she noticeably less concerned about his proximity. When they had swum enough, she climbed aboard first and went below to dry herself. Rawlins stayed on the deck and dried in the sun until she called out that a cup of tea was waiting. He didn't want to go below but, to his surprise, she joined him. They sat a little apart, their legs dangling over the side of the barge, as though they were holidaymakers. Neither spoke, each looking across the lagoon to where the endless reeds stirred gently in the languid breeze. It was as if coming out of a reverie that Mrs Kingsley eventually broke the silence.

'When do you think we should leave?' Her voice was little more than a murmur.

Rawlins considered for a while. 'I imagine the Army has arrived by now, even if the telegraph wires were cut at the outset. That alone would be enough to prompt a reconnaissance party. The smoke would have told them all they needed to know.' He looked at her. 'I suppose we have to assume it's safe to return.'

'Yes, that seems to make sense.' She sounded a little distracted. 'How will you go about it? I'm assuming we can't be seen together.'

'Most definitely not.' Rawlins set himself to reveal his master-plan. 'I have in mind to leave here tomorrow morning while it's still dark - still night, really – and row downriver to a disused landing stage. It was meant for unloading building materials but the development never took place. It's out of the way, unseen from the river but close to the town. I shall leave you then, but you should wait there in the skiff, out of sight until at least midday. You must give me time to get home, which might be tricky if there's a curfew. I have to shave off this stubble, change and then put myself where other people are bound to see me. If they ask where I've been, I'll say I've been following the story from a safe distance. At least two or three hours must pass before you row down to the main quay. After that, I will simply be another reporter anxious to hear your amazing story.' He checked and looked at her. 'But I shan't ask for an interview, or anything that might bring us face-to-face.'

She stared into the water. 'I don't know that I can do it. You make it all sound so plausible, but I don't even know if I can row.'

'Of course you can – look at me, Isobel – I'll show you how to row, and you must practise until your hands are tender. It will help if you have blisters when you return, good background detail for your story.'

'No wonder you are a journalist.' She looked up at the heavens. 'I don't know...'

'You do know, Isobel; you know you can't stay here. You will have been missing for three and a half days. You just have to say you waited for the smoke to disappear before venturing back, which sounds perfectly reasonable to me, since you were sheltering here on the barge. Tell the truth; simply edit out any mention of Rawlins the journalist.'

She looked at him, resigned to the inevitable. 'I suppose I really have no choice.'

For the rest of the afternoon, Rawlins showed Isobel Kingsley how to row. She practised with endless circuits of the lagoon until they were both sure she could manage on her own. It also made her hands tender, although she insisted on making their meal. In the evening she tried to read, while Rawlins checked every inch of the barge for any evidence of dual occupation. He remade the bunk-bed as he found it and disposed of more than half of the empty tins and packets by throwing them deep them into the reeds. Her bedding received particular scrutiny; it was the one place where there could be incontrovertible evidence of co-habitation: he found nothing.

When he had finished, he returned to the galley and began to read. Mrs Kingsley, struggling to concentrate on her own book, studied Rawlins from under her lowered brow. She was acutely aware an extraordinary episode in her life was drawing to a close and another, perhaps equally challenging, was soon to begin.

'You have never spoken about yourself.'

Rawlins looked up, surprised at her intervention. 'You've never asked.'

'I'm asking now.' She sounded strangely determined.

'What would you like to know? Would you like to hear how a cabal of planters tried to get me dismissed? They didn't like my reporting of conditions on some of the plantations.'

'No, I didn't know that.'

'The proprietor would have seen me go, but my editor prevailed. I've no idea whether your husband was one of the cabal but, since I'm still gainfully employed, it really doesn't matter. But I would like to move on from this reporting backwater; I do have ambitions.'

And so their conversation continued, Mrs Kingsley endlessly curious and Rawlins willing to fulfil her curiosity, such a world away from her own experience. They talked for a long while, just as they had in the church, and just as easily until, soon after nine-o'-clock, Rawlins suggested it would be advisable to try and get some sleep, as they would have to be up by four in the morning. Mrs Kingsley took his advice and retired.

When he saw her lamp was out, Rawlins went to her again. She exhibited no surprise, nor did she seem much discomfited. He took her light cotton coat and made her lie on it. For the first time he undressed her, to which she made no objection. Then Rawlins made love to Isobel Kingsley just as he had previously, with tenderness and care until she responded in kind. Then more urgently, both understanding this was the last time. When it was finished, they lay side by side, Rawlins finally falling asleep. Mrs Kingsley did not sleep, her own thoughts revolving around her conviction that she would never experience anything like it again.

Rawlins woke when it was still inky dark outside. Beside him Mrs Kingsley lay unmoving, asleep at last. He groped his way to the galley, lit a lamp and checked the time on his pocket-watch; a little after three-o'-clock. Opening the door to the companionway, the night bore down on him, starlit except where a few light clouds drifted on the faint breeze. There was no moon. Returning to the galley, he laid out their over-familiar breakfast and began the slow process of boiling water for tea. Before it was ready, Mrs Kingsley appeared, dressed but with her hair untidy. When she saw her reflection, she grimaced and began putting it right. Neither felt the necessity to speak.

Soon after four-o'-clock, when both had checked yet again for any ill-left signs, they climbed the companionway, returned the key to its hiding place and edged down into the skiff. Rawlins rowed at first, feeling his way beyond the lagoon in picturesque but feeble starlight. Beyond the lagoon Mrs Kingsley took over, which slowed their progress but reassured them that she would manage when alone. She continued rowing when they reached the river, while Rawlins acted as coxswain, with frequent instructions to correct their course.

By now, a faint band of pre-dawn light was visible in the

east, so that the reed margin became increasingly defined. Rawlins, anxious not to miss the narrow channel entrance to the landing stage, at one point halted briefly against the reeds until the light gained a little. Aided by the current, Mrs Kingsley's occasionally erratic rowing kept them moving, until Rawlins suddenly pointed and whispered urgently, 'There it is'. A decrepit sign, almost hidden in the reeds, announced the existence of the landing stage in sun-faded capital letters, a painted arrow pointing into the cut.

Carried by the current, they missed the channel entrance, and Rawlins had to take over to pull them back against the flow. Once in the channel, rowing was hindered by thin patches of reeds, slowly reclaiming man's temporary excavation. The wooden landing stage emerged from the gloom, skeletal in its stark outline. He nudged the skiff alongside until it bumped into a piled support, Rawlins urging Mrs Kingsley to hold them fast while he tied up. That done, he settled back on his seat, somehow reluctant to look at her. It was a few moments before he spoke.

'I must go. It will take me at least an hour to get home, and I want to do it in what's left of the night. I can skirt much of the housing but, even so, the street-sweepers will be about, assuming all is quiet. But no Europeans, even if the Army is in charge.' He changed tack. 'Will you be all right here on your own? You have some food and drink, and I see you've brought a book. Fine, but best dispose of the book in the reeds before you leave this cut. Otherwise, it may look as though this has been a bit of a jaunt.'

'Yes, I will do as you suggest.'

'Right, I must go,' he repeated, but it was obvious he was reluctant to leave.

'May I ask you something?' She was very solemn.

'Yes, if it's quick.'

'How did you happen to come by my house at the very start of the trouble?' It was a question she had considered often, but not articulated until now.

Rawlins looked at her, a shade uneasily. 'I saw one of your servants – I won't say which – who told me you were there, alone.'

'So you came to rescue me.'

He nodded. 'Yes; I had a job crossing the bridge, the looters were already heading for the rich pickings of your Avenue. I only got through because I speak the language and some of them know me.'

'And did you always expect to attach conditions to this rescue?' She seemed more curious than angry.

'Please don't expect me to answer that' He hesitated, then felt impelled to add, 'We've survived the riot, haven't we? Come through with scarcely a scratch – while I'm sure others have not. Can't we part now without acrimony?'

When she failed to answer, Rawlins clambered out of the skiff onto the jetty. He turned to speak and found her upturned face looking at him. It was impossible to judge her mood in the ghostly light. He thought she looked beautiful.

'Don't forget what I've told you; keep the story simple, the truth but without Rawlins. And you know where you're going? The town quay is hardly ten minutes away, once you get back in the current. There will be plenty of people about by then; you won't be swept out to sea.'

'I hope not. I should have plenty of blisters by then, too.' It was the first time she had made a joke, if such it was. But it sounded like a joke.

'Goodbye, Isobel. And remember to live your life.'

Without waiting to see if she replied, he turned and set off, his footsteps muffled on the damp boards. At the end of the jetty he stopped, a dark figure hardly discernible against a darker background. But she heard him distinctly enough, although it was hardly more than a murmur.

'I wish we could have stayed on the barge.'

Isobel Kingsley did not trust herself to reply, and then he was gone.

Having dismounted from the train, Rawlins made his way along the platform and handed his ticket to the collector. Waterloo station was not overly crowded for the middle of a Wednesday afternoon and, being in no particular hurry, he was sauntering absent-mindedly through the concourse when he heard a voice.

'Mr Rawlins, I believe.'

He stopped but did not immediately turn to the speaker, although he recognised the voice. 'Mrs Kingsley, I'm sure,' he replied, and then did turn to look. She was changed, but not greatly. A little fuller in the face, lighter hair than he remembered, perhaps due to a few strands of grey. Still effortlessly poised, and retaining that obscure beauty which had so captivated him.

'You have a good memory for voices, Mr Rawlins.'

'Yours is not a voice I am likely to forget, Mrs Kingsley, or would want to.'

She gave a thin smile at this, although Rawlins thought the Mona Lisa could hardly have been more enigmatic. 'I saw you and wondered whether to...' She hesitated, before suddenly continuing, 'Do you have time for some refreshments?'

'Why, yes, of course. I'm just returned on the train, so... it would be a pleasure.'

Once seated in the cafeteria, neither seemed anxious to be first to resume conversation until Mrs Kingsley made the effort. 'I see your name in the paper quite often, "Our Special Correspondent". Quite the successful journalist.'

'Yes, I have been fortunate. I went to South Africa at the outbreak of the war, wrote some articles and sent them to various editors as a speculation. It was successful, and now it seems I have become the fount of all knowledge for everything east of Suez, yet it's some years since I was out there. It's rather absurd, but who am I to complain?' He checked, studying his companion. 'But you, Mrs Kingsley, please tell me of yourself. You look wonderfully well; please tell me that you are.'

She smiled again, more naturally this time. 'I am well, and with every reason to be, for I am recently a grandmother, a baby girl to my daughter. They live only six miles away; I drive myself there in the trap.'

'Excellent,' exclaimed Rawlins, delighted. But he continued in a more serious vein. 'I was sorry to read about your son.'

'Yes, a tragedy, but he would insist on an adventure. None of them were ever found, nor the boat, although some wreckage was thought might be theirs. The sea is a dangerous place, Mr Rawlins.'

'Yes.' Rawlins ruminated on this self-evident truth for a moment. 'And your husband?' he added, hoping to lift the mood.

'He is quite well, although occasionally ill with recurrent malaria. We bought a house in Hampshire, near where I was brought up. We also have a house here in London; he stays there frequently for business purposes. I do not, being more at home in the country, and near my daughter. I spend a good deal of time on charitable works, and the resulting friendships.'

Rawlins smiled his pleasure but was not inclined to probe further, so Mrs Kingsley continued. 'And you, Mr Rawlins, are you back here permanently?'

'Yes, my roaming days finished after South Africa; I've seen enough for a lifetime. Now I have a wife – better late than never - and two children, with another on the way.' His hands were clasped together on the table as if in prayer, or nervousness. 'Living abroad, all that travel, some unwholesome climates; somehow it already seems like another life. Family has proved a better substitute.'

'I'm pleased to hear it. Marriage must suit you well; you've lost that lean and hungry look.'

'I can't deny I've put on a pound or two; I find my wife's cooking very difficult to resist.'

'Yes,' responded Mrs Kingsley, 'I remember you as a man with a strong appetite.'

This remark, delivered so innocuously, rendered Rawlins silent. He searched her face for any other meaning, detecting nothing. But Mrs Kingsley was a mistress of self-control, as he well knew, and as she now made plain.

'Do you ever think back to those days, to that time when circumstances threw us together?'

Rawlins tried not to flinch from her steady gaze. 'Yes, nearly every day.'

'Really? Even after twelve years?" Her expression became quizzical. 'I would have thought you were far too busy for such introspection.'

'No, I can assure you it is the truth. How could I forget? It left an indelible mark upon me, and I am sure on you, too. I often wonder how you are, whether you were able to shake off that great depression. You seem content now, but to hear that you have really found true happiness would go down very well with me.'

She made as if his statement went unheard. After a short silence she began again, very quietly. 'I think of that time quite often. My husband was the only one who found my supposed adventure impossible to believe. In the months afterwards he questioned me again and again about what happened, and was never convinced. He knew me too well, or thought he did. But it was cathartic for me: suddenly I found the strength to say I was going home, and he could stay or follow. The children were at school in England, my family was there, and that was where I wanted to be. He did follow eventually, but it took three years.'

'Some good did come of it, then,' ventured Rawlins, unsure of her reaction.

'Yes, you could say it was my salvation for, as you determined, I was very unhappy out there.' Mrs Kingsley looked at him frankly. 'Don't think that excuses your behaviour, which was unforgivable. But I am reconciled with it. That is why I spoke to you.'

'Thank you,' said Rawlins, like a man receiving absolution. 'Thank you. It is some comfort to hear that, although I cannot but agree with your sentiment. It was a strange time, and I was a man obsessed. But I am truly sorry for what I did, although words can never put it right.'

'Nonetheless, I'm pleased to hear them.' Mrs Kingsley had not taken her eyes from his, assessing his sincerity. 'But don't be too critical of yourself. You were also kind to me, kinder than you perhaps realise. I desperately needed a friend at that time, but circumstances could never have allowed it to be you.' In the ensuing silence she glanced up at the cafeteria clock. 'My train leaves in a few minutes; I must be going.'

Rawlins nodded in acknowledgment, not knowing how to take his leave. They both stood, Mrs Kingsley picking up her bag before making for the cafeteria door. Rawlins followed her outside, where both paused.

'Goodbye Mr Rawlins, it's been interesting meeting you again.' Her smile conveyed satisfaction rather than cordiality.

'May I walk you to the barrier?' It was suddenly important to him.

'Thank you, but that won't be necessary.' After a swift, enigmatic glance at his face, she turned and began the walk to her platform.

'Isobel, wait!'

She stopped. 'You must not call me that.'

'Too late, I already have.' Rawlins, a man dependent on words, struggled to find the right ones. Failing, he could only say, 'I will never forget you.'

'Goodbye, Mr Rawlins.'

He watched her walk to the barrier and beyond, until the carriages hid Isobel Kingsley from view.

Attending a writers' retreat, our mentor devised an exercise which required each of us seven 'students' to contribute a single element of a plot-line to include two named people (one a foreign national), jobs for each, a location, a mystery object and a drama. Time did not allow for actual writing but, wanting to see this through to completion, I later wrote ...

Brief Encounter (in Garsdale)

EDGAR GAVE A brief wave as his brother-in-law's car departed. Hardly waiting for the car to disappear, he crossed the minuscule car-park and walked up the incline to Garsdale station platform. He was not surprised to see just one other passenger waiting. In fact, he felt two waiting passengers would have constituted a crowd, for Garsdale is a scattered hamlet set deep in the Cumbrian hills. The fact that it had a station made him smile, for Edgar was a train driver used to more populated routes.

Edgar's fellow passenger was a woman, observed surreptitiously from under his brow. From her profile, Edgar could see she was not young but a mature attractiveness was present. She had not made use of the bench seat or the waiting room, evidently preferring to stand on the exposed platform and brave the brisk wind that was chasing cloud shadows across the dappled hills. A wheeled suitcase waited patiently by her side.

A gust of wind caught Edgar, causing him to turn his head away. But the damage was done, for his right eye was suddenly painful. For perhaps a minute, he conducted a series of rapid blinks, squints and other facial contortions to try and eject the foreign body. He could hardly see through the flood of automatic tears, so he missed her approach.

'Are you all right?' enquired a quiet but confident voice.

'Yes, I think so. It's just something in my eye, thanks to this wind. I'll probably live.'

'You seem to be struggling. Would you like me to have a look? I am a nurse; I'm used to dealing with such emergencies.'

With difficulty, Edgar focussed on her luminous blue eyes. 'Well, if you don't mind. It is a bit uncomfortable.'

She lived up to her calling, the offending particle nudged to the corner of his eye and then deftly removed.

'Ah, that feels better,' said Edgar, still blinking but trying to do so in a manly fashion. 'Thank you. Is there a charge for your services?'

'Not today. Another time perhaps, if you make a habit of it.'

'In that case, would you care to massage my calf muscles? I was climbing in the hills yesterday and they feel really tight.' Sometimes Edgar overcame his natural reticence in pursuit of humour.

'I'm sorry to tell you I am not paid enough to be a mobile NHS clinic, particularly on self-inflicted injuries. I'm afraid you will just have to suffer.'

'Oh, that's a shame,' grinned Edgar. 'Whatever happened to the Hippocratic oath?'

She gave a wry smile. 'I'm beginning to think that piece of grit has done more damage than I suspected.'

Edgar returned her smile. 'I doubt my brain can be scrambled much more.'

Silence fell between them, although Edgar was pleased that she did not immediately move away. 'If you don't mind me asking, what brings you to Garsdale? It's hardly a conventional tourist centre.'

She hesitated before answering, choosing her words carefully. 'It has been a holiday, although a little unconventional. I have been to a writers' retreat. It's just down the way, but you can't see it from here.'

'A writers' retreat,' replied a surprised Edgar. 'Well, that sounds fascinating. So should I presume you are a writer?'

'An aspiring writer,' she corrected. 'I have written some bits and pieces but I wouldn't dream of calling myself a writer. But I've learnt a lot and come away determined to carry on writing, and to do it better. Just as important, I've made some new friends.'

'Well, that's a bonus in itself,' said Edgar, still absorbing the retreat concept. 'My name's Edgar, by the way.'

She looked at him closely before replying, as though considering the wisdom of this burgeoning relationship. 'I'm Jessie.'

'Well, Jessie, if you've a mind, please tell me more about your writers' retreat. And what sort of writing you do.'

'Very well, although you may regret asking. But, before that, will you help clear up a mystery for me?'

'Yes, of course, if I can. What sort of mystery is it?'

'It's over here,' said Jessie, leading the way back to where her wheeled suitcase still waited. 'There,' she said, pointing to the tracks, 'what is that?'

Edgar peered down, a puzzled frown creasing his brow, quickly turning to incredulity. 'D'you know, it looks like a golf ball.'

'I thought so.' Jessie pulled a face and drew back from the platform edge.

'Oh, dear; don't you like golf?'

'No, I loathe it. It was the cause of my divorce. I was a golf widow to my ex-husband's obsession and now I go queasy at the very sight of those hideous white balls.'

'I see,' ventured Edgar cautiously, uncertain whether her dislike was being exaggerated for comic effect. On balance, he was inclined to think not.

'Are you a golfer, Edgar?'

Edgar pondered this ominous question, acutely aware his answer might be crucial. 'Well, I have been known to play a round or two. But only at a friend's invitation,' he added quickly, as he saw Jessie's face darken. 'I'm not a regular by any means. A good walk ruined, as Mark Twain said.'

Perhaps it was this literary reference that saved Edgar, for Jessie's face immediately softened. 'Ah, Mark Twain. Now, there is a writer. Have you read "Huckleberry Finn?"'

'No, but I love Huckleberry Hound cartoons. If you say it's as good as them, I'll certainly give it a read.'

Jessie gave him a penetrating look. 'Is that one of your peculiar British jokes, Edgar?'

'Well. I'm not sure it's peculiarly British, but I like to believe it was a joke. If it's in doubtful taste, it probably is British.' Edgar could not restrain another smile. 'I have detected a faint accent, Jessie, so please enlighten me before I drop any more clangers.'

'I'm Icelandic, although I've lived in Britain much of my life. We have our own humour, usually featuring volcanoes and apocalyptic events. Perhaps we're not so different after all.'

Edgar nodded his agreement, but he had been struck by a sudden urge. 'I know I shouldn't, but I've a mind to fetch that mystery white thing, just to see what it is.'

'No, you shouldn't, Edgar. The train is due any minute and we're not allowed on the tracks. There are notices everywhere saying so, and you will be fined, quite a lot, actually.'

'I'm a train driver, Jessie; I'll get away with it. Treated with respect, trains are perfectly safe. Besides, I'm curious to see what it is. If it is a golf ball, it must be the longest mis-hit in human history.'

'No, don't do it, Edgar.'

But, after a swift glance to left and right, Edgar was already lowering himself over the platform edge. He scrambled across the rails and granite chippings, picked up the golf ball – it was a Maxply; very good quality - and set off on the return. But Edgar was no longer young and had never been athletic, so it may have been this debilitating combination that caused his fall. Nor was it a graceful fall, more akin to a sack of potatoes falling off a lorry. Then, to Jessie's mounting horror, Edgar seemed content to lie unmoving across the rails for some considerable time.

'Edgar! For God's sake, Edgar, are you all right? Can't you move?'

Grimacing, Edgar looked up to see the attractive Icelandic nurse hovering anxiously above him. 'I'll live, Jessie, although I wish you hadn't seen that. What a pratt!' He struggled to his feet and, with Jessie's assistance, hauled himself back over the platform edge. Standing unsteadily, Edgar began rubbing his bruised knees.

'What an idiot,' exclaimed Jessie, equally furious and frightened at his stupidity. 'And you've torn your trousers. My God, here comes the train, too. You stupid man; you could have been killed.' She turned from Edgar to seize her suitcase. 'Come on, I'll help you on the train and then see what damage has been done.'

'Thank you, Jessie, you really are an angel of mercy. Florence Nightingale would be proud.'

'Yes, I'm sure I deserve a medal.'

With the present-day nurse firmly grasping his arm, Edgar hobbled painfully towards the carriage. 'After you've sorted my knees, Jessie, you might as well massage my calves while you're down there.'

Jessie's reply was lost between a fresh gust of wind and the closing carriage doors.

Beyond a Joke

THE SYNDICATE HAD jogged along happily for several years. A small group, their common interest was shooting but the social side was equally important, the six members enjoying both giving and taking the inevitable banter during their sporting day. Character traits were a popular subject for humour, as well as shooting ability or their luck during a drive. William, who had been privately educated, suffered on multiple fronts, as he was not a very good shot and any gamebird hit was deemed particularly unlucky. But William took it in good part, as did they all when they became targets in their turn.

So the reluctant resignation of Terry – he was moving away - caused a frisson of concern among those remaining, for they did not control who might replace him. Their landlord-cum-shoot manager had the final choice, and they knew he had a candidate in mind. And that is how Greg arrived at the beginning of the new season, an unknown quantity but who the established members were more than willing to welcome into the syndicate fold. Indeed, all went well at first, Greg proving affable and keen to fit in, asking numerous questions about the backgrounds of his fellow Guns and joining in the general conversation with forceful gusto. But perhaps that forceful gusto was a warning shot, if you'll excuse the metaphor.

There were eight shoots during the season which, at the end of the day, were always celebrated with tea or coffee and a slice of cake in the 'gunroom'. Since this was a roughly-converted former stable, facilities were adequate rather than luxurious, although an infra-red heater provided some warmth in cold weather. Here the day was conversationally dissected and the bag discussed, along with numerous other unrelated topics. After half an hour or so, the syndicate members would begin to leave for home and, since Greg lived furthest away, he was usually one of the first to leave. It was after Greg's departure at the end of the third shoot that William first voiced a concern. Somewhat diffidently – as befits a privately educated man – he mentioned to Ken that the newcomer seemed to have quite a lot to say. Ken agreed, and said that one or two of the others had already expressed the same view. Nothing more was said at the time, but it seemed something of a minor cloud now hung over the syndicate.

As the shoots passed, this amorphous, distant cloud steadily developed into a dark, towering cumulonimbus. Pursuing the analogy, what might be described as the sound of thunder rumbled discontentedly in the background, growing gradually louder as if heralding an approaching storm. Only Greg, the proximate cause, remained blithely ignorant of this unrest although, had he been more perceptive, there were subtle clues in the reactions of his fellow Guns. However, Greg was not subtle and his conversation had developed beyond loud into deafening, and with added questionable humour. John, whose surname was Wilde, became 'Oscar', with the nudges and winks often associated with the playwright's sexuality. Richard became 'Dick', with the obvious allusions. William was renamed 'Posh' and frequently asked to 'spice up the day'. No-one was spared, however tenuous or puerile the connection. Apparently delivered in the bantering spirit of the day, it simply grated.

By the start of the final shoot, there was a sense of desperation among the old guard. The prospect of another season with Greg – he was looking forward to it, he said – was enough to prompt Arthur and William to question their willingness to stay in the syndicate. The others were unhappy but at a loss what to do. Ken, who often acted as the syndicate's unofficial spokesperson, had mentioned their concerns to the landlord but too circumspectly to ram the point home. And it was this failure that bore down on Ken on the season's last day, shooting poorly, his mind on weightier issues than the occasional pheasant. However, during the day, he resolved upon a stratagem.

The last drive concluded and another season drawn to a close, the members repaired to the 'gunroom', where cake and coffee awaited. Seated comfortably within range of the infra-red heater, they listened to yet another punchy anecdote about Greg's successful business life. At its conclusion, Ken leaned back in his seat as if deep in contemplation. 'You know, Greg, I've been thinking. You're always keeping us amused with your jokes and stories, and I'm aware I contribute almost nothing by comparison. And it's been playing on my conscience. Although I can't hope to match your wit, I feel that I ought to make an effort and tell a joke.'

Greg grinned. 'That'll be a first, Ken; you're not the most natural comedian I've ever heard.'

'No, indeed I'm not,' agreed Ken, 'but I'm willing to give it a go, if only to salve my conscience.'

'It doesn't sound too promising,' said Greg, 'but I'm all ears.'

The other four members remained silent but keenly attentive. This was not like Ken at all, whose humorous contributions were frequent but dry and understated.

'Right, then,' continued Ken, 'here we go. This joke concerns an Irishman. We're not told his name, so I'll call him Paddy, although we shouldn't really fall back on stereotypes, not in these more enlightened days. But it is important to remember that Paddy is Irish, because it's fundamental to the joke. Anyway, Paddy has arrived in England, fresh from Ireland. We don't know why he has come, but he might well be an economic migrant, which was the cause of much Irish emigration, if you remember, particularly after the potato famine, although that's a long time ago now. But, in some ways, economic migrant would be a little surprising, since per capita income in Ireland is now pretty much on a par with the UK, if not better.'

'Could he be an IRA infiltrator?' interrupted Richard, guessing Ken would welcome some support.

'That's a good point, Richard, although the Good Friday agreement is still in force after all these years and seems to have obviated the need for any such drastic action. I can't think of any recent IRA bomb incidents over here, unless I haven't been paying attention, which would be a dereliction on my part. I imagine none of us want to confront the notion that we're too busy with our own lives not to notice a major bomb outrage. But never mind that; on the whole, I'm still inclined to believe Paddy is an economic migrant but I'll allow that he may well have Irish nationalist sympathies, although these may well have been allayed by the recent Windsor Accord.' Ken suddenly gave a puzzled frown. 'Thinking about it, I've just realised we don't know where he actually landed. It could be Liverpool, of course, which was a favoured destination in the bad old days of Irish immigration, very much reflected in the make-up of that city's demographics to this day, I believe. Or, who knows, he might simply have washed up on our shores in a small boat, although then he'd more likely be Albanian, or something.'

Ken paused to take a breath, allowing Greg to ask, 'Is there much more of this? I'm beginning to lose the will to live.'

'Oh, sorry Greg. I know I'm not the greatest joke-teller. It's just that I believe in setting the scene, as it were, for added verisimilitude.'

'Quite right,' added William, picking up on Richard's lead. 'I often find a joke considerably diminished, if not ruined, if there is inadequate background.' The other members nodded sagely.

'Well, that's heartening to hear,' said Ken, before continuing, 'anyway, let me quickly recap so that I can get back into character, as it were. Right, Paddy the Irishman has just landed in England, probably as an economic migrant and quite possibly in Liverpool. I think we've got that clear now. Anyway, Paddy is walking down the street – I'm afraid I don't know Liverpool, so I can't name any likely thoroughfares – when he comes to a building site.'

'That would probably be near the waterfront,' interjected Richard. 'They're doing a lot of redevelopment there, which has lost them World Culture status or something similar.'

'World Heritage site, actually,' corrected Arthur, as Greg's expression lapsed into a grimace. 'UNESCO has stripped Liverpool of that title, although I don't think many Liverpudlians will lose any sleep over it. I'm not sure they asked to be a World Heritage site in the first place. It was probably thrust upon them, as is the way with so many of these supra-national organisations. And don't get me started on the EU.'

'No, we won't,' was Ken's firm response, 'not if I'm to finish this joke before midnight. Although, since you mention it, I do wonder whether the Northern Irish Protocol would now affect Paddy's status. But that Protocol is an absolute minefield so, to avoid confusion, I think it's safer if we assume Paddy arrived before Brexit.'

There was a murmur of agreement from the others, except for Greg, who slumped further in his chair.

'To continue,' said Ken, frowning as if to remember where he should resume. 'Ah, yes; Paddy's walking along the street past a building site when he sees, hanging there on the security fence, a sign saying "Builders Wanted". Now, bearing in mind Paddy is probably an economic migrant, it can hardly be viewed as surprising that he thinks to himself, "I could use a spot of cash; I wonder if there's a job for me". Oh, by the way – just coming out of character again – I'm afraid I don't do an Irish accent. I've given up trying. It just wanders off into some sort of previously unknown mumbo-jumbo dialect which only detracts from the joke. I can do a passable Welsh, or English with a hint of Scots, but Irish eludes me. It's a shame but there you are: you'll just have to imagine.'

'You did Indian once, I remember,' offered Arthur, 'that wasn't too bad.'

'Did I? Well, thanks for that, Arthur, but a touch of Hindi won't sit too well with an Irishman, will it? Not this Paddy anyway, although I think the Irish are much more cosmopolitan nowadays, since the advent of the booming Celtic Tiger economy. Which rather begs the question, why has Paddy come to England if things are going so well at home? But we'll have to ignore that for the purposes of this joke.'

'Is there actually a joke?' muttered Greg, slumping dangerously from the vertical.

'There certainly is, Greg,' responded Ken. 'Just hang in there a bit longer and all will be revealed. It's really clever, as well as very funny.'

Greg forced a smile, adding, 'I'll be the judge of that.'

'That's true, but I don't think you'll be disappointed. You may even decide to add it to your repertoire.'

''Somehow, I doubt it.'

'Well, let's wait and see, shall we? Now, where was I? Oh, yes; Paddy's walking down the street, sees the sign 'builders wanted' and thinks this might be just the job for him. So he goes into the site and asks for the foreman. The foreman's a very busy man, he's told but, not a whit discouraged, Paddy sets off to find him. He walks all over the site, asking for the foreman, who really is very busy apparently, not hiding away in some convenient corner smoking a cigarette and leching at page three of the "Sun"...'

'I don't think they do topless on page three any more,' ventured John. 'They yielded to the forces of Woke. A shame in my opinion but, in this day and age...' John's interruption petered into silence.

'Really? I didn't know that but thanks for putting me right,' said Ken with a wry laugh. 'I haven't seen a copy of the "Sun" for years, and then only to look at the cartoons, Andy Capp in particular.'

'Wasn't Andy Capp in the "Mirror"?' queried Richard.

'Was it? Well, it hardly matters because it turns out the foreman wasn't hiding away reading some tabloid; he was simply very, very busy. Anyway, Paddy eventually finds him...'

'Thank God for that!' came the heartfelt interjection from Greg.

'... and asks him for a job. Look, says the foreman, I'm a very busy man. I've no time to spend interviewing every Tom, Dick and Paddy who happens to drop by; I've got a building site to run. I'll ask you just one question. If you answer correctly, then you've got the job. Fair enough, says Paddy, fire away. Right, says the foreman, what's the difference between a joist and a girder? Oh, says Paddy, that's easy; Joyce wrote "Ulysses" and Goethe wrote "Faust"'.

A wall of laughter, deep, sonorous and apparently spontaneous, greeted the end of Ken's joke. Thighs were slapped, nudges exchanged and cries of 'well done, Ken' and 'that's a good one' echoed around the converted stable. There was only one exception; Greg, who appeared more bemused than amused.

'Do you know,' continued Ken, 'that joke has been voted "Joke of the Year" by the Erudite Society every year since the society's formation in 1786.'

'That's very prescient of them,' observed William, 'since Joyce wasn't born until 1882.'

'Brilliant,' said John, 'with pointless knowledge like that, I can see private education is worth every penny.'

And so the reverberations of Ken's joke continued to roll around the gunroom, although propelled by just five of the six men present. Unusually, Greg did not contribute, preferring to leave for home a few minutes later. The goodbyes were friendly enough, well-meaning in their expressions of 'safe journey' and 'mind how you go'. But no-one, not even Greg, said 'see you next season'. And it's possible the other members may have misjudged Greg. Maybe he was more perceptive than they realised because, for some reason – never explained - he decided not to renew his syndicate membership, perhaps believing his fellow Guns were beyond a joke.

The Mrs Choudhury Affair

PERHAPS IT WAS destiny that introduced me to Mrs Choudhury. I was at a loose end for a few days when Derek phoned, one of his team had gone sick and he had a job underway with a rather demanding customer; could I help him out? A lovely man, Derek; retirement age but says work keeps him young, persevering with his little landscape gardening business although I can see he's slowing down. Anyway, the job in hand was to install a summerhouse and an orangery as well as renewing paths and fences, and Derek was temporarily a man short. I'll be honest, it wasn't my first choice of an idle few days but, softy that I am, I couldn't say no to a friend in need. And a stint of physical labour wouldn't do me any harm, either.

Derek had boxed a bit clever when he phoned. He mentioned the customer was 'rather demanding' when he should have said 'she's a right cow'. One of his regular crew, Mick, was more forthcoming when the four of us squeezed into the pick-up the next day. When I berated Derek for being economical with the truth, a gentle smile suffused his kindly face, which reminded me why we were friends.

We arrived at a large mock-Tudor detached house, a typical suburban product of the 1930s of which Betjeman would have been proud. There was clearly no shortage of money, the new works being embellishments rather than necessities, in the nature of vanity projects. But good for Derek and his crew, this so-called trickle-down of wealth. I was just the dogsbody labourer but I didn't mind. Occasionally, it's a nice change to have someone else in charge, taking responsibility. And that meant dealing with Mrs Choudhury, who certainly made her presence felt. Her husband seemed to work from home but was rarely seen, which left Mrs Choudhury to oversee progress, and often it wasn't quite to her satisfaction. She was a right pain, forever querying whether Derek was complying with the plan, which seemed very flexible on her part. I wouldn't have minded if her consultations with Derek were conducted reasonably – I mean politely- but they were hectoring to the point of rudeness.

It was a shame because Mrs Choudhury was a handsome woman. It was difficult to attribute an age but I guessed she was somewhat older than me, perhaps just the wrong side of forty. She looked exotic in a sari and, although I'm no expert on sub-continental clothing, a close-fitting bodice caught my eye. I expected to hear a distinctive accent but there was none unless she became animated, which was not infrequent. I felt sorry for Derek as she spouted on, and wished he would speak up for himself, but that is not his nature.

All would have remained just about tolerable if only Mrs Choudhury had kept merely hectoring. But on my second day she overstepped the mark. A concrete base had to be laid in one go, so we were late beginning our lunch break. Mrs Choudhury appeared beside the pick-up at two-fifteen, furiously demanding to know why we were not working. Derek's explanation leaving her stranded, she stood visibly seething for a moment before turning on her heels and striding off. But she should not have muttered, quite audibly, "Lazy English bastards".

The four of us heard, although no-one said anything, least of all Derek. But I wasn't too pleased, not so much for myself as for the others. And Bryn was Welsh, but I think she meant him as well. Of course, their jobs depended on keeping relations sweet – it's too easy for a customer to withhold payment and make a business sweat. But it grated on me.

It was Mrs Choudhury's habit to appear at any time during our working day, presumably to catch us idling. Other than those unwonted visits, we hardly saw the woman except if she went into the utility room, converted from a former attached garage but now part of the house. We were constructing the orangery, which was at the back of the property where it would catch more sun. I had been sent to fetch an angle-grinder from the pick-up, parked under a lime tree just across from the utility room. As I walked to the truck, I glimpsed Mrs Choudhury through the single window. She did not see me, being busy setting up the washing machine or some such housewifely task. A personal door opened from the utility room to the garden, only a few yards from where I stood.

I shouldn't have done it, but she had really needled me. Walking quickly to the door, I opened it with silent care, although the noise of the washing machine drowned any sound I might have made. Mrs Choudhury was facing away from me, absorbed in some unknown thoughts. A few swift paces brought me up behind her. I think she must have heard something or half-seen a movement, because she began to turn but not before I put one hand over her mouth and levered her right arm behind her back. Off balance, it was easy to push her a yard or so to a clear section of wall and hold her there, face pressed against the plasterwork.

'Best not to struggle or make a fuss, Mrs Choudhury, but please listen carefully to what I have to say.' In fairness, she was hardly in a position to struggle or make a fuss, which made life much simpler for us both. 'Earlier this afternoon you called us "lazy English bastards". That is not true; my colleagues work hard and are doing a good job, despite your constant moaning. I don't understand why you don't treat them better instead of being a permanently miserable, objectionable cow. A little humility would make life better for everyone, even you.'

I was speaking quietly into her left ear from a distance of about two inches, so I was fairly sure she could hear me well enough. She remained absolutely still. I knew I was coming to the tricky part. "Right, I've said my piece and, in a moment, I will let go. Now you must decide what you are going to do. You can run to your husband, make a big drama, cancel the job, perhaps try and involve the law. But four of us heard what you said and I suspect you've expressed similar sentiments before. Your husband may not be too pleased to be involved a row initiated by his wife's bitter tongue. So I offer you this deal: my colleagues know nothing about this, it is solely my affair. I will say nothing to them, that I risked their jobs. And if you say nothing to your husband, no-one but us will be any the wiser.'

I paused there, to let it sink in and give myself a breather. But it was time to finish. 'I can't understand why you're not better tempered. You have every advantage, plus you are a good-looking woman. Here's a suggestion: why don't you bake a few of your special goodies and bring them out to us one lunchtime? Surprise us with your better nature.'

With that, I let go and quickly stepped back, making

sure I was out of arm's reach. She turned on me, eyes narrowed in fury. For a moment I thought she was going to come at me, but she must have thought better of it. I waited a few seconds, hands up, palms forward, the classic gesture of conciliation. She was still furious but uncertain what to do. When I believed she wouldn't attack my back, I turned and exited the utility room with what I hoped was a measure of assurance.

That episode took place quite late Tuesday afternoon. I don't mind admitting I was on tenterhooks for the last hour until we finished, but all remained quiet. There was no sign of Mrs Choudhury or her husband. When we arrived next morning and still nothing untoward, I began to relax a little. Perhaps she had heeded what I said. I hoped so, because I didn't want to be explaining to Derek and the crew why the job had come to a sudden halt and with little prospect of payment. We certainly saw less of Mrs Choudhury. In fact, she didn't appear until after lunch, and then only walking to her car, some distance away. I followed her progress for a few seconds, but she didn't look across.

Thursday was equally quiet, even the crew cheerfully remarking on her absence, although they could not begin to guess the reason. I did not enlighten them, still concerned something might blow up, even though time was diminishing that prospect. Anyway, I was rather edgy, forever looking out for an appearance by either of the Choudhurys, although I could hardly expect them to be invisible around their own home. But there was a moment, just before lunch, when I caught a movement at one of the first-floor windows. It wasn't a good view, but I'm sure it was Mrs Choudhury. Perhaps she had taken to more circumspect viewing of our progress.

Friday was my last day and, by then, I was breathing a little more easily. Lunchtime came and, as usual, we lounged around the pick-up, eating our sandwiches and yarning. The appearance of an unsmiling Mrs Choudhury was an unwelcome surprise, and conversation suddenly lapsed. But she came bearing gifts, a tray of jaggery cake she informed us. It was a popular Indian cake, very light and moist, she explained, and contained cinnamon for added flavour. She hoped we would like it. We all thanked her, me included, and I tried to catch her eye but she avoided mine, giving nothing away. She didn't dwell, quickly returning to the sanctuary of the house. My mates were stunned, and there was some revision of their previous opinions. I was slightly less surprised, but very relieved.

Later that day, the orangery largely finished and me more of a handicap than a help, I was directed to digging holes for fence posts. Not a very exciting job but I was happy working at my own, none too vigorous, pace. I will never know whether Mrs Choudhury saw me there, away from the others, although it seemed an odd coincidence that she chose this moment to take a stroll round the garden. She would have passed me perhaps fifteen yards away – presumably a safe distance – but I made a point of speaking, thanking her again for the cake. She stopped and turned to face me.

'It was kind of you to go to that trouble,' I continued, 'we all enjoyed it.'

She stood unmoving, watching me with no expression that I could determine. And there are moments when you have to take the initiative. 'It's my last day working here. I've been filling in for one of Mr Bland's staff who's off sick, but he'll be back on Monday. Your cake was the highlight of my week.'

'What do you do, your usual job?' Still unreadable, but at least she was talking.

'I'm a financial adviser.'

A slight frown became evident. 'Then why do you do this? Are you a failure as a financial adviser?'

I put on my most charming smile. 'I like a change, the contrast. I find manual labour good for the soul, provided it doesn't go on too long. And you meet interesting people.'

It does no harm to signify interest, but she made no reply and her expression had reverted to inscrutable. I made one last effort.

'Are you pleased with the work so far? The orangery really looks the part.'

She made me wait for an answer, her eyes never leaving mine but giving the impression of assessment, like searching for the best cabbage in the display.

'Yes, I'm quite pleased.'

'And Mr Choudhury?'

'What sort of financial adviser are you? Do you specialise in business or personal asset management?'

'Business, mainly. But I sometimes advise on personal investments.' This was true to the extent that I look after my own finances.

'Do you have a business card?'

'Not on me, no. But I can give you my contact details before I go.'

'Leave them in the utility room, on the worktop. And you should always carry a business card, otherwise you will miss opportunities.'

With that injunction ringing in my ears, Mrs Choudhury resumed her stroll, although it led straight back to the house.

It was nearly a month before Mrs Choudhury called. It was short and began oddly, asking if I knew who it was. I did know, because I recognised her voice, aided by the trace of an accent which seemed amplified on the phone. She would like some financial advice. Very well, when would be convenient to meet? This evening, come to the house at seven-thirty. She rang off without waiting for my reply.

I was in Nottingham when I took the call, in a workaday café enjoying a ham, egg and chips lunch. I had an appointment in the afternoon, which I would have to keep short if I was to return to Hertfordshire dormitory land in time to spruce myself up. And a faint warning bell was ringing in my head: what was the woman up to? I could hardly believe she needed financial advice from me, a name and number scribbled on a scrap of paper and left on a utility room worktop. And with a certain history between us. I was aware Mrs Choudhury was setting the agenda, which made me cautious but curious. But isn't that what killed the cat?

It was dark by the time I parked the car in the front driveway, where Derek's pickup had not been allowed. An impressive oak door, set back under a tiled porch, was the obvious access, and an illuminated bell-push invited pressing. A feminine footfall preceded the door opening and the appearance of a woman I hardly recognised. This Mrs Choudhury was dressed in a dark skirt and jasmine silk blouse, black hair cascading down over her shoulders.

'Come in and shut the door,' was the less-than-effusive greeting, and I followed her swift progress along the hall until she turned into a plush living room. No-one else being present, I quickly returned the pepper-spray to my pocket, my worst suspicion not realised – not yet, anyway. She indicated an armchair but I preferred the one beyond, with a better sight of the door. A very surprising sight sat down on a sofa opposite, but none the worse for that. Transposed into conventional European dress, Mrs Choudhury sat straight-backed, upper legs modestly covered and angled away from me. She remained silent, assessing me again in what I now dubbed 'the cabbage selection syndrome'.

'How can I help you, Mrs Choudhury.'

'Do you really work in finance?'

I took a deep breath, leaned back and studied the elaborate plaster cornice over the doorway. 'Yes, I really do work in finance. I advise certain people to pay what they owe my client, Mr Kalogeras, or it will be the worse for them.'

A suggestion of satisfaction played on her face, as though her judgment had been vindicated. 'And does your role involve violence?'

'Sorry to disappoint you, Mrs Choudhury, but, no, almost never, and then only to escape from a difficult situation. Resorting to violence would represent complete failure on my part.'

'Then why did you resort to violence with me?' She seemed genuinely curious.

'I'm really not sure. You certainly annoyed me, more for my friends than me. Normally, I would have just spoken to you at an opportune moment, but something told me you wouldn't listen. I could not imagine us having a reasoned conversation. My instinct was for a short, sharp shock.'

She did not answer this point, which told me I might well be right. 'Do you take pleasure in frightening women?'

'Absolutely not. And I took no pleasure in what I did to you, which was simple bullying. But it makes me wonder why you asked me here. And why I came.'

'Tell me about your work.'

I shrugged my shoulders. If that was what she wanted... 'Mr Kalogeras is an entrepreneur with many complex interests, among which he also supports other businesses. But some are poorly managed, or the economic cycle works against them; whatever. When required, I act as Mr Kalogeras's agent. I visit the business concerned and advise on courses of action. You have to bear in mind, a business with debt problems is almost always owed money by their customers. I help expedite those outstanding payments so that Mr Kalogeras can be paid his due. Sometimes he settles for a share of the business rather than cash. There are many variables.'

'How are you paid?'

'That's my business.'

Mrs Choudhury paused to reflect on this, and I wondered whether we were finished. But she wasn't, going on to ask so many other questions about my work that it began to feel like an inquisition. I answered some and deflected others but, after an hour, I'd had enough. I thought I would upstage the woman by leaving quite abruptly but, damn it, she beat me to it.

'That's all I want to know,' she said, standing up and walking out of the room, leaving me to follow like some lap dog being taken for walkies. The front door was opened and Mrs Choudhury stood beside it, a study in enigmatic Indian beauty. Her eyes were not on me as she uttered, 'Thank you for coming.'

'Thank you, Mrs Choudhury, although a cup of tea and a biscuit would have been nice.'

I heard the door close smartly behind me.

It was ten days before she phoned again. Recognising

the number, I was ready for her this time. However, she sounded subtly different, a fraction more amenable, although still wanting to give the orders. She gave no reason for wanting to meet, and I didn't ask. But I wouldn't attend the house, which led to stalemate until she relented and agreed to meet at a suitably out-of-the-way gastro-pub. I was on time, and waited in the car-park. Of course, she was twenty minutes late – almost certainly deliberate - and made no apology, which tested my patience. Mrs Choudhury was again dressed Western-style, a dark jacket over an ivory satin blouse this time. Very smart, but she wore too much eye make-up for my taste. There were few preliminaries, since she seemed to have mastered the art of saying very little. Not having eaten, I was confounded when she did not want a meal. Before ordering drinks, as a little test, I said I assumed we were going Dutch on the evening's expenses, which she affected not to hear.

We sat opposite each other, a small table between us. When, after a minute or two, she deigned to look at me, I thought it was time one of us spoke.

'What exactly do you want from me, Mrs Choudhury? Certainly not my limited financial expertise. You can afford proper, expert advice, not the ramblings of some do-it-yourself investor with the losses to show for it. So, what is it that you want from me?'

There was no immediate reply, only another long, level look into my face, head tilted slightly to one side. 'You interest me. What you do for a living, it's unusual. And you make strange choices, like working as a labourer in your down-time. Not to mention your criminal approach to personal relationships.'

'Hardly criminal, surely. I like to think it is simply direct. "Let your communication be yea, yea, nay, nay. For whatsoever is more than this, cometh from evil". Matthew five, verse twenty-three, if I remember correctly."

For the first time that I could recall, Mrs Choudhury smiled. Well, more a half-smile, really, and rather sardonic, but I thought it was definitely progress.

'Quoting the bible to justify your actions? You are hardly qualified to be the advocate of the non-violent Christian message as I understand it.'

'Hmm, best not to get into a deep theological discussion. I suspect you have a wider knowledge than I do, which wouldn't be difficult. And you still haven't answered my question: what do you want from me?'

Nor did she answer me. Once again we entered the inquisition arena, this time about my personal life. Was I married? No? Then a partner, surely? A girlfriend? What were my interests, hobbies? Where was I educated? Did I have a degree? Seizing an opportunity to escape from relentless questioning, I said, 'No I don't, but you've reminded me of an interchangeable Indian-Jewish joke. A mother and adult son are walking beside a river when the son falls in. "Help, help," cries the mother, "my son – the doctor – is drowning."'

I laughed and, to be fair, she smiled again, rather dismissively, as though humouring a small child. More than an hour had passed, pleasantly enough if you like one-sided inquisitions but I had come to the conclusion I wasn't going to learn any more of Mrs Choudhury's motives during this conversation. And I had long-finished my pint and didn't want another, for I am not much of a drinker. Strangely, she forgot to ask about my drinking habits, perhaps drawing her own conclusions as she sipped her way through a single glass of red wine.

'Right, I've had enough of questions for one evening,

Mrs Choudhury, so I'm going to toddle off now and wash my hair, or watch TV.' It was my turn to give an interrogatory look. 'I can't say I've particularly enjoyed our chats so far but, if you really want another date, you are going to have to be rather more forthcoming. Please bear that in mind if you decide to call again. Oh, and there's no need to pay me for that glass of wine; take it as my treat.'

I felt her eyes boring into my back as I walked to the door.

There's a saying, isn't there, about men being from Mars and women from Venus? Well, I'll certainly go along with that but, in my experience, a few women are not so much from Venus as the Planet Zog. Mrs Choudhury, for example. I had no idea what to make of this woman, and I sensed the feeling was mutual. Which made our association interesting but also baffling, frustrating and plenty more adjectives if only my vocabulary was wider.

When three weeks passed with nothing heard, I began to believe I had over-stepped some undefined mark and that was the end of the business. And I had no intention of phoning Mrs Choudhury. This charade was entirely of her making. She wanted to be in charge, setting the rules and I was content to go along with that, although I had my own boundaries. Our association to date reminded me of the gavotte, the courtly French dance where the couple circle each other for ages before ending with a kiss. That was my fond hope. Only Mrs Choudhury knew what was in her mind, and it increasingly looked as if it had been abandoned.

At least, such was my thinking until she called late one afternoon. I recognised the number and her voice, which was just as well because, as was her habit, she did not say who it was. Where did I live? She would come to my flat that evening, I was informed. Our shortest ever telephone conversation, and it left me precious little time to get home and tidy the place up. Not that there was much to tidy, as Mrs Choudhury pointed out when surveying my living room.

'Is this all the furniture you can afford?'

'I rent this flat so that I can move at short notice. There is no point in cluttering it up with unnecessary belongings.'

'You have quite a lot of books.'

'It's a modest collection, limited to one hundred books. If a new one comes in permanently, another must go. It's a useful self-discipline.'

She peered at the bookcase. 'Some of these are quite heavyweight reading; history, politics. And a book on collecting silver.'

'Yes, behind this carefree mask I am not entirely frivolous. And my collection of silver comprises precisely four items.' But it was time to take control before she began another inquisition. 'Why don't you sit down instead of prowling around like an over-active panther.'

To my astonishment, she laughed. 'Is that how you see me; a prowling panther? A dangerous wild beast?'

'It seems apt; beautiful, feline and who knows how dangerous?' As I say, it does no harm to let them know you're interested. 'Would you like a cup of tea, or something? And possibly a biscuit?'

She settled for a cup of tea, but no biscuit. We sat on the only two easy chairs, adjacent but more than an arm's length apart. She had overdone the eye make-up again, otherwise looking very cool in an emerald green blouse and the habitual dark skirt. I saw her knees for the first time as she crossed her legs, and wondered at the sexiness of such a minor revelation.

'I hope you haven't forgotten it's your turn to speak this time.'

'What do you want to know?'

'Why you are here, sitting in a dingy flat drinking own-brand supermarket tea. This is not your milieu, nor am I your natural acquaintance.'

Mrs Choudhury studied me yet again, as if further scrutiny could possibly tell her any more. 'Why do you think I'm here?'

Wearying of this particular gavotte, I responded rather sharply. 'I think you are unhappy, despite all the trappings. I can imagine no other reason. But one of those heavyweight books over there - possibly the bible – says happiness can't be bought. Am I on the right track?'

The mistress of non-answering swerved again, but at least a new channel of communication opened. 'I am my husband's second wife, although we've been married twenty years. He has two sons by his first wife, and I have given him a daughter. She is at university in the United States. My husband and his brother have been successful in business, with the results that you have seen.' She drew breath here, considering what to say next. 'My husband has always been interested in Sanskrit. Do you know what Sanskrit is?'

'An ancient Indian language?'

'Yes, but more than that, it's the language of the Hindu scriptures and classical Indian epic poems such as the Mahabharata. That is what my husband now spends an increasing amount of his time studying.'

'It sounds very worthy.'

'Yes, but I do not share his interest.'

'So are you the classical neglected wife?'

Mrs Choudhury frowned, as if uncertain of her own feelings. 'If only it were that simple. I have my own interests, of course, but they are mainly social, which I do not find very fulfilling. It may be a cultural problem, although it seems to affect me in particular. I do not feel wholly at ease with either Indian or British culture; at times, both drive me to distraction. And then came your episode, which really made me focus. Don't flatter yourself that I find you irresistible. I've been courted by better-looking and vastly more successful men than you. And some of your remarks make me squirm.'

'I'm under no illusions.'

'Good.' She gave a wry smile, having put me in my place. 'But there is something different about you, that is what I noticed. You also seem to straddle two different worlds, and we may have that in common. That is why I am here, to find out.'

It was my turn to take a deep breath. 'Well, thank you for sharing that with me. By the way, that's a quote straight from the HR touchy-feely handbook, but I do appreciate what you're saying.'

A disapproving look accompanied, 'There you go again, saying something you think is clever, just to irritate me.'

'Yes, it's an annoying habit, apparently. It may explain why I'm unattached.' I gave a deep sigh of mock humility, but it was a defensive measure. The woman was perceptive, I had to give her that. 'You're quite right, Mrs Choudhury; I don't fit in easily. I don't like city life, but my living is there. I don't like crowds, except in football stadiums. I am restless and dissatisfied but in a way which I can't even explain to myself. There, does that help you?'

A satisfied smile gave its own answer before she added, 'Yes, that is very useful. It's good to have one's instincts proved right.'

'Does that mean we're friends now?'

Mrs Choudhury favoured me with a stark, disapproving look. 'That would be going altogether too far.' And then she laughed, pleased to have caught me out with a joke of her own. Yes, the stern, unbending Mrs Choudhury actually made a joke; she really did possess a sense of humour. It proved something of a breakthrough, too, because conversation flowed more easily after that, a more balanced exchange of questions and explanations. Rather like a good first date, if you ignored all our previous encounters.

Around nine-thirty Mrs Choudhury announced that it was time for her to leave, which was a pity because I was enjoying our chat. She stood up and put on her jacket, but I could see something was on her mind, perhaps wondering how to take her leave. After a moment's consideration she said, 'You should arrange where we next meet. It must be within twenty-five miles, of a suitable standard and discreet. If I find the venue unacceptable, I shall immediately return home. It should be for Thursday week, meeting at six-o'-clock.'

'Should I book just the restaurant, or a room as well?'

'Use your judgment.'

'My judgment says "expensive". Are we going Dutch?'

'That's for you to find out.'

'Very well, Mrs Choudhury; how should I contact you?'

'Leave the details on your kitchen worktop. Give me a spare key and I will call and collect them when convenient. You will know I've been because I shall leave the key on the worktop.'

'How do I know you won't burgle the place?'

'Because you have absolutely nothing worth stealing.'

This conversation had taken us to the door, where we both stopped. I don't mind admitting I wasn't sure what to do next, this being unlike anything I'd experienced before. I decided to play safe. 'May I kiss you?'

'You haven't given me your spare key.'

'If I do, will you let me kiss you?'

'Give me the key first.'

I took that as a yes, went outside and retrieved the spare key from behind an airbrick. She followed, which wasn't what I'd hoped. The kiss, in full public view – although there was no-one about – was simultaneously loveless, passionless and unerotic, like kissing your mother goodbye, although I don't make a habit of kissing her on the lips. Mrs Choudhury seemed similarly unmoved, and I seriously hoped things would improve soon.

That was the start of the affair, if such you could call it. We rendezvoused at a small, bijou hotel in the Hertfordshire countryside. It met with Mrs Choudhury's approval but, hell, it was expensive. I met the whole bill on that occasion, although she paid half on subsequent visits, always in cash. This amused her for some reason, always counting out the notes in front of me, paying with exactitude right down to coins. But, even with this subsidy I wasn't sure how long I could maintain the expense.

That first visit was instructive in that I discovered she was shy when undressed, which I found an endearing trait in such a forceful woman. A less endearing feature was her insistence that I continue to call her 'Mrs Choudhury'. I cavilled at this, pointing out that her name was Prisha, discovered from public records which listed her as a joint director of three companies. Nonetheless, she remained adamant so, not wanting to fall out over such an oddity, I complied. Perhaps it helped her feel she retained control. It would be ungentlemanly to describe her performance as a lover, but occasionally she did seem a tad distracted, as though wondering what to have for supper.

We met four times in eleven weeks, hardly an indication of obsessive passion by either party and strongly influenced on my part by my bank balance. On that fourth occasion, at the stage where, if either of us had smoked, cigarettes would have been lit, she began another interrogation. Was I satisfied with my life? Since she already knew I was mildly dissatisfied, I felt we were going over old ground, and said so. But she persevered. What would make me happy? Eventually I fell back on that hoary old chestnut about marrying a beautiful millionaire nymphomaniac who owned a brewery. For some reason that displeased her, accusing me of not taking it seriously – not her sharpest piece of deduction, in my view. She went quiet for a while, although we made up before we left.

It was nearly a fortnight before we met again, and everything seemed fine until we reached the cigarette-lighting stage. Then she started again. More probing about happiness and fulfilment. Of course, she explained, although money wasn't essential for happiness, it certainly provided a key to that particular door. Did I agree? Well, it gave you the freedom to choose, I couldn't deny that. There followed much discussion, mostly on her part, about the benefits of wealth, which I found odd; a monied woman spouting on to a man whose bank balance dwindled substantially every time they met. It irritated me to the extent that I told her so. She was dressing in front of me now, no longer quite such a shy maiden.

'Don't you have any ambition to change your life?' Her voice was familiarly close to hectoring.

'Yes, but I don't see the point of endlessly hypothesising over it.'

Mrs Choudhury fixed me with a penetrating stare. 'What if I told you I have the solution. That I know a way both of us can realise our ambitions, perhaps even our dreams.'

'Come on then, fantasy woman; let me in on the secret.'

She had the most beautiful brown eyes, but her unwavering look was suddenly anything but soft. 'My husband has a weak heart. If you were to do to him what you did to me, I'm sure that would be the end.'

Too shocked to reply, she took my silence as an opportunity to continue. 'It would simply be advancing a natural development. He's going to die anyway, but sooner would be more convenient. And if you are concerned about a possible police investigation, I could arrange a trip abroad, where police investigations are rather more lax. But with his medical record, I can't believe it would come to that.'

At last, I managed to find my voice. 'I can't believe what I've just heard, Prisha. Or are you just kidding me? Because, if you're serious, it would be murder, although I notice you prefer euphemisms.'

'Oh, don't be so holy with me. We both know you have a violent streak, which you put to good purpose when it suits. It could be put to good purpose now. I would make it worth your while, give you the means to realise your dreams. I would be able to make it a very substantial sum. You're used to dealing with money and investments; you could...'

'Stop, Prisha, stop.' I held up my hand to bring this nonsense to an end. To my surprise I was quite calm, although an icy coldness had settled over me. 'I won't hear any more. And I'm prepared to file what you've just said in the "unmentionable" box in my brain provided you give up this crass idea. As before, no-one else will hear it. But please tell me you are not serious.'

She had stopped dressing, her blouse still unbuttoned. 'You should regard it as a rare business opportunity; minimal risk for maximum reward.'

'Minimal risk; the chance of a life sentence?' I shook my head in disbelief. 'You have seriously lost the plot, Prisha.' Then something obvious occurred to me, which I delivered quite matter-of-factly. 'I won't listen to any more. And you have to understand this is the end of us. This is where we go our separate ways.'

It seemed to take a moment for this to register, then her stare hardened into anger. 'You're a fool. Not only a fool; a coward. You haven't the balls to take an opportunity when it's laid on a plate for you. No wonder you're a failure. I can't believe you are such a miserable coward.'

'I'd rather be a coward than a murderer, Prisha, although you should be careful directing either word too freely at me.'

A tense silence fell as we both took stock of the situation. I read somewhere that murder is almost always banal, and it struck me then; Prisha half-dressed and me propped up on one elbow among rumpled bedsheets. After an unconscionable time, there was a sudden resumption of movement, Prisha hastily buttoning up her blouse and me rousing myself from the bed. Ready to leave, she turned to me, eyes familiarly furious. 'Call yourself a man? You're just a snivelling dog.'

Then she picked up her bag and left.

I've been called worse. And in the aftermath, I spent some

time considering our strange association. Had murder been on her mind from the outset? The thought chilled me to the bone. Was the love-making simply a means to an end, for I had never been convinced she was a natural adulterer? As expected, no definitive explanations offered themselves. And it was not the slightest surprise to hear nothing from Mrs Choudhury. As the weeks passed, the strange affair began to recede slowly into memory.

Here's another cliché; what goes around, comes around. I'm not even sure I understand exactly what it means but, like a revolving carousel, Mrs Choudhury disappeared from my life, and then suddenly reappeared. A telephone call one afternoon, a number I didn't recognise, otherwise I may not have answered. As usual, she gave no name, just, 'I have a difficulty, I need your advice.' Problems with her directorships was all she would say on the phone. Would I call at the house and help her? The word 'please' did not cross her lips. Jesus, I'm a softy, I even went that evening.

She looked well, back in a sari, although there was a faint tension in her demeanour. At first I thought it was because of our meeting but that idea was quickly banished as I was updated. Her husband was dead, she announced; two months ago, while in India. Heart failure. I can't pretend I didn't find this deeply suspicious, but she rattled swiftly on to the nub of her problem. Her imagined inheritance was nothing like anticipated. Yes, she gained the house, but her daughter received a twenty-five percent share. However, it was her interests in the family companies that bore the heavy hint of chicanery. She showed me some papers detailing a multiple capital raising which diluted her shareholdings in all three companies to just ten percent. The changes were all recent, around the time we had been frolicking in the boutique hotel. Was this a coincidence? The main beneficiary was Mr Choudhury's brother but the two stepsons also became shareholders. Prisha swore blind she had never been consulted, which would have made the changes illegal. But the advisory documents were found in her husband's office, in which she filed her personal papers and to which she had free access.

It bore all the hallmarks of a family stitch-up. And the more I heard from Prisha, the more certain I became. Her brother-in-law had never taken to her, she said, and he was the main driver of their property business in the latter years. Crucially, relations with her husband had cooled, too, although remaining amicable. Mr Choudhury's private assets were considerable, but divided between their daughter, the two step-sons and Prisha, her share was not adequate for the lifestyle she had envisaged. The house would have to be sold, if she was to live comfortably.

I was on the verge of pointing out she would still be pretty well placed – there were regular distributions of company dividends – when she cut in and asked whether I would help fight her case. Now, there are times when the truth is difficult, and this was one. I'm pretty sure you have been cheated, I explained, and have moral and legal right on your side. But you have no evidence. You would need to prove a conspiracy; difficult, expensive and uncertain. And they are in a position to do you far more harm than you can inflict on them. Under those circumstances, it is almost certainly best to settle for what you've got.

This did not sit well with her. Once again, I was subjected to those inscrutable looks that somehow conveyed deep displeasure. Feeling I had done my duty, I made to leave. To my surprise, Prisha was suddenly more amenable, insisting we have a drink while talking about less contentious topics. It was easier to agree. During this half-hour, and knowing my interest in silver, she showed me a beautiful amulet set with rubies. Indian silver is not my field, but it was easy to admire the superb workmanship. Soon after that, we parted on what I regarded as reasonably good terms.

A couple of days later I arrived back at the flat in the late afternoon. Having only snacked for lunch, my priority was something to eat, but hardly had my ready-meal been placed in the microwave than the doorbell rang. Displeased at this untimely interruption, I opened the door to find three men outside, none looking at all friendly. I can't deny my heart skipped several beats because I carry a deep, nameless dread that something from my past will catch up with me one day. A shortish, thickset man held up a police warrant card while announcing my name and looking at me questioningly. After careful study, I deemed the card genuine, so answered 'yes'. This same detective sergeant also had a warrant to search the flat, so we adjourned inside, my meal abandoned as I sat, baffled but resigned, observing a police search.

A short while later, the officer searching the second bedroom put his head round the door and called the sergeant. Moments later they both emerged and the sergeant arrested me on suspicion of the theft of a silver bracelet set with rubies. He meant Mrs Choudhury's amulet, I realised, as everything became clear. This was revenge.

At the police station I declined legal representation, saying that I was very willing to co-operate but only if provided with a meal. Eventually I was given an indifferent pizza and a mug of tea. Then it was down to business, a recorded interview. Where was I on the evening of two days before? At the home of Mrs Prisha Choudhury, by her invitation. Did I recognise the amulet that lay on the table between us in a transparent evidence bag? Yes, it looked identical to one Mrs Choudhury showed me during the visit. If it was the same, they would find fingerprints from my right hand only, since I had soon handed it back. How did the amulet come to be in my possession? No idea, but someone, perhaps even Mrs Choudhury herself, must have put it in my flat. Why would she do that? Because I had failed to help her or give advice she wanted to hear. How would someone gain entry to my flat? Mrs Choudhury knew where the spare key was kept. And so on. I think it was when I said there were at least two CCTV cameras covering my block of flats that they realised this was a charge going nowhere. It was nearly eleven before I arrived home.

Late the following morning I received a phone call from the detective sergeant. They had checked the CCTV; it showed Mrs Choudhury entering my flat on the day after my visit. They were minded to charge her with wasting police time and, apparently, I had good grounds for a private prosecution. I urged against any prosecution, spinning a story about her bereavement and how upset she was. Bereavement counselling would be a better option.

Most of us are creatures of habit, and Mrs Choudhury was no exception. She believed Tuesday afternoon was the quietest time for shopping at her preferred supermarket, and made it her regular habit. Typically, she kept me waiting, although this was understandable because I had not let her know we were meeting. Loitering between the drop-off bay and the ATM, I eventually spotted her saried figure crossing the car-park. Closing in, I approached from behind as she was about to withdraw a trolley from the rack and spoke quietly into her left ear. 'Leave that for a moment, Mrs Choudhury; let's go and have a coffee.'

If she was startled, it hardly showed. A brief moment of inaction, then, without a glance at me, she set off for the café. There were only two spare tables and she settled for the nearest while I joined the queue for our coffees. Service was commendably quick; in a couple of minutes I was sitting down opposite the familiar figure. Too much eye make-up again, and I thought she looked a little thinner in the face.

'I expected you to come to the house to confront me but, of course, you prefer to attack from behind.' This was delivered quite matter-of-factly, and not calculated to make me smile.

'Do you ever get the feeling, Prisha, that we've never quite got the measure of each other? I do, all the time. But never mind that; did you enjoy your little joke?'

'I knew you'd soon talk your way out of it.'

'Yes, but you could have been prosecuted. Didn't you think of that, or did your anger make you blind beyond caring?'

She studied me intently. 'Why should you care what happens to me?'

'I haven't the faintest idea, Prisha. Really, not a clue. But something keeps prompting me that you are someone who could use a sympathetic voice. You've seemed unhappy from the moment we first met, and it's no better now. It's beyond me, and you seem unable or unwilling to say why. Even worse, I suspect you may not know yourself. But if you do know, I wish you'd tell me, so that I can close this particular chapter a shade more satisfactorily.'

True to form, she went off at a tangent. 'You have not asked about the circumstances of my husband's death in India. And yet you must be curious, suspicious even.'

'And are you going to enlighten me?'

'No, I leave it to your judgment.'

'You make my point for me, Prisha. I said nothing to the police, by the way, or I think they might have followed it up.'

She made no response, certainly not a thank you. 'I'm going to the States, to see my daughter. I shall stay there for a while. When I come back, I shall sell the house; that's what has been agreed. The will, probate, all that business should be settled by then. As you know, everything was left very tidy, stitched up as you so elegantly explained.'

I nodded, a vague gesture of acknowledgment. 'And after that?'

'I might return to study, an MA, although I haven't settled on a subject.'

'Well, that sounds positive, Prisha. I really hope everything works out for you.' These pious banalities indicated it was time for me to leave, and we both sensed it. She kept her eyes on mine and I was surprised to see a softer look.

'Why don't you come to the house this evening and I'll cook us dinner.'

It was one of the few pleasantries I ever heard Mrs Choudhury utter, and yet my first instinct was, 'she wants to poison me.' It must have showed in my face because she laughed, and I had to follow. And I can't say I wasn't tempted, but an inner voice spoke for me.

'Thank you, Prisha, but I won't risk darkening your doors again.'

That was the signal to leave and she picked up her

shoulder bag. 'Do you expect me to go Dutch on this?' she enquired, indicating the coffees, neither of which were finished. She had a dark sense of humour.

'Please accept it as a parting gift from someone who tried to be your friend.'

Whether this touched a nerve, I don't know, but she gave me a long look that seemed to reflect... what? Bafflement? Frustration? Or was this a mirror of my own feelings? Then, without another word or glance in my direction, she walked off to secure a trolley. I waited by our table until she disappeared into the vegetable zone – to choose a cabbage? – and then made my way out to the car-park. It was only as I drove to the exit that I felt a sharp stab of regret.

The Sergeant Major's Bull

REGIMENTAL SERGEANT MAJOR Beech had completed his morning rounds of the battalion by 11.30. He had overseen muster parade and then proceeded to drop in on the guardroom, the motor pool and sundry other units including the cookhouse, where he had obtained a mid-morning cup of tea and established what was on the menu for lunch at the sergeants' mess. Now he had just arrived back at HQ Company office to find there was a crisis.

A uniformed clerk was clutching a telephone to his chest while casting enquiring looks around the office at several other soldier clerks, all of whom looked nonplussed. 'What is going on here?' demanded the RSM, in a voice both authoritative and penetrating. Only the bespectacled lance corporal holding the telephone ventured a reply.

'It's a call from Featherbys the auctioneers, sir, in town. A bull has escaped from its pen and is running loose around the sale-yard. Featherbys want to know if we have a marksman available to shoot the bull if it can't be recaptured.'

The RSM considered for a moment. He was a man of action, after all, and they were not too thick on the ground among the HQ company clerical staff. In contrast, RSM Beech had wielded a rifle on behalf of his country for more than twenty years, in both war and peace, and had the medals to prove it. Maybe this was an opportunity to add a little more glory, albeit without much chance of a medal. However, a grateful letter of thanks from the auctioneers to the colonel would go down well, not too dissimilar, perhaps, from a 'Mention in Dispatches'.

'Tell them we shall be there in half an hour.'

The RSM waited until this was relayed to the auctioneers and the call ended. 'I shall need a driver. Can you drive, corporal?'

'Yes, sir.'

'Very well, you will come with me.' He turned to an officer sitting across the other side of the room. 'I take it you have no objection to my borrowing this man for an hour, Mr Harrold?' Nineteen-year-old second lieutenant Harrold, having kept his head down ever since the call came through, showed not the faintest inclination to countermand the RSM's order. Beech turned back to the corporal.

'Go to the armoury and draw a rifle and five rounds of ammunition. I want a bolt-action Lee Enfield, not one of the new semi-automatics.' The RSM was a strong traditionalist. 'Sign in your name but give my authority. Then meet me at the motor pool.'

At the motor pool, readily available transport proved in short supply but RSM Beech soon solved the problem. 'The colonel is away; I'll take his car. This is an emergency; people's lives are at stake.'

The impressive Humber staff car, complete with regimental pennants fluttering from the wings, was immediately made available, and the RSM and his de-facto corporal-driver soon ensconced within. As the car left the barracks, the two guards mistakenly presented arms, although RSM Beech declined to stop and point out their error.

'What's your name then, corporal?' Beech wanted to know.

'Hallett, sir.'

'Right, Hallett, I don't suppose you've been on a jaunt like this before?'

'No, sir.'

'Well, we'll be representing the Army and, more particularly, our regiment, so we need to be soldier-like and efficient at all times. I will do the shooting but you will be my number two. Follow me closely and do as I say.'

'Yes, sir.'

There followed a pause in the conversation, although RSM Beech was a strong believer in being able to engage with his soldiers. It occurred to Beech that his driver was a little older than the usual National Serviceman. 'Are you doing your National Service, Hallett?'

'Yes, sir.'

'Did you get a deferment?'

'Yes, sir. I was able to finish my college course.'

'I see. Got long to do?'

'Three months, sir.'

'Then back to Civvy Street, eh? Got a job lined up?'

'Not yet, sir, but I'm just starting to make enquiries to prospective employers. That's why I wanted to get some qualifications before being called up, so that I could go straight into a job afterwards and, hopefully, a career.'

Hallett's explanation unsettled RSM Beech. It reminded him that his own – already extended – service would finish in fifteen months' time, and he had no plans whatsoever regarding his future. It was made more troubling by hearing of a former warrant officer colleague who had left the army a year ago and was now working as a railway porter. He was only too aware his service friends and contemporaries were steadily dwindling away, there remaining only two currently serving who could call him 'Twiggy' to his face, and neither served in his present battalion. The very thought of leaving the army's all-embracing structure had begun to seem more alarming than any German panzer-grenadier he had faced.

But the army was changing, Beech acknowledged; his era drawing to a close. The talk was of ending conscription, that reliable supply of young men, albeit most of whom did not want to be soldiers anyway. He tended to be dismissive of conscripted soldiers for that reason. A fully professional army would be good, but it would be much smaller, with fewer opportunities for promotion. Not that it would affect RSM Beech, but he worried for those remaining in the service.

There was no mistaking the sale yard, a mixed press of farmers, vehicles, tractors and even a few horses. A small, scruffy man emerged from the crowd and knocked on Hallett's window, which he lowered a little.

'Follow me,' were his only words before setting off through the crowd. He led the way beyond the throng to an empty grassy patch beside a large, dilapidated shed. 'Park here. The bull is round the corner.'

RSM Beech was not impressed with this terse relay of instructions and information, despite their concision being worthy of any sergeant-major's orders. 'Bring the rifle, Hallett,' was his only response as they alighted from the car.

Without another word, their guide disappeared through a door into the shed, and the two soldiers were left to follow. The shed proved to be open on the other side and had clearly housed livestock earlier that morning since the straw floor-covering was liberally dotted with cowpats, some very liquid. Both Beech and Hallett trod carefully, while their guide strode along as though heedless of the peril. They left the shed and turned into an area which, had it been a university or cathedral, would have been called a quadrangle. This quadrangle was not so illustrious, being smaller and bounded on three sides by yet more utilitarian sheds. Against the clapboard wall of one of the sheds stood a bull.

It was a magnificent animal. As well as being formidably muscular, it sported a charming dappled grey-brown hide and its massive head bore two short, curved horns surmounted by a dainty twist of hair. On the appearance of the three men, it raised its head and viewed them with belligerent suspicion.

'Have you shot a bull before?' asked the stockman.

'No,' replied Beech tersely, 'only men.'

If this statement was intended to impress the stockman, it failed. 'The owner doesn't want the carcase ruined with a body shot, so it has to be the head. Between the eyes is too low but if you stray too much above, you'll hit the bony boss and that will only annoy him even more. Two and a half inches above the eyes will do the job.' He paused, squinting at the restive bull. 'I'll leave you to get on with it.'

With that injunction he turned about and retired back into the shed, taking up a position behind a low breeze-block wall which offered a panoramic – and safe – view of the proceedings. Beech stood for a moment, apparently assessing the tactical situation. Hallett, standing a little behind the RSM and peering round his substantial frame at the agitated bull, wondered whether he should offer the rifle to his superior. After all, should the bull charge, they would look a trifle foolish with an unloaded weapon still in the hands of the number two.

'Right, Hallett,' began the RSM, presumably thinking along the same lines, 'give me the rifle.' The rifle changed hands.

'There is no magazine fitted,' observed Beech, his face tightening. 'Therefore, I cannot load the weapon. Do you expect me to beat the animal to death with an unloaded rifle, Hallett?'

'You took the magazine and rounds, sir. They're in your left-hand pocket.'

'Ah, yes; so I did.' There was a short hiatus while the RSM handed the rifle back to Hallett, took the errant items from his pocket and pushed the clip of five rounds into the magazine. Taking the rifle back from Hallett, he fitted the magazine and worked the bolt to put a round into the breech. Now he was ready for action.

Beech assessed the range at between twenty-five and thirty yards. 'I think we'd best get a bit closer, Hallett. It's got a big head but I want to make sure.' The two men edged slowly forward, Hallett wondering what on earth his role now was, other than providing moral support. At twenty yards the RSM stopped, not least because the bull was becoming ever more restive, raising and lowering its head with increasing menace. Beech spoke over his shoulder to Hallett.

'I'm going to shoot from the standing position,' he explained, as if instructing a platoon of recruits, 'so that the round has a safe downward trajectory. The bullet may well pass clean through its skull and we can't be sure what's beyond that shed wall. We don't want any unintended casualties.'

Out of the RSM's sight, Hallett threw up his hands in

frustration. Why didn't the bloody man just get on with it? But, ever mindful of fire control discipline for deliberate shooting, Beech raised the rifle only when he had found a comfortable standing position, feet fifteen inches apart but dangerously close to a large cowpat. Hallett covered his ears and there was the sharp report of a shot.

The bull blinked. Hallett blinked. The RSM blinked, and then stared at the bull in increasing disbelief. Was it possible he had missed? But he was not a war veteran and RSM for nothing. Hallett heard a short harrumph and the sound of the rifle bolt working. Beech dropped to one knee and in one fluid movement raised the rifle and fired. The bull instantly slumped to the ground. There followed a moment's silence between the two soldiers.

It was the stockman who broke the silence. He approached the two men, a sly half-grin on his face. 'What the hell happened there, then?'

There was no reply from either of the soldiers, the silence becoming more awkward by the moment. Gravitas became even more difficult to maintain with the realisation that the RSM had knelt in the cowpat. Suddenly, Hallett spoke up. 'The miss was my fault, I'm afraid. Stupidly, I spoke to the sergeant-major just as he was about to shoot.' He sounded very contrite.

The stockman gave Hallett a sardonic look. 'Is that so?' The sly grin still lurked around his weather-beaten features as he glanced at the RSM's trousers. 'That won't look too good on the parade ground. Still, at least it's a dead bull now; I could tell by the way it went down. I used to work in an abattoir,' he added, by way of an explanation. He led the way to examine the bull, and quickly pointed to one of the horns.

'That's your first bullet, you can see where it's grazed

the horn. The second shot did the job, though, spot on.'

'Yes,' said Hallett, 'your advice was very helpful. We're used to rather a different sort of bullseye in the army.'

The stockman nodded in acknowledgement, not displeased that his role had been recognised. He waved his hand at the bull. 'All right, you can leave me to deal with this.' For the first time since the shooting, he addressed RSM Beech specifically. 'I expect Featherbys will want to show their appreciation of your marksmanship in some way; maybe a prime cut from this old boy. Or they might be willing to meet your laundry bill.' The sergeant major did not deign to reply.

There was no conversation in the car when it left Featherbys saleyard. In fact, RSM Beech had not uttered a word since shooting the bull, apparently absorbed in solving a most difficult, and pressing, problem. A problem that it was essential to resolve before their return to barracks, namely; how could he prevent the story of his missed shot – at an actual bull! – circulating around the entire battalion, and far beyond? If this got out, he would be a laughing stock. Pondering in silence amid the pervasive aroma of cowpat, he realised there were only two plausible options: threats or promises. Which was it to be?

The camp entrance and guardroom were in sight before Beech spoke. 'You did well back there, corporal; kept a cool head. Number two is an important role, in support.' There was a moment's hesitation before he continued. 'I've heard your name mentioned more than once in the office; a good worker, very reliable. If you can keep it up for the remainder of your service, I will be advising that your discharge papers rate your conduct as exemplary,'

'Thank you, sir.'

But the RSM had evidently not finished. 'You know, I'm a bit puzzled why you are still only a lance corporal. The army is not always quick enough to recognise talent. I know you only have three months to go, but it would look better in Civvy Street if you left with two stripes on your arm, rather than one. I shall be making some enquiries.'

Prospective full corporal Hallett turned the car into the camp entrance. 'Thank you, sir.'

Daughter of Darkness

HAVE YOU NOTICED how Life has a way of biting you when least expected? Sometimes it's just a light nip, others distinctly more noticeable. On this occasion I was returning to my flat after a day spent visiting businesses which owed my client money. Since most of them were owed money themselves, a sense circular futility was hard to shake off, but I am paid for results, so a certain perseverance is required. The working day over, my brain pleasantly in neutral, I climbed the stairs, walked along the open-sided walkway to my flat and opened the door. Even then, standing in the lobby, it took a moment to realise the quiet voices I could hear were coming from my living room. Since a professional assassin was hardly likely to commit such a basic error, I was more curious than alarmed as I eased the door open and peered into the room. Like a spectre at the feast, there she sat, comfortably ensconced in the better of my two easy chairs, purporting to watch TV.

'As I live and breathe; Mrs Prisha Choudhury, you really do haunt me. What do you want now?'

She deigned to look at me, dark eyes as lovely as ever but giving nothing away. 'Is that the best greeting you can manage after a year's absence?'

'Oh, I'm sorry. Hello, Mrs Choudhury, the woman who caused me to be arrested. How perfectly wonderful to see you. My word, you're looking well; have you been on holiday somewhere nice? You seem to have picked up quite a tan.'

'That could be viewed as very offensive.'

'It was meant to be offensive, Prisha. I'm sure you expected nothing less.'

The mistress of not replying did not reply but sat studying me with apparent concentration, reminiscent of her former 'cabbage selection' syndrome. In the absence of a response my irritation began to slip away. 'I see you've made yourself a cup of tea. Since you seem to know where everything is, why don't you make me one while I take off my shoes and jacket? Only half a spoonful of sugar, mind, or I shall send it back.'

Five minutes later we sat facing each other in the living room. She had turned off the TV and I had moved my chair so that I could look her in the face although, since she was also the mistress of inscrutability, I doubted whether I would learn much. Western style dress, I noticed; an emerald green satin blouse coupled with a dark skirt that came just above her crossed knees. So simple, yet it was my favourite Mrs Choudhury outfit, as she well knew.

'What do you want, Prisha?' I asked, more gently this time.

'Your security is bad. I could hardly believe you still leave a spare key behind the air-brick.'

She clearly wasn't ready to answer my question, side-stepping instead to a one-sided review of the twelve months since we'd last met, which wasn't her style at all. Four months had been spent in the US, much of the time near her daughter who was at university there. On her return, she had moved home and been busy getting the new place as she wanted it. When she began to get into the problems of installing a new bathroom suite, I held up my hand. 'Riveting stuff, Prisha, but what do you want?'

There was a long silence, as though reluctant to come to the point. 'My daughter is missing.'

I was quiet for a moment, wondering where this was going. 'Your daughter, Riyah, if I remember correctly. Right, what exactly has happened?'

'She was living at home with me, after coming back from the US. Ten days ago, she left and I haven't heard from her since.'

'Have you argued?'

'We had a disagreement, not an argument.'

It wasn't difficult to imagine Prisha Choudhury's kind of disagreement, as I knew from experience. But, behind the mask of inscrutability, the situation had clearly rattled her sufficiently to seek me out. Given our history, I guessed it was not a step lightly taken. 'Have you any idea where she might have gone? Staying with a friend? What about a boyfriend; is there one?'

Another lengthy pause, which spoke volumes. 'Yes.'

'OK, what is the problem there?'

'He is the problem.'

'Oh, dear.' I find this old-maidish expression often emerges unbidden when conversation takes a turn for the worse, and I wish it wouldn't. 'A problem in what way?'

'He is unsuitable.'

'Aren't we getting onto tricky ground here, Prisha? Your view of what may be 'unsuitable' for your daughter, for example.' This bringing no response, I had little choice but to press on. 'Unsuitable in what way?'

'You are wrong to think I am imposing my views on my daughter. It's his character I don't like. I met him only twice; charming, plausible and without regular employment, a dangerous combination when my daughter has means of her own.'

'You think he has that in mind?

'She is young and sometimes foolish.'

'Age is no bar to foolishness, as we well know.' We both sat contemplating this truism for a moment, me thinking it was particularly true where Prisha Choudhury was concerned. I sighed inwardly before continuing, 'But I understand your concern. And you've really heard nothing for ten days, not even a text?'

She gave the faintest shake of her head. 'When she was in the States we spoke every week. Here, if she went away, she would phone every few days.'

'What about your two stepsons or your brother-in-law: have they heard anything? They are family after all.'

'We have very little contact since my husband's death. You know the circumstances; it should come as no surprise.'

'Perhaps not, but they are close relatives. It's surely worth asking.'

'I will not give them the satisfaction.'

'Very well, Prisha, have it your own way. Have there been any enquiries from Riyah's friends, concerned they haven't heard from her?'

'No.'

'If they're not worried, it's probably because Riyah is still in touch with them, which is reassuring to some degree. Are you able to contact any of these friends?'

'No; Riyah has taken her laptop and her phone – not that I would know how to hack into them. I think she lost touch with some of her friends while in the States. Since she's been back, she's become involved with this boy and I don't have a number for him, or an address.' Pausing for a second, Prisha added, 'She worked part-time at a restaurant, and was friendly with one of the girls there, named Bryony, I believe. She might know something.'

'I hope so, Prisha, otherwise there's precious little to go on. Which brings me back to where I began: what do you want of me?'

'You are being deliberately obtuse.'

'Am I? And I thought I was merely asking you to be specific.'

'You are a very annoying man.'

'So I understand.'

This exchange ended in silence and, on my part at least, a strong sense of déjà vu. We sat looking at each other, mutually uncertain and equally unwilling to speak next. But she was better at this game than me, so I said, 'Do I infer that you would like me to look for your daughter?'

She kept her eyes on mine. 'Yes,' she replied, very quietly, before relapsing into silence.

'You realise I am not a private detective. I do not spring from the pen of Raymond Chandler, even less am I Sherlock Holmes. Nor do I specialise in finding missing persons.' This last was not entirely true. I sometimes had to track down reclusive company directors who were not anxious to discuss their business affairs. But finding a girl with a dubious boyfriend via a single possible friend who worked in a restaurant... And there was another factor. 'I also have a living to earn, so my time may be limited.'

'How much money do you want?'

That annoyed me. 'Are you trying to goad me, Prisha? If so, you are succeeding. Have you come here as a friend, or are you still obsessed with past baggage?'

I saw a flicker of... what? Her expression registered something, possibly regret or even remorse, although that might have been wishful thinking on my part. Whatever it was, she clearly felt the need to say something. 'I trust you to help me.'

At last, a clear, unambiguous statement from the impenetrable Mrs Choudhury. I felt like saying, "See, you can do it if you try" but instead offered, 'Thank you; I will do my best to find Riyah.'

Three-quarters of an hour later I had extracted as much background information from Prisha as she could muster. She did her best but it was thin stuff, largely based on recalling conversations with Riyah. I made what notes I could, although it wasn't a large notebook and there was still space at the bottom of the single page. But at least Prisha seemed to relax a little and conversation flowed more easily, which was a relief. When she came to leave, we walked to the lobby together and I opened the door. An awkward moment, neither of us sure what words or actions were suitable. As she went to walk through, I took hold of her arm.

'Whisper it quietly, Prisha, but I'm actually quite pleased to see you.'

Her eyes met mine and there was the ghost of a smile. 'I knew you would be.'

Not quite what I expected, but about par for Mrs Choudhury. I wondered whether she expected me to kiss her, hesitated, and then didn't. But I can't deny I would have liked to.

During what remained of the evening, I reflected on the task in hand. Prisha had provided several photographs of Riyah from her phone; a strikingly good-looking young woman, with a strong dash of her mother visible. I had only Prisha's description of the boyfriend, Kyle Jordan, plus a few other details such as he had dropped out of Cambridge University. Why, I wondered? But there was only one place to start; Bryony, Riyah's friend from the restaurant, and I didn't even know what she looked like.

It turned out to be a restaurant with a bar and small motel attached. It looked as though the business had expanded from an original, older building, presumably just a pub. Tucked round the back of the main building were the six chalet-style motel rooms, a succession of identical plastic doors and windows hiding beneath a covered walkway. They were separated from the car park by a wooden pole fence of the type more often seen in Westerns complete with hitched horses. As I set off for the bar-restaurant entrance at the side of the building, a tall, youngish man emerged wearing a grey jersey bearing the establishment's logo in gold lettering.

'Is Bryony in this evening?' You would have thought we were bosom buddies.

'Haven't seen her, but I've been in the cellar. I think she's on the roster, though.' He didn't stop to elaborate, perhaps late for his cigarette break, so I walked on. The bar was opposite the doorway with the restaurant off to one side, although access was governed by a sign on a small table which read, 'Please wait here for service'. Since I had already eaten, I made for the bar. It wasn't busy, eight or nine people scattered among the various tables plus a wistful-looking man seated at the bar nursing a pint. This was a nuisance because I wanted to speak to the girl who had appeared behind the bar.

She began serving up my pint while I looked for a name badge on her blouse, but there wasn't one. Late twenties, a big girl, overweight, which she ought to do something about because she was not unattractive. An indecipherable tattoo decorated the visible part of her neck.

'Are you Bryony, by any chance?'

'That's me,' she acknowledged, eyes fixed on the pint glass because it was about to overflow.

'Have you heard from Riyah?'

She looked up at me sharply. 'Who wants to know?'

'I'm a friend of the family'. I coupled this with a bland smile but didn't volunteer more because I wanted to see her reaction.

'Has the mother sent you by any chance?' Guarded, bordering on hostile; Prisha had received a bad press from her daughter.

'Yes, she's rather concerned about her. Nothing heard for nearly a fortnight, although we think she may well be staying with Kyle.'

'Well, then, that's the answer. Speak to Kyle.' Eyebrows raised, she cocked her head to one side, implying that was her last word on the subject.

'Unfortunately, it's not that easy, Bryony. You see, we don't have any contact details for Kyle, no address, not even a town where he might be living. It could be Timbuktu for all we know. All we want is some reassurance that Riyah is ok. For example, it would be very reassuring to know if she's been in touch with you since she left home, in the last ten or twelve days, say.'

Bryony did not in immediately reply, her brow furrowed in confliction. I waited, but when nothing was forthcoming I added, 'Look, I understand if Riyah has cast her mother in a poor light. She can certainly be an awkward beggar, as I know to my cost. But, like any mother, she loves her daughter, Bryony, and just wants to know that she is safe and well.'

She gave me a long look from under her plucked eyebrows before murmuring, 'I had a text saying she'd left home. We were supposed to catch up but I've heard nothing since and her phone is switched off most of the time.'

A couple had come to the bar and Bryony broke off to serve them. How much more did she know, I wondered, and what could she be persuaded to divulge? The couple went off to find a seat but another man arrived for a refill. They were a nuisance, these customers, I decided. When he left the bar, I was disappointed to see Bryony stay where she was, evidently not anxious to continue our conversation. Irritated at having to start again, I eased along the bar.

'You must be a bit concerned yourself, Bryony, if Riyah hasn't been in touch. I intend to carry on looking for Riyah, so would you like me to let you know if I hear anything or, even better, if she turns up at home? In fact, it seems to me we could help each other. Here's my card, and if you care to give me your number...'

'Riyah wouldn't thank me for that. I don't think she wants to be found.'

Time for a dose of intuition. 'Do you think that's Riyah's wish, or Kyle's?' That seemed to strike home, for Bryony gave me a sharp glance. She did not reply, so I reinforced her concern. 'Kyle is a very plausible young man, but do you think he has Riyah's best interests at heart? What do you make of him?'

Something must have registered because her expression lost its hint of suspicion. 'He came here quite a few times, to pick up Riyah. This won't sound good but I was a bit jealous at first, because he's good looking and clever – not the sort of boyfriend ever likely to fall my way. Riyah was happy but I noticed she always paid for his drinks, even a bar meal if he had one. He had a knack of forgetting his wallet, if you know what I mean, until it just became a habit for Riyah to pay. I know she has some money but I thought she was too soft, though she was prickly when I mentioned it.'

I gave a wry smile. 'Well, Bryony, you may not have a great opinion of Riyah's mother, but you share the same scepticism of Kyle Jordan. Do you have any idea where he lived while he was coming here to pick up Riyah?'

We were interrupted again for another refill. Couldn't they wait until we'd finished? When it was completed, I was pleased when Bryony came back to join me.

'I went to his house once, well, Riyah and me. It was meant to be a party but it wasn't my scene; not many people, not much drink and a lot of talk I didn't understand. They all seemed to work with clever technical stuff and were talking shop. It was house near Cambridge, a place called Waterbeach. Kyle was one of four in the house-share. I only remember the name of the road, not the house number.'

'Can you remember where the house was?'

'Not really, but next door had a Father Christmas gnome stood by the gate, even though it was nowhere near Christmas. That might help if you want to find it.'

Deeply thankful for anything of use, I made a note of the road. Bryony took one of my cards but would not give her phone number. If she heard from Riyah, she would phone me. Between further interruptions, I asked a couple more questions but nothing useful was forthcoming, so I thanked her, said I hoped to hear from her soon, and left. If we weren't exactly engaged, at least Bryony and I were now acquainted, and that was something to report to Prisha.

Where the hell is Waterbeach, I asked myself? It rang a bell but not very loudly, one of those towns I felt I ought to know but, shamefully, can't place. Or was it somewhere so obscure that Google Earth has yet to track it down? Somewhere near Cambridge, Bryony said, and my phone quickly confirmed that Google Earth had indeed found it. North of Cambridge, a village nestling on the banks of the river Cam although, with a name like Waterbeach, it was hardly likely to be far from water.

Waterbeach is one of those Fen villages swept up in the great Cambridge development, with the wartime airfield disappearing under a welter of business parks and new housing that will double the population. As satnav guided me through a maze of new roads, I wondered at what point a village grows sufficiently to become a town, and whether the older inhabitants had objected to this sudden transformation. If they had, no-one had taken much notice.

In the early evening there wasn't much traffic and even fewer pedestrians, lending an air of commuter dormitoryland. After squeezing into a parking place at the end of the road, there followed the surreal experience of walking along a residential road looking for a Father Christmas gnome in late March. I hoped it was still there, or it would mean a lot of door-knocking. And he was there, wedged beside a gatepost and holding a parcel proclaiming 'Welcome' in block capitals. There was a hole where his left ear should have been, as though some dissatisfied parcel-recipient had taken umbrage. Since Santa was more visible from the right, I opted to start with the right-hand neighbour.

The front garden didn't amount to much, shingled over for easy maintenance and housing three differently-coloured wheelie bins. There was no doorbell, so I knocked on the door and then stood well back and side-on, the text book way of minimising any perceived threat. It was just as well, because a young woman's wary face appeared around the barely opened door, which was still security chained. She did not speak, so I had to.

'Oh, hello. I know this is a bit of a long shot but does Kyle still live here?'

Her thin face was partially obscured by hair falling across her brow. 'No, he doesn't – and you should stop bothering us.'

The right house, evidently, but it seemed I wasn't the first to enquire. 'I'm sorry, I'm not sure... I'm a friend of Kyle's, you see; we worked together at Zeniths, and he gave me this address. But I've been away for a while and he must have changed his phone.' Make it confusing, an explanation but with gaps, nothing too pat. Even so, she still looked suspicious, more so than Bryony.

'That's like the others said, until we let them in.'

'Who is it, Bev?' A young man's irritated voice from somewhere in the house.

'He says he's a friend of Kyle's.'

'Tell him to fuck off, then. We don't want a repeat of yesterday.'

At any moment the door was going to close. 'I'm sorry; I seem to have come at a bad time. I don't want to come in, if that's what's worrying you, but do you have a contact number for Kyle by any chance, or forwarding address? Only he said he could find me work when I returned and, to be honest, I need to start earning.'

'We've got a pile of threatening letters you can have.' Her voice softened slightly, and the door remained ajar. 'We don't know where he is. He cleared off owing money for rent and other stuff, not that we'll ever see it. And we're not the only ones.'

'I'm sorry to hear that. How long has he been gone?'

'Not all that long...' Bev began, but she suddenly disappeared, to be replaced by an angry young man's face disfigured by a purplish bruise above his right cheek. 'Just fuck off and look for Kyle somewhere else. That bastard has brought us nothing but trouble.'

A heartfelt diatribe followed, not intended to let me speak. As it continued, I became aware another young man had dismounted from a bicycle and was pushing it across the shingle. Distracted by this new arrival, I heard the door slam shut, leaving me little option but to turn to the cyclist. I played the perplexity card.

'Well, I've no idea what that was about, but your friend seems very upset.'

'Yes, he's a bit touchy after yesterday.' He was looking at me from under an untidy mop of fair hair, not all due to wind-blown cycling. An expression of resignation rather than anger, which was a relief.

'I was just enquiring after Kyle, but it seemed to set him off. I did notice the bruising, though.'

'Yes. Two men called yesterday, looking for Kyle. Said they were friends, so Bev let them in, even made coffees. We don't know where he is, and that's when it began to go wrong. One of them became a bit... not aggressive, exactly, but very pushy, as though we were hiding something. Nigel has a short fuse sometimes, and you saw the result.'

'Didn't you call the police?'

'No, it wasn't worth it. His pride is hurt more than anything.' He paused, eyeing me closely. 'I take it you're nothing to do with them?'

'No, definitely not, although I am looking for Kyle. Or rather, his girlfriend, Riyah. We – the family, that is - think they're living together, hence my interest in Kyle. I believe she came here sometimes.'

'Occasionally, yes. They looked a good couple at first, but I can understand her family's concern now.'

'I'd like to find them before your friends from yesterday,

if you understand. I don't want her involved in any of Kyle's goings on, if she's with him. Have you any idea where he might have gone?'

'None, I'm afraid.' He shook his head, further disturbing his ruffled hair. 'Kyle has quite a few contacts around Cambridge who might put him up, but I don't know about a couple. He's clever at anything to do with computers, though, and he likes Cambridge, so I'd be surprised if he moved far. If he put his mind to it, he could make a good living, but he keeps devising get-rich-quick schemes which don't end well.'

'Yes, that's the impression I'm getting.' Then curiosity got the better of me. 'Out of interest, these get-rich-quick schemes; any idea what they were?'

'They involved stock markets, options, forex, spread betting. I heard the words but they mean nothing to me. The trouble is, they haven't done much for Kyle, either.'

Since I couldn't think of anything more to ask, I judged the conversation was coming to a close, but it does no harm to try and make friends. 'Thanks for that; you've been very helpful...' I held out my hand, which he took.

'Roger.'

'Well, thanks, Roger. Would you take my card, you never know if you might think of something? Anything at all, even the most insignificant-seeming detail. Could I take your number, too, just in case? And, look, when I was taking to Bev, I spun her a bit of a story because I could see she was nervous. I meant no harm, so would you apologise to her on my behalf?'

As I set off back to the car, I reflected on the fact that I can be very humble when required.

On the drive home, I called Prisha. I just wanted to give

a quick update but she asked me to call in. It would be my first visit to her new house and it wasn't that far off my route, but I could have done without. When I arrived, she appeared her usual inscrutable self, although I caught a hint of tension. She led the way to the living room - markedly more modest than her previous exotic affair – where we sat down opposite each other. Before I could begin my briefing, she announced that she had heard from one of her stepsons.

I took a moment to absorb this information. 'Did he call you, Prisha?'

'Yes.' She sounded dubious, which did not surprise me. 'My stepson, Ishan, the younger of the two, and the more amenable. He enquired after Riyah, although I suspect he knows she has gone. He said he had changed his phone and lost Riyah's number but I don't believe it. He sounded as though he wanted to find out what I know.'

'Did he ask to speak to Riyah?'

'Yes.'

'And what did you say?'

There was a telling hesitation. 'I said she was away for a few days, staying with friends.

'Hmm. Don't you think you ought to come clean with your family, Prisha? I know you're not keen but what if they've heard from Riyah? And it sounds as if they might, otherwise, why the call?'

'I don't want them involved. It's none of their business.'

'I'm not so sure about that, particularly if they are in touch with Riyah. Why don't I speak to Ishan and find out what he knows?'

'You are supposed to be on my side.'

'I am on your side, Prisha, but I worry about your blind spots. I want to get on and find Riyah, and I'm making some progress. But I'm stuck at the moment, so we have to follow every possible avenue, even if it means speaking to your family.'

A long silence told me this was not well received. I wondered whether she was going to be difficult but I dare not explain why it was now more urgent to find the Kyle-Riyah combo before other, less well-intentioned, searchers.

'Very well, I trust your judgment.'

From Prisha Choudhury, this was a positive paean of praise, so I obtained Ishan's telephone number before she changed her mind. After that I brought her up to speed with regard to Bryony and my trip to Waterbeach, although I carefully omitted any mention of another search team. She heard this without comment. Wanting to get home, I began to make my excuses, genuinely enough, because I hadn't eaten since lunchtime and Prisha hadn't even offered me a cup of tea. We walked along the hall before pausing while Prisha unlatched the front door. As she turned and faced me, I was struck by a disquieting sense of *déjà vu*. Prisha Choudhury possessed the most seductive lips of any woman I've known but, once again, I hesitated, even though her upturned face was only inches away from mine. Somehow, the moment did not feel quite right. As I went to step through the doorway, she spoke very quietly.

'I'm sure you are doing your best.'

'Yes, Prisha, I am, but I worry whether my best will be good enough. And you are not noticeably tolerant of failure.'

'I have confidence in you.'

'Thank you, Prisha. Those words will ensure I sleep soundly in my bed tonight.' She didn't smile, but then I'm not sure irony is quite her kind of humour.

I called Ishan the following day. A confident recorded voice twice asked me to leave a message but I would not, and he answered at my third attempt. I gave my name and explained who I was in a concise, rehearsed statement. I then asked if it meant anything to him. Yes, he was vaguely aware of my existence as a friend of his step-mother. I detected no irony and, as his tone was cautious rather than hostile, I pressed on.

'You may be aware Riyah has gone away for a while without leaving a forwarding address. And her phone is switched off most of the time or asks to leave a message, which is a little concerning. Prisha has had no contact for some days, so she has asked me to call some of Riyah's friends just to find out that she is ok. As a family member, have you heard from Riyah recently, particularly within the last fortnight?'

There was a delay while he decided what to tell me. 'Has it occurred to you that she might not want to be found?'

'Yes, I'm aware there has been a disagreement between mother and daughter, although that is hardly unique. Prisha is keen to mend fences but her main concern is to hear that Riyah is fit and well. That is the priority. There is no insistence that Riyah return home.'

'You have a lot to learn about my stepmother.'

I didn't like this, an assumption that I was naïve in my dealings with Prisha. Perhaps it needled because it was true, at least in part, but I wasn't about to say so. 'She can be a little difficult at times, but she loves her daughter, Ishan, and just wants to know she's ok. Anything else can be sorted out later. That being so, have you heard from Riyah within the last fortnight?'

There was another long pause before he began, 'I don't

know why I should provide comfort for that woman. She's done nothing but cause trouble within this family. But I take your point. You can tell Prisha that I had a text from Riyah about ten days ago, saying she'd left home and was now enjoying a life on the ocean waves.'

'A life on the ocean waves? Is that what she said?'

'Yes, exactly that. It was a very short text, ending "catch up later".'

'And has she caught up? Any follow-up message since?'

'No.'

This monosyllable conveyed a hint of concern. Perhaps that side of the Choudhury family were more worried than they cared to let on. 'How often does Riyah usually contact you?'

'Look, I've told you as much as I know. And it's a pity Prisha can't bring herself to do her own dirty work instead of getting some boyfriend to do it. But then I suppose she's afraid of the reception she'll get, like hearing a few home truths. That's all I've got to say, and a business that doesn't run itself.'

The line went dead. Not, I reflected, my most impressive communication breakthrough, although I had learnt something. A life on the ocean waves? Were they staying on a boat? That would make sense, if you wanted to become elusive. It seemed likely Riyah was stretching a point about being at sea. Much more likely a canal boat or cruiser, there being plenty of scope on the rivers around Cambridge and the Fens. On the other hand, if they really wanted to get lost, those rivers gave access to a network of canals that stretched over half the country.

But a waterborne lifestyle is not cost free. Food, fuel, mooring costs – all have to be paid for. Was it Prisha's worst nightmare, with Riyah funding it all? Or was Kyle contributing, working his contacts around Cambridge to earn some money. Something Roger had said came back to me: he would be surprised if Kyle left the area. I went along with that, unless he was desperate. And one course of action now seemed obvious.

It took Roger a moment or two to place me, my call catching him at an inconvenient moment judging by the hint of irritation. I quickly apologised for troubling him again and his tone mellowed.

'Something has occurred to me, Roger, where Kyle might be staying. Do you know if he had any dealings with boats? You know, houseboats, or any sort of boat that provides living accommodation?'

'Well, I know he's a big fan of being on the water. He stayed on a boat a couple of times. For the odd weekend, that kind of thing; never too far from a pub. I don't know whose boat it was. It might have been hired; you can hire a boat by the day or for a weekend, particularly out of season. But Kyle is clever at exploiting people if they have useful connections, like someone who owns a boat.'

'Does he have a favourite area, or stretch of river?'

'Not that I know of. He could be a bit secretive at times, and we weren't best buddies while he was here. He started off friendly enough – after all, we were house-mates - but once he realised I wasn't likely to be much use to him, he became more distant, if you know what I mean.'

'Well, no surprise to hear that, Roger.' Which was true, although I said it while wondering what more I could usefully ask. But I was forestalled.

'He's been in touch, by the way. With Bev.'

Just like that, out of the blue and completely casual, as though telling me my fly was undone. Taken aback, I could only query, 'Who? Kyle?', which made me sound a bit dim.

'Yes. He texted Bev asking if the rest of his clothes were still at the house.'

'When was this?'

'Yesterday.'

I could hardly believe what I was hearing. 'Did Bev reply?'

'I'm not sure. She might have done.'

'Can you ask her? Are you at home?'

'Yes, hold on a moment.' There followed a succession of noises off; muffled footsteps, a door being opened, a scraping sound, more shuffling footsteps, then Roger's faint voice and Bev's indistinct reply.

'Yes, she told him the clothes were still here, in a holdall.'

'Is he coming to collect them?'

There was another indistinct exchange before Roger's voice returned. 'No, he won't come to the house, which is hardly surprising. He wants us to drop them off somewhere.'

'Do you mean Bev has got Kyle's address?'

More muffled conversation before Roger replied, 'No, it's not where Kyle is living, apparently, but he says we can leave the bag at this place and he'll pick it up later.'

'So where is this drop-off?'

'Somewhere called Hilgay, bloody miles away. But Bev doesn't have a car and nor do I, and I'm certainly not traipsing all the way up there on my bike for his convenience. Nigel can borrow a car, but he won't, not for Kyle.'

'No, I understand that.' But I needed that address, the only lead to finding Riyah, if they were together, and I was sure they were. 'Can I speak to Bev, Roger?'

More delay, before Roger said, 'No, she doesn't want to speak to you, or say any more. Hold on, I'm going back to my room.'

I held on, because what else was I going to do? Roger came back on the line. 'Bev's a bit awkward about Kyle because they were close at one time, and I don't think it's entirely gone away on Bev's part. That's why Kyle contacted her rather than me or Nigel.'

'Fine; I get that. But I wish Kyle no harm, Roger; he is merely a means to an end, finding Riyah. It sounds very much as if they could be on a boat somewhere. If so, I imagine Hilgay or whatever it is won't be far from a waterway.'

'It's near the Great Ouse, apparently. But it's quite a way from Cambridge, although I suppose he could work from a boat provided there was electricity and a signal.'

I took stock for a moment, becoming more convinced by the second that Kyle and Riyah were living on a boat. The only problem was - where?

'Look, Roger, can you get that address from Bev? I can do the drop-off and use it as an excuse to ask a few questions of whoever lives there. It's best you ask, since she doesn't want to speak to me. But you can assure her I mean Kyle no harm; I just want to find Riyah. Even better, would it be possible to arrange a day and time with Kyle for the hand-over?'

It was asking a lot of Roger and I didn't like it. And my fears proved well founded.

'I don't know. I thought we'd seen the last of Kyle but no; he and his problems just keep coming, and now this is just more of his crap. Really, I'm sick of the whole frigging Kyle business.'

'I understand what you're saying, Roger; totally. Kyle has

left a trail of mayhem and you're left with the consequences. Nobody wants that. But I simply want to find Riyah, and then you won't hear another word from me. Look, if you would leave the bag outside the house with the drop-off address attached, I could pick it up without even knocking on your door. How does that sound?'

A long silence indicated this suggestion was at least being given some consideration. I was wondering what further reassurance I could offer when Roger spoke.

'We could do that, I suppose, if Bev gives the address. There's a lean-to on the side of the house, where I keep my bike. I could put it there; out of sight and in the dry.'

'That sounds ideal. I can collect it tomorrow, although I don't know quite what time. But if you put it out first thing, it won't matter. To keep it simple, if I hear nothing more from you today, I'll assume Bev has provided the address, and the arrangement stands.'

There was another delay before Roger answered, 'All right, I'll see what I can do. Anything to be shot of the bloody man.'

The negative principle: simple, effective, brilliant at cutting out needless communication. Mind you, it assumed Roger and Bev would each play their part, otherwise it would be a wasted journey. But, having no other option, it was surely worth the risk.

I had to postpone a business meeting at short notice to free up the following day, which I always deem unprofessional, but needs must... Leaving home after the commuter rush made the journey to Cambridge tolerable and, from there, only another ten minutes to reach Waterbeach. I parked in my previous spot and walked to the house, the neighbourly Santa still offering his battered welcome. The house showing no twitching curtains or signs of life, I crossed the shingle and passed through an unfinished archway. A makeshift lean-to revealed itself, without Roger's bicycle but with a holdall. Attached to one handle was a tie-on label displaying, in girlish writing, an address. Well done, Roger; you talked Bev round.

I did not dwell. Picking up the holdall, I made my way back to the car and began extricating myself from Waterbeach. Back on the A10, I became trapped behind a funereal-paced articulated lorry, allowing ample time to survey the countryside. Sadly, the Fens it is not a landscape that appeals to all, the flatness allowing magnificent cloudscapes but, on a dull March day, there was little magnificence on offer. Bounded by watery ditches, endless regimented fields looked fertile in their spring greenness, although hardly beautiful - unless you are a farmer.

The artic and I eventually bypassed Ely and then circled around Littleport before crossing the river Great Ouse, two occasions when he might have turned off, but didn't. We continued our way north, running adjacent to the river and its occasional boat traffic. This set me off again: were Kyle and Riyah actually on a boat and, if so, where? Surely my instinct was right? But what if they were on the move? Seeing these few craft meandering along mile after mile of a river with links to a maze of other waterways was enough to make me doubt the sanity of this search. And what would Prisha say if I returned empty-handed?

After a few miles, the road diverged from the river and I began to wonder where it was taking me. But Hilgay was still there, suitably bypassed and squeezed between the church and a water tower. Google search showed the location of my road, a lane to nowhere on the outskirts of the village. There were still some gaps between an odd mix of old and new properties, perhaps waiting for house prices to rise sufficiently to make development worthwhile. Having only a house name rather than a number, I was reduced to something of a crawl while trying to spot, let alone read, various house names. Failing to find it by the time I had run out of properties, I parked in a field gateway, hoping the farmer did not require access in the next twenty minutes.

I did not have to carry the holdall far before I found my destination. 'Minerva' declared a rickety wooden sign, hardly visible from the lane. A 1930s style double fronted bungalow in a plot wide enough to accommodate a large garage-workshop, made of what looked suspiciously like asbestos panels. The bungalow itself looked reasonably well maintained but the garden was neglected, the lank grass not cut since winter. A solitary bramble bush was thriving beside the garage.

There being no doorbell, I knocked vigorously on the wood-panelled front door. No answer. Of the two front windows, one had curtains drawn, so I moved along to look through the other. It revealed a small living room of notable ordinariness but giving no indication of recent occupation. Following the concreted path around the side of the bungalow, a translucent window and external pipework indicated the bathroom, beyond which was the kitchen with a door opening to a scruffy back garden. Then another bedroom, curtains open, showing a single made-up bed. All in all, a brief search that unearthed nothing of significance that I could see.

Not so, when I extended my search. The concrete path did not run to the garage, and the ground was soft beneath the thin grass. I'm no Jungle Jim but even I could see someone had walked across before me. In a muddy patch in front of the garage personal door, I saw that it was two people, the imprints large enough to indicate both were men. They had entered the garage, and then left, according to the footprints, which looked fresh enough to have been made that day. Was this Kyle and some unknown friend – hardly Riyah, unless she had exceptionally large feet – checking for the holdall? Or was it somebody else, also looking for Kyle. If so, how did they know about this place?

The garage was empty of any vehicle or boat, but was professionally fitted out with a block and tackle hoist above a pit sunk in the concrete base. Two large metal cabinets, both padlocked, were mounted above a scored wooden workbench. Padlocked, presumably, to keep safe an array of tools, for the occupier was evidently a practical man. I wondered whether to leave the holdall suspended from the hoist but eventually settled for the workbench. Back outside, I went to the double doors at the front, but there was no sign a vehicle had recently left the garage.

It always pays to ask questions, and it's amazing what people will tell you. I went next door, a more modern bungalow partially screened from its neighbour by a couple of straggling buddleia bushes. There was a doorbell this time, which I pressed. The sound of shuffling feet preceded the door being opened by an elderly woman, her grey hair wound in a tight bun. I started to speak as she blinked at me through plain, round spectacles but she cut in, announcing 'I'll just get my husband', and shuffled off. I heard a brief exchange before an elderly man came into view, more sure-footed and rather more alert. He gave me a questioning smile, an invitation to explain this intrusion.

'I'm sorry to trouble you, but I'm supposed to be meeting him next door' – I indicated with my thumb – 'but he doesn't seem to be here.' I left the query hanging in the air.

'What, you mean, Martin?'

'Yes, I arranged to meet him here, but there's no sign. Have you seen him?'

He gave a little chuckle. 'No, he's still in Portugal as far as I know. Won't be back until the middle or end of April.'

'Oh, that's a bit odd; I'm sure he said he'd be back by now.' I thought for a moment, and tried a long shot. 'I'm supposed to see him about the boat, and I was under the impression it was here. You know, laid up over the winter.'

His look of puzzlement deepened as he shook his head. 'No, he leaves it at the marina, as far as I know. They might lift it out, but it's too big to go in his workshop. Is he thinking of selling it, then?'

'It's just a possibility at present; very tentative. Well, it looks as though Martin and I have well and truly crossed our wires somewhere, but I'd like to take a look at the boat while I'm in the area. Do you know the name of the marina, and where it is?'

At last, the look of puzzlement dissipated somewhat. 'I'm not sure it has a name, but it's not one of the big marinas, you know, with lots of boats. It's a private cut, only a dozen boats, about half a mile downstream from the town. Martin knows the owners, I believe. We've been there a couple of times, out on the river for the day, when Martin invited us. Littleport; only a few miles if you're in a car.'

'Of course, Littleport; that rings a bell now you've mentioned it. And the mooring is downstream, you say. But I still can't remember the name of the boat, if he's ever told me.'

'You've seen it already, if you've been to the bungalow – Minerva.'

'Ah, yes; that makes sense, his two places of abode. A

bit confusing for the postman, though.'

I smiled at my own joke, but it only induced a return of puzzlement to my man. Some fall on stony ground, which is always disappointing. There remained one other query.

'I was meant to meet a couple of friends here. You haven't seen them by any chance, have you?'

A shake of the head. 'Our living room is at the back, so we don't see much out here. Not that there's much to see; it's very quiet. Which is why we like it,' he added, and I wondered whether it was a hint for me to depart.

'Yes, I must leave you in peace. Thanks, anyway, for trying to help, and my apologies for disturbing you.'

He gave a nodded acknowledgment before withdrawing across the threshold, oblivious of the debt I owed him.

My informant was right; it was only a few miles to Littleport, but I knew that already, having driven past the place earlier. I found a small public car-park and managed to squeeze into a place as someone was leaving. Then I had a job finding the right coins for the pay-and-display and had to ask another motorist for help with change. In the end he donated fifty pence towards the cost of two hours, which was good of him. At least I knew roughly where the river was, and set off walking in that direction.

This took me through the old part of the town, founded long ago when the river was the key element in its development, providing the means to transport heavy goods. Near the river, two rail tracks of the London to Kings Lynn line necessitated a level crossing, beyond which was a riverside pub and access to a footpath running along the top of the flood defence bank. As I stepped out along the path, it struck me that the Great Ouse is very much an engineered river, straightened and confined between two substantial banks, hardly an example of riverine beauty despite its popularity for cruising. Beyond the opposite bank, I could see traffic on the main road I had now traversed twice that same morning.

In the distance, half-hidden among a rare clump of leafless willow trees, was a clutch of buildings, a house with two workshops adjacent. Drawing closer, patches of white proved to be boat superstructures, their hulls hidden from view behind the flood bank, so it looked as if I was on the right track. The cut forced the main path to deviate around the buildings but a lesser track led down to the moorings; six boats on the near bank, five on the opposite, where there was one vacant space.

There being nobody to stop me, I walked round to the far bank, scrutinising each boat as I went. None seemed occupied, nor was anyone visible around the house or workshops, but then it was midweek and not yet Easter, so hardly high season. I found no 'Minerva' but, on the near bank, one cruiser had oddly shaped fenders covering the bow where a name might be displayed. Was this suspicious, or did the vacant space mean I was too late? I stopped by the house because, if I could find somebody, I had questions to ask. As I glanced around, someone arrived at the moorings from along the footpath. Dressed in a long, shapeless coat, head surmounted by a woollen bobble-hat, the figure made to board the nameless cruiser. I arrived as she was in the companionway, unlocking the door, but perhaps hearing my footsteps, she looked up and saw me.

'Hello, Riyah.'

A long stare from tired eyes, a little nervous. 'Do I know you?'

'No, you don't. But I'm a friend of your mother's, and

she's asked me to find you and see that you're ok. She's been worried about you.'

Riyah grimaced at this, and muttered 'that's all I need', more to herself than me. I told her my name and asked if we could sit down, have a cup of something and agree what message I could give her mother. There was one other burning question.

'Is Kyle here?'

There was a telling silence before she answered, 'No, he's not.' Then she looked up and said, 'You'd better come aboard.'

It was a sorry story that Riyah recounted, of disillusionment, regret and, in all probability, abandonment. The novelty of living on a cramped boat had soon begun to wear off, and she was meeting all the bills. When she began questioning what the future held, their relationship had become strained. Then, yesterday afternoon, Kyle had asked her to walk into town and post a pre-paid letter, some sort of official return, he said. Oh, and would she leave her phone, which he sometimes used for purposes known only to himself? She went, glad of the prospect of a walk. On her return an hour later, Kyle was gone, as was her phone and bank card, although he had left over twenty pounds in notes and coin in her purse. She had no idea where he might have gone, or what she ought to do.

I made sympathetic noises, but there was a more pressing question I wanted answered. 'Are you aware other people are looking for Kyle? I suspect he owes them quite a lot of money, because they're going to considerable trouble to find him.'

'He's in debt, so it's no surprise to hear that. He's clever at parting people from their money, a great opportunity to join his brilliant share-trading system. Investors, he calls them. Except his system doesn't seem to work, and if they're not getting the promised return, I suppose they want their money back.'

'Were you an investor, Riyah?'

'No, thank God. My money is tied up in a trust fund, for which I am truly grateful. Even so, he's cost me plenty.'

It wasn't the moment to go into all the gory detail, and I wanted a swift conclusion. 'Ok, Riyah, shall we talk about your options, such as they are. Look, your mother wants you back home, and if Kyle was the cause of you leaving, well, it seems he's history now. She'll welcome you with open arms.'

I wasn't totally convinced of this, and nor was Riyah. 'I don't know how well you know my mother, but she's the reason I left.'

'Yes, I know she has her moments, but this is too important for that sort of nonsense. I've seen how worried she's is. It will be fine, I promise.'

Riyah hesitated, her expression suddenly strained as she muttered, 'I don't know.'

'Honestly, Riyah, it will be fine. Of course you're concerned, tired and fed up as you are. But a few days at home will do both you and your mother the world of good.'

'Oh, yes; I'll be positively blooming.' She stopped, staring into the middle distance before muttering, 'but it doesn't seem I have much choice.'

Hearing this, my heart sank, although I hoped it did not show. 'Right, that's decided, so can I help collect your things? Then we can be away from here.'

'I didn't bring much, leaving in a hurry and all that. I bought this awful coat from a charity shop but at least it's warm.'

A smallish wheeled suitcase still had room to spare

when Riyah had finished packing. Nor was she in a hurry, suggesting we might have a bite of lunch before setting off, and even tidy up, but I vetoed the idea, keen to get away. 'Leave everything. It's just possible Kyle might come back, so do you have a place to put the key? Good. We'll cancel your bank card once we're away from here.'

A phone call to Prisha could wait, too, at least until we were back at the car. Then I heard Riyah say, 'God, not more visitors?'

Two men had appeared beside the cut and were surveying the boats. I did not need to ask who they were. 'I'm pretty sure they're looking for Kyle. I'll go and speak to them. When you leave the boat, make sure you stay a yard or two behind me. Let me do all the talking.'

Not waiting for a reply, I headed for the companionway and climbed onto the deck. They saw me as I stepped off the boat. We were some yards apart, which was how I wanted to keep it. One was late twenties, quite tall and very solidly built. The other was perhaps a decade older but with an open, intelligent face. He proved to be the spokesman.

'Are you the mystery man we've heard about?' A pleasantly modulated voice, for a hard man.

'I wouldn't know, but if you're looking for Kyle, I'm afraid you've missed him. He left yesterday afternoon, leaving no forwarding address. But I don't suppose that's much of a surprise to you.'

This was received with a sceptical smile. 'No, I can't say it is. Even so, we'd like to make sure, just in case. And speak to this young lady, of course.'

Riyah had emerged from the boat and was taking up station behind me. I said, 'No, really, you can take my word for it; he's gone. And I'm only here to take this young lady home. Whatever remaining interest she had in Kyle died yesterday when he took the opportunity to run off with some of her property. Not a great character reference, but it suits him.'

'He's a bit slippery, I grant you that.' Spokesman gave me a long, questioning look, while Burley simply looked blank. After due consideration, Spokesman added, 'Look, we've had a very busy morning, driving about, visiting places. You may have done the same. There's obviously common cause here, so why don't we all get on the boat, our hostess can make us a coffee and we can exchange information that will help us both?'

'I'm not sure you're hearing me. I've lost all interest in Kyle now; he was merely a means to an end. My only job was to find this young woman and take her home.'

'And I'm just as sure we can still help each other; and a civilised chat over a cup of coffee is the way to do it.'

We were getting nowhere like this and I was running out of ideas, and patience. 'Thanks for the offer, but we must get on. Besides, your friendly chats have a way of inflicting injuries. I've seen Nigel's face. You know; Nigel of the Waterbeach trio.'

The mood changed instantly. Spokesman's face hardened and Burley looked as if he'd suddenly been woken up, glancing around to see if anyone was about. There wasn't.

'You should be careful what you say. Nigel, as you call him, was very disrespectful. Beverley was more helpful, in the end. We've been to the house twice today. No answer first time, but we found a holdall with an address attached and a note from Beverley inside. It was meant for Kyle, but it proved a wild goose chase. Beverley was more helpful when we went back and saw her just now.'

The knowledge that we must have passed each other on the road to Hilgay lent an ironic twist to the morning. And it hadn't occurred to me to look inside the holdall. But it was the realisation that Bev had known about the boat all along that annoyed me. When this pair returned from Hilgay – had they broken into the house to find her? – she must have given the boat details, almost certainly in the knowledge that Kyle had gone. She was evidently less concerned about what might happen to Riyah when they visited.

'You have been busy. And what state is Beverley in now, I wonder?' I saw no point in prolonging the conversation. 'Anyway, it's been very pleasant chatting to you both, but we must get on. If you'll just stand aside...'

Neither moved as I stepped forward, until Burley squared himself to block my path. I kept going, he braced himself, clenching his fists as he did so. Two paces apart, I whipped up the pepper spray and let fly. A choking cry as he clutched his face while I swivelled to Spokesman and fired again. He was almost out of range but ducking away threw him off balance. Back to Burley, and a hefty kick to his right knee, hoping for a dead-leg. Half an eye on Spokesman, but he wasn't rushing to his mate's assistance, and I wanted finished with Burley, so punched him hard on the temple. He went down, still groaning.

Turning to Spokesman, his eyes blinking uncomfortably, I offered some advice. 'Best you step aside and help your mate'. He hesitated, but then moved off the path. I turned to Riyah. 'Come on, let's go.'

She did not need to be told twice, half-running past the stricken pair. I took Riyah's case and hurried her along the track, sometimes breaking into a short-lived jog. Looking back, there was no sign of pursuit, but I wasn't inclined to wait and find out. Reaching the pub, I had one final look, saw nothing, so dropped our speed to regain breath. Nor did I dwell once we reached the car, quickly hitting the road. Riyah had hardly spoken a word but, with her breathing easier, her first question was, 'What was that spray?'

'I carry it in case of tricky situations. I only carried it today because I thought Kyle might be on the boat, and be difficult.'

She still looked a little shaken. 'I didn't imagine anything like that could happen.'

'I've seen an example of their methods. Kyle has got himself into fairly deep water, borrowing money from unforgiving sources and then dodging off. They will be hard to shake off, particularly if he stays in the area. Anyway, you are well out of it.'

She did not reply, a familiar trait presumably inherited from her mother. Or she might simply have been very tired, because she settled her head back in the headrest, closed her eyes and appeared to sleep. I took the opportunity to phone Prisha, saying we were on our way. As ever, there was no great show of emotion. She asked to speak to Riyah but I fobbed her off, saying she was asleep, although I saw Riyah watching me through half-closed eyes, listening to the conversation.

As the journey reduced to the last few miles, there remained one last question to be asked, and answered. I wasn't looking forward to it, but it couldn't be dodged.

'Forgive me for asking such a personal question, Riyah, but are you pregnant?'

She turned away, suddenly interested in observing the bland Hertfordshire countryside. 'What makes you think that?'

'Oh, just something you said about positively blooming. I may be wrong, of course, or you could tell me it's none of my business, which would be perfectly true. We've hardly known each other five minutes, so there's no reason why you should tell me anything.'

Her gaze remained somewhere beyond the car window. 'I'm about ten weeks.'

'Ok, and does Kyle know?'

'No.'

We both considered the situation for a moment, until I asked, 'When best to tell your mother, do you think? For what it's worth, my instinct is the sooner, the better.'

There was no reply, and I could see her lips tightly pursed.

'Look, I have an odd relationship with your mother. There are times when we strongly disagree, but we seem to survive these differences. If you prefer, I can go in first and prepare the ground.'

'Whenever she finds out, she'll go mental.' Her voice sounded unsteady, on the verge of tears.

'Don't underestimate your mother's love, Riyah. It's there all right, even if it's not always obvious. But I'm willing to tell her, if you wish. You know, be a lightening conductor.'

'I would have thought you'd done enough.'

'Well, let's just say I like to see a job through to the finish.'

She switched her gaze to the dashboard, although I doubt she saw it. While I waited for a reply, drops of rain appeared on the windscreen, so I flicked the wipers, leaving a greasy smear which was no help at all.

Then a very small voice said, 'Would you mind?'

I parked the car in the driveway, beside the house, where it couldn't be seen from the front door. Prisha answered the door, greeting me with her enigmatic half-smile which, as usual, conveyed little. She glanced beyond me, looking for her daughter.

'Riyah's asleep in the car, Prisha. She's very tired; it will do her good to sleep for a while. She'll be with you shortly, but it gives me a chance to bring you up to speed.'

Prisha Choudhury was watching me closely, a little too much eye make-up again, I noticed, although I was prepared to forgive her that.

'Riyah and Kyle have been living on a boat, on the Great Ouse north of Cambridge. They fell out and he took an opportunity to sneak off with Riyah's phone and bank card. There may be other stuff, too; Riyah will know. She was left on her own, abandoned, which is when I found her, too tired and upset for me to learn much more. She'll be fine when she's rested.'

Prisha made no reply, only a slight nod of her head in acknowledgment.

'There's something else I have to tell you.' I waited until Prisha's eyes were locked onto mine. 'Riyah is expecting a baby.'

Her eyes narrowed, she looked away and made a noise deep in her throat. 'A daughter of darkness.'

'Stop, Prisha; don't say another word.' Fighting an urge to shout, I held up my hands. 'I won't listen to any more of that nonsense. Listen to me: your daughter is outside, exhausted, upset, fearful. She knows she's made a mistake, been foolish, but this is when she absolutely needs her mother's love. And it must be unconditional, Prisha, because, if you can't find it in your heart, then I'll drive that girl away and find another solution. And don't make the mistake of thinking I won't.'

Turned away, head bowed, I couldn't see her face. Determined to say nothing more, I stood and waited, and then waited some more. It seemed an age before she straightened up and turned to face me. To my surprise, she seemed quite calm, looking me directly in the eye.

'I know you mean what you say, but it won't be necessary. Riyah's home is here with me. There will be no recriminations, I promise you, only this mother's love.'

'Good. That's what I expected to hear, Prisha.' I even managed some kind of smile. 'Shall we go and fetch Riyah?'

'Yes, I need to see my daughter.' Suddenly, she reached out and clutched my arm. 'Just a moment, I have something to say. I made a promise to you just then; now I want one from you. I want you to promise you will not turn away from me again. I know we are a strange pair, but you speak the truth to me as you see it, and I need that. It's why I want you to promise.'

For the first time since I had known her, Prisha Choudhury suddenly looked vulnerable, and it was as though a mask had been removed. Disconcerting, but I felt better for seeing it.

'We are an odd couple, Prisha, but that's for us to know and others to find out. I don't make a habit of bandying promises about, but you have made me an offer I can't possibly refuse,' Although I did have one after-thought. 'Does that mean we're friends now?'

She studied me intently, gave a small, rueful smile and observed, 'You make some really stupid remarks.'

'Yes, I'm told it's part of my charm.' I linked my arm through hers. 'Come on, let's go and see your daughter.'

The Majesty of the Law

NOTHING SO EPITOMISES the greatness of England as the rule of law. Well, I suppose we have to include Wales, but certainly not Scotland, with their Procurator Fiscals and suchlike. Goodness knows what happens up there, and best not to ask. Anyway, imagine if you will, a perfectly normal day in a county court somewhere in England. A trial is due to start. The low murmur of conversation comes from the half-full public gallery occupied by idle voyeurs, the homeless, pensioners cutting down on their heating bills and a smattering of people with an actual interest in the outcome of the trial.

Below the public gallery, prosecuting counsel Neville Bodkin is idly shuffling through his case papers. Youngish, besuited and bewigged, he believes he is an impressive sight, projecting an air of competent malice by which he hopes to intimidate both the defendant and the defence counsel even before speaking a word. Bodkin is assisted by a pupil from his chambers, Charlotte Mandible, who is halfway through her pupillage and, incidentally, very pretty.

Across the courtroom sits Reginald Ragwort, an elderly solicitor conducting the defence. He conveys an air of bumbling ineptitude, carefully honed over many decades to delude gullible opponents into believing he is a brick short of a full load. Even as he sits gazing vacantly into space, no-one has ever determined whether this is true or not. The defendant, Henry Stote, sits close by. His weatherbeaten face is difficult to age but he is dressed, unusually but smartly, in plus-fours and a Norfolk shooting jacket, an ensemble offset by a tie featuring a motif of a weasel. Only Stote knows whether this is a subtle play on words with his name and the Mustelidae family, or mere coincidence. He is a gamekeeper.

Bodkin casts a dismissive eye on the defendant's advocate and turns to the lovely Charlotte. 'The man's only a solicitor; it shouldn't be allowed. What were they thinking, letting solicitors act in a county court? We barristers deserve better. How can we expect a decent intellectual tussle from a man taking a day off from conveyancing?' His lip curls in righteous contempt.

'You're not keen on solicitors then, Neville.'

'Oh, they're all right in their place, I suppose, sorting out probate and suchlike mundanities but certainly not here. This is for grown-ups.' Bodkin, whose own pupil inexplicably abandoned a legal career after only four months of his tutelage, is keen to establish a better rapport with the lovely Charlotte. 'Did you know that a bodkin is a pointed arrowhead designed to pierce armour? Rather appropriate, don't you think?'

'Really? I thought it was a blunt needle my granny uses in hemming.' Bodkin looks askance at the attractive Charlotte, scowls briefly and resumes reading his notes.

As the jury files in and take their seats, the sound of muttered conversation in the public gallery rises and then falls away, the regulars understanding this is the equivalent of the theatre lights dimming. The clerk of the court demands, 'All rise', and there follows a general shuffling as all bar one in the public gallery, too drunk to respond, comply. The entry of His Honour Judge Eustace Popplecock invites comparison with the entry of a Roman emperor into the gladiatorial arena; only the crowds, the lions and the certainty of imminent death are missing. Nor is Judge Popplecock an imperious figure: think Roman emperor inclined to vote Liberal Democrat. Tall, gangling and bespectacled, he seems somewhat burdened by his wig and gown, glad to reach the security of his seat. He makes himself comfortable, gives a barely perceptible nod to the court clerk, and the metaphorical curtain rises.

The jury has been ushered in, the charge read out and the defendant, Stote, has entered a plea of 'not guilty', thus ensuring an adversarial conflict. It is time for the prosecution to outline its case and Neville Bodkin rises to the occasion. 'This, your Honour, is an unusual case brought by my clients, the Poddymoor-on-the-Wold Clean Green Energy Group. It concerns a malicious conspiracy by the defendant and other person or persons unknown to prevent the development of an approved electricity generation farm at Poddymoor-on-the-Wold. As we will demonstrate, the defendant and others have conspired to introduce two protected wildlife species to the proposed site, namely; newts and orchids, for the express purpose of preventing the development.'

Bodkin pauses for dramatic effect. 'You will be aware, your Honour, of the seriousness of a conspiracy charge. We will prove that this is not an inchoate conspiracy but one with actual and profoundly deleterious consequences for the already parlous state of this country's energy provision.'

Judge Popplecock ruminates upon this latter statement,

making a mental note to look up the meaning of 'inchoate' when he gets home, and perhaps 'deleterious' while he has the dictionary to hand. He nods sagely. 'Very well, Mr Bodkin; proceed.'

Neville Bodkin proceeds to outline his case. 'Your honour, I intend to show in detail how a comprehensive environmental survey was correctly and professionally carried out on the site as required by law before planning permission can be granted. No protected newts or orchids were present. Only two days later, the defendant, Henry Stote, was seen at the site, burdened with backpack and bucket, visiting every ditch, pond and meadow in the vicinity. Then, the following day, two protected species were discovered by members of the public who are, by an extraordinary coincidence, all members of the 'Save our Poddymoor' group. Conspiracy is too kind a word for such a craven and despicable act, your Honour, as we intend to prove'

Bodkin resumes his seat with a theatrical flourish, at which Judge Popplecock invites the defence counsel to respond. The careworn, crumpled figure of Reginald Ragwort rises uncertainly to his feet and mutters, 'All will become clear, your Honour.'

A bewildered silence falls on the court, swiftly followed by muted tittering in the public gallery. Judge Popplecock, frowning incredulously, stares at defence counsel. 'Is that all you have to say, Mr Ragwort?'

'Yes, your Honour.'

'Well, brevity may be the soul of wit but in a trial...' His voice tails away in perplexity. 'It must be your witness, then, Mr Bodkin.'

Somewhat sooner than anticipated, Bodkin begins calling his witnesses. What is unusual – indeed, noteworthy

– is that Reginald Ragwort never once questions the succession of prosecution witnesses on behalf of the defence. As the witnesses come and go, all confirming the damning presence of Stote at the site, he remains unmoving, eyes focussed on some unknown distant object, apparently oblivious to the proceedings. At first this pleases Bodkin no end, confirming his profound belief in the superiority of barristers. But, as time goes on, and Ragwort still unmoving, seeds of doubt begin to percolate through Bodkin's mind. What is the fellow up to? Could there possibly be some diabolical counter-argument lurking in ambush? A surreptitious glance at Ragwort's mummified countenance lends some reassurance, but even so...

The denizens of the public gallery, almost comatose after the procession of untested prosecution witnesses, rouse themselves when Henry Stote is called to the stand. This is Bodkin's moment; the lethal application of a keen legal mind.

'You are a gamekeeper, are you not?'

'That's right, sir, in the employ of Sir Ambrose Bunyan these last fifteen years.'

'But gamekeeping is not your sole employment or source of income, is it?'

'No, sir.'

A faint smile plays across Bodkin's lips at this unexpectedly naive reply; the fellow really must be a simpleton. 'Then please enlighten us on your other occupation.'

'I am a financial adviser to the Bank of England.'

Uproarious laughter erupts in the public gallery, Bodkin recoils as if struck by one of his arrowhead namesakes, while Judge Popplecock is almost apoplectic.

The latter rounds on Stote with all the severity of the law. 'Attempts at humour have no place in these proceedings. If repeated, I will regard it as contempt of court and you will be punished accordingly.'

At this point, Ragwort stirs to make his first intervention. 'If I may, your Honour, I can confirm that Mr Stote is indeed consulted by the Bank of England, via the person of Sir Peregrine Peseta. Being public spirited, my client accepts no payment for conveying his views on the nation's economy, although failure to follow his urgent advice to restrain quantitative easing has cost the country billions and embedded serious inflation. We can obtain an affidavit to that effect if you wish, your honour, although I believe Sir Peregrine is in conference with the Chancellor of the Exchequer this morning. But I could request a special intervention if you deem it necessary.'

Judge Popplecock is rocked to his core. Why, he had dined with Sir Peregrine only last week, and tapped him up for some fail-safe investment opportunities. The idea that Peseta might get these ideas from some wretched gamekeeper is deeply shocking. He will sell those bonds at the first opportunity. Suddenly remembering he is required to speak, he manages, 'On reflection, perhaps that won't be necessary. Carry on, Mr Bodkin.'

Bodkin, still somewhat taken aback, tries to rally. 'Notwithstanding your gamekeeping and, er, financial roles, you do have another source of income.'

'I do, sir.'

But Bodkin is becoming cautious of Stote's seeming admissions. 'Well, pray divulge its nature, unless it is a matter of such importance to the state that it is subject to the Official Secrets Act.' Bodkin is pleased to hear a titter run round the public gallery.

'Oh, no, sir: it's nothing like that. No, I go beating on neighbouring shoots. Thirty-five pounds for a day's beating, and all the game pie you can eat lunchtime. And a beer. Very enjoyable, unless it rains.'

'I think you're being deliberately obtuse, Mr Stote,' cries Bodkin. 'You know very well you possess a stock of great-crested newts and green-winged orchids, and that you supply these protected rarities at advantageous prices to persons desirous of stopping approved developments vital to the country's infrastructure.'

'Oh no, sir, that would be quite illegal. However, I am very fortunate in the wildlife that abounds around my cottage.'

'And would that bountiful wildlife include great crested newts and green-winged orchids, by any chance? The very species so recently discovered at Poddymoor-on-the-Wold?'

'Yes, sir; I am very fortunate.'

'Indeed you are, Mr Stote.' Bodkin grasps the lapels of his suit, an impressive gesture he has copied from TV court dramas. 'And how far from your front door might be found these rare newts and orchids?'

'Oh, I should say about twenty-five yards, sir.'

'Twenty-five yards! How wonderfully convenient. Then you are ideally placed to look after every aspect of their welfare, ensuring they and their valuable offspring thrive under your beneficent eye. Indeed, they prosper so well that supplying a few surplus specimens when requested would hardly affect your core breeding stock, thus providing the basis of what might be described by some as a "nice little earner".'

'Oh, no, sir; that would be completely illegal.'

Bodkin draws himself up to his full five feet eight

inches, a not particularly impressive sight. Having laid the foundations of his case, it is now time to build upon it. 'You have heard a number of witnesses state that you were seen at the Poddymoor-on-the-Wold site burdened with a backpack and a bucket. I think we can all speculate on the contents of the backpack – multiple rounds of bacon sandwiches, perhaps, with green-winged orchids for dessert – but pray enlighten us as to the purpose of the bucket?'

'It's a pet bucket, sir.'

Unseemly laughter again erupts from the public gallery – this is exactly the kind of exchange they've come to hear. Judge Popplecock, on the other hand, is not amused, rounding on the public gallery delinquents and shouting, 'Silence in court!' with unsuspected, and very unliberal, venom. Nor is Neville Bodkin amused, the slowly-diminishing laughter drowning out the sound of his grinding teeth. With some caution, he continues his cross-examination.

'You claim it is a pet bucket? In what way is it a pet?'

'Oh, no, sir; the bucket is not a pet – that would be ridiculous. No, I keep certain pets in it. The rigid sides prevent the creature from being crushed should I trip over.'

'And we should assume these pets are great-crested newts?'

'Oh, no, sir; you mustn't move any sort of newt about the country, that's completely illegal. No, I was carrying an orphaned baby stoat named Susan. She has to be fed milk very frequently through an eye-dropper, so I have to carry her everywhere.'

'Then why is Susan the mysteriously orphaned stoat not with you today?

'Well, sir, somebody else is looking after her. But I could

bring her tomorrow in the bucket if you'd like to see her. She's a lovely little thing, like quicksilver and not at all ferocious...'

'I don't think that will be necessary,' interrupts Bodkin. 'However, given your onerous stoat nurse-maiding duties, what exactly was the purpose of your extensive, time-consuming visit to Poddymoor-on-the-Wold?'

'Well, sir, someone had advised me – quite anonymously – that there were rare newts and orchids on the site. Being very keen on amphibians and orchids, I was pleased to go and have a look.'

'And, amazingly, although a painstakingly thorough, professional survey had found nothing only two days before, you immediately stumbled on not one, but multiple examples of these rarities.'

'That's right, sir. But what made the trip even more worthwhile was my surmising that the newts might well be a new sub-species; a pale-breasted great-crested newt.'

A new outbreak of stifled laughter from the public gallery was immediately silenced by a venomous look from Judge Popplecock. Bodkin's eyes narrowed.

'May I ask what qualification allows you to pronounce upon such a matter?'

Reginald Ragwort rises to make an intervention almost as rare as the newly-discovered newt. 'Your Honour, Mr Stote is a much-respected member of the Amphibian and Orchid Enthusiasts' Society. Indeed, he is a founder member. There is some suggestion that, should this be confirmed as a genuine sub-species, it be called Stotes newt. But my client, modest to a fault, would prefer it to be known as the Poddymoor-on-the-Wold pale-breasted great-crested newt.'

Bodkin is incredulous. 'Surely it's not usual for a new

species to be named merely after the place of its discovery?'

'Oh, yes, it is, sir,' adds Stote helpfully. 'The Orkney vole, for example, or the St Kilda wren.'

'And the Manx shearwater,' echoes a voice from the public gallery.

'Don't forget the Dartford warbler,' says a measured voice, which may have emanated from the court clerk.

'Enough!' shouts Judge Popplecock, his patience stretched beyond endurance. 'What is going on here? We have a pet bucket, an orphaned stoat named Susan, a green-winged orchid that might fly for all I know and now a newly-discovered newt with an incorrigibly long name. Whatever next: the Lundy lark? The Rockall robin? The Anglesey aardvark? At least these names would be short and comprehensible.' Judge Popplecock shifts furiously in his seat. 'Will you get a grip on your case, Mr Bodkin, before we all sink beneath the verbiage of strange – and possibly mythical – creatures.'

Swallowing hard, Bodkin addresses the judge in a tone trapped somewhere between pique and self-pity. 'I'm sorry, your Honour; it is deeply regrettable that the language of taxonomy so frequently lends itself to ill-judged mockery. However, in the interests of justice I feel we must persevere.'

'Very well, Mr Bodkin, carry on, but do try to keep things simple and relevant.'

'Yes, your Honour, thank you.' Bodkin turns back to the defendant. 'Mr Stote, let us return to your excursion to the proposed electricity generation site at Poddymoor-on-the-Wold. You say that your visit was the result of information received anonymously about the afore-mentioned protected species. Yet only two days before your visit, a comprehensive and professionally conducted wildlife survey found not a single trace of the species so strangely discovered immediately after your visit. How do you explain this anomaly?'

'I don't know, sir. You would have to ask the ladies and gentlemen concerned. Perhaps they just weren't up to the job, too much time spent behind a desk. You need very keen eyesight and know where to look. I haven't mentioned this before, sir, not wanting to disparage their efforts and get them into trouble, but I also noticed a rare dragonfly – more accurately, a four-spotted libellula darter as it happens – and a dead bat which seemed to resemble a greater mouse-eared bat which was actually believed extinct...'

'Enough!' shouts Justice Popplecock, scarcely audible amid a renewed outbreak of unseemly laughter from the public gallery. As the hubbub dies away, the judge rounds on prosecuting counsel. 'Mr Bodkin, the prosecution has singularly failed to provide anything other than the most anecdotal of circumstantial evidence and I will not allow this court to descend further into a place of public entertainment. Case dismissed.'

The discharged jury members file out, the public gallery slowly empties, its occupants well satisfied with the day's entertainment, while Judge Eustace Popplecock is able to leave early for his dinner date with the charming, recently-widowed Marjorie Stewkley-Fothersgill. Reginald Ragwort remains inert in his seat until an usher prompts him to leave. No-one sees Henry Stote depart, his gamekeeper's gift for moving like a phantom amply demonstrated. The lovely Charlotte Mandible tidies away her papers before turning to the forlorn, slumped figure of Neville Bodkin.

'Well, Neville; how do you think that went?'

On their departure the courtroom is now empty, brooding and silent, an apt testament to the majesty of the law.

Riding the Tiger

THE SPECIAL TASK came as a terrible shock to Second Secretary Vladimir Chernikov. The more so because, until summoned by the Deputy Director, it had seemed such a routine day, seated at his desk in the Soviet Economics Ministry. In his own eyes, Chernikov was a man of considerable importance, his superior status continually reaffirmed as his pale gaze roved over busy underlings, heads bowed in work vital to the current five-year plan. Indeed, Chernikov's career was a perfect example of how success can be achieved with minimal talent, having risen to his position by a judicious mixture of sycophancy and slavish observance of rules.

But mediocrity is no bar to ambition, which coursed through his veins like a strong, silent river. There was just one check to Chernikov's ambition: an ongoing purge. This was necessary to explain the USSR's systemic failures to the proletariat. Why were there shortages of such basic commodities as eggs and butter when the Party's successive five-year plans should have provided bounty for all? To account for these failures, countless heads had rolled, and were rolling still as a new state trial of former Party grandees had been recently announced. If there were traitors at that level, no wonder there were shortages.

Haunted by the purge, Chernikov drew meagre comfort from his status as second secretary. Although enjoying importance within the limited bounds of the Economics Ministry, he took some reassurance from the knowledge there were three, more senior, heads in the hierarchy above him. Thus, Chernikov reasoned, his relative anonymity provided a precious margin of safety, for he could hardly be held responsible for any failures while he was directed by those more senior. And yet, ambition only temporarily restrained, it remained his dearest wish that the Director and his deputy be found wanting on the final day of the purge.

Chernikov's summons to see the Deputy Director had come as a surprise, for communication between the senior post-holders was now quite limited. All were afraid their words, however carefully chosen, might eventually require explaining to the NKVD while enjoying their hospitality at the notorious Lubyanka prison. When admitted to his senior's more prestigious office, he found Deputy Director Orlov seated behind a large desk. Orlov always reminded him of a toad; squat and fat, with a face pock-marked by the scars of some dread disease inflicted in his youth. But something was different about Orlov today, and it took Chernikov a few moments to realise why. Normally rubicund, Orlov's complexion was now an unhealthy shade of grey. He motioned Chernikov to a chair beside the desk.

'Comrade Chernikov,' he began, his deep voice echoing around the office as though seeking a means of escape. 'You have been selected to carry out a very important task.'

Chernikov's heart raced. No-one wanted a 'very important task'; it meant increased visibility, scrutiny and hence greater danger. But he didn't say so.

'This task is instigated by the very highest authority, the

General Secretary of the Communist Party of the Soviet Union.'

Poor Chernikov's heart went instantly into reverse, screeching to a stop. 'The General Secretary,' he managed at last, 'Comrade Stalin himself?'

'Yes,' said Orlov, in no mood for mercy. 'This comes direct from the General Secretary himself, a personal instruction.'

Another long silence followed, Chernikov unable to speak and Orlov somehow reluctant to divulge the exact nature of the task. At last Chernikov found a tremulous voice.

'But what is this task, comrade, what am I expected to do?'

Orlov leaned back in his chair and studied the ceiling. After long deliberation he finally addressed a cobweb woven around the central lampshade. 'You are to investigate and report on the presence of tigers in Georgia.'

If Orlov was embarrassed to relay the instruction, it was nothing compared to Chernikov's incredulous horror at its receipt. Were his ears playing tricks? Was Orlov playing a cruel joke? Had he fallen asleep at his desk and this was a nightmare? Nothing made the slightest sense, even when he asked Orlov to repeat the instruction.

'But I know nothing of tigers, comrade, in Georgia or anywhere else. There must be some mistake. How is it possible I have been chosen? I work with economics, not tigers.'

Orlov's oversized head swayed from side to side, his heavy brow knitted in mystification. 'It seems to be one of those extraordinary coincidences, comrade, with even stranger consequences. You may recall Foreign Secretary Litvinov was recently on a mission abroad, Germany or

Sweden, or some other country; it hardly matters where. During this important mission, he was obliged to attend a social event, at which some functionary of the hosts happened to ask Comrade Litvinov whether any Caspian tigers still existed. It appears a zoo of theirs had exhibited one many years ago, and they wondered whether it might be possible to obtain a replacement. Of course, Comrade Litvinov expertly avoided answering the question or making any rash promises regarding fulfilling their request. And so far, so innocuous.'

Orlov turned his neutral gaze from the ceiling to Chernikov. 'On his return, reporting to the General Secretary, he pointed out the frivolousness of the capitalist world, asking about tigers when world peace hangs in the balance. But it had evidently stirred something in Comrade Stalin because, just like the foreign functionary, he too enquired whether tigers still existed in Georgia. After all, he is a Georgian, from the Caucasus, and it seems tigers were known there in his youth.'

Pausing again, Orlov screwed up his eyes as if trying to make sense of what came next. 'Sadly, nobody knew the answer and an awkward silence descended. Now, among others present at Comrade Litvinov's briefing was our esteemed Director. Perhaps concerned about the progress of the five-year plan and anxious to present himself in the best possible light, he boldly stated that this Directorate would quickly determine the exact status of the animal, and report back to the General Secretary accordingly. That is how the task arrived here, at the Ministry of Economics.'

'But...' began Chernikov, only to be waved down by Orlov's podgy hand.

'I understand your bafflement, comrade, but there is yet more. All this was relayed to me by the Director on his return from the meeting late yesterday afternoon. You may imagine the diligence we applied in selecting a suitable candidate to carry out this task, only too aware the reputation of the Directorate – indeed, it's very future – may hinge on the outcome. We considered a number of candidates but discarded most, as we felt only someone with sufficient official status would have the authority to obtain results. We finally settled on First Secretary Kirin.'

Chernikov's overworked heart leapt. 'Then I am not...'

'Patience, comrade,' interrupted Orlov, 'there is yet more. It was seven in the evening by the time we had agreed on candidate Kirin. We arranged to inform Comrade Kirin this very morning, but there has been a development. The Director has not arrived at work. I am given to understand he is suddenly unwell. Now, here is a strange thing, comrade: I was informed not by his loving wife but by an anonymous man telephoning from I know not where. Furthermore, in his absence, I am instructed to become acting Director and First Secretary Kirin to become my Deputy. An unexpected situation, and by no means congenial to me. I am, of course, extremely concerned about the health of our Director, and wish to see him return to the Directorate with all speed. But, in the meantime, the situation now requires you to fulfil the General Secretary's request.'

Orlov slumped back in his chair, his sickly grey pallor now explained by this turn of events. Chernikov was equally stricken, although for entirely different reasons. He sat as though stunned, struggling to comprehend all the ramifications of this ghastly task, and failing. His desperation made him bolder than usual.

'Surely there is some mistake, comrade. Are you not able to query the directive with someone in the Politburo

Secretariat? Ask them for confirmation - preferably in writing – of the exact nature of Comrade Stalin's enquiry?'

Orlov's expression became incredulous. 'You expect me to query a task ordered by the General Secretary himself? No, comrade; your brief could not be clearer: are there any tigers in Georgia? I recommend you see this as a golden opportunity, reporting directly to Comrade Stalin, perhaps even in person, if your report finds favour. Your name will be become known in high places.'

A wave of nausea almost overwhelmed Chernikov, quickly replaced by a fainting lightness in his head which caused him to grip the sides of his chair. There was no escape.

'Surely there is some guidance on how I should go about this enquiry?'

'Alas, no,' replied Orlov. 'In the absence of any precedents, you will have to use your initiative. I wish I could help, comrade, but I fear I will be fully occupied with maintaining the work of the Directorate.'

When Chernikov managed a reply, it was little more than a whispered appeal. 'But how will I know what outcome the General Secretary wants?'

Orlov's face reverted to grey inscrutability. 'Alas, comrade, no-one knows.'

Back in his office, Chernikov sat in stunned contemplation. If his situation was absurd, it was also deeply, grossly, appallingly unfair. After all, he had served the Party and his country with unsparing devotion for what seemed a lifetime. After the revolution, it was true, he had briefly followed the Mensheviks, but only because they held sway in his provincial town for a short time. As soon as he saw the Bolsheviks gaining the upper hand, he had been only too willing to join the Party and place his services at their disposal. During the civil war and the Anarchy, had he not demonstrated his loyalty by remaining safely in Moscow, trying to make order out of chaos in food distribution? Everything in his career illustrated unswerving commitment to the Party and country. And now this; a life-or-death task on a subject about which he knew precisely nothing. Chernikov choked back a sob.

Where to start? Against every fibre of his being, Chernikov was forced to consider Orlov's injunction to use his initiative. This almost abstract concept had lain dormant in Chernikov's brain for so long that it had not so much rusted as completely seized up. The very thought of using initiative was anathema to him, fraught with consequences for which he would be held solely responsible. Chernikov felt the General Secretary's breath on his neck.

Who might know about tigers in Georgia? His mind remained blank until he suddenly remembered the zoo. Of course! The zoo would know. Animals were their *raison d'etre*. Hugely relieved at this breakthrough, Chernikov found the relevant telephone number in the directory. His call was answered with a monosyllabic, 'Yes?'

'This is Second Secretary Chernikov of the Ministry of Economics calling.' He paused to allow the full import of his status to register.

The response was a gruffly suspicious, 'What do you want?'

'I want to know whether tigers are still to be found in Georgia?'

'What the hell are you asking us for? This is Moscow, if you hadn't realised.'

'But you are a zoo; you deal with all sorts of animals.

Surely you have some idea?'

'Look, we have a pair of marmots, a Siberian hamster and a giant rat named Igor who lives under the floor where I'm sitting.' Somewhere in the background muffled sniggering became audible. 'Understand this, comrade; zoos are not a Party priority at present; too many bourgeois connections. We count for nothing, and know nothing. If you want to find out about tigers in Georgia, you'd better go there and count them.'

Chernikov was deeply shocked. 'I don't think you realise the seriousness of this enquiry. It emanates from the General Secretary himself and your attitude is a gross breach of inter-departmental protocol. Who am I speaking to?'

'Igor the rat. Goodbye.'

Chernikov's fury was unbounded. To speak to a Second Secretary so. The impudent fellow should be denounced and sent to the Gulag for a few years. He'd soon learn some manners there. He would denounce the man himself... Now, what was his name? Igor the rat was clearly meant to mislead but had he mentioned another? He could not recall one. Nor, he realised, was the telephone call recorded. It would be his word against the Director of the zoo, if that was who had answered the phone. More likely it was some minion, a counter-revolutionary hiding among marmots, hamsters and a giant rat named Igor. As Chernikov considered these difficulties, he alighted on one small crumb of comfort; none of his staff had overheard the conversation. Perhaps it would be better to let the matter drop.

Where next for help? Somehow reluctant to telephone another source, even if he could think of one, Chernikov fell back on a safer alternative; the State Library. Such was his task's priority, Chernikov decided he must visit the library in office time. Summoning his deputy, Chernikov outlined the vital importance of a project that would require his full attention for the foreseeable future. Mention of the General Secretary was prominent, if not the explicit nature of the task, which he implied was secret. He was pleased to see a flicker of concern when his deputy was informed he would be left temporarily in charge. And a useful defence for him, Chernikov, if ever held to account.

The journey to the State Library took only twenty minutes. The building was impressive, as was the collection, founded in Czarist times. He tracked down the zoological section and found a book which looked promising; a record of Russian fauna. It proved a technical volume, particularly when it came to tigers. Chernikov was confounded to discover *Panthera Tigris* covered multiple species including Bengal, Javan, Malayan, Siberian and, to his relief, Caspian. It seemed the Caspian tiger was also known by other names such as Turanian, not least because its range was so vast. Countries rolled past Chernikov's pale eyes in profusion: Turkey, Persia, China, even Korea. And, in Russia, the wretched animal was listed in a bewildering array of minor countries such as Azerbaijan, Armenia and many more ending in 'stan', areas which Chernikov always found deeply confusing. Fortunately, Georgia was also listed. That was some comfort; at least Comrade Stalin was not playing some grotesque joke.

As he read, Chernikov became aware of the book's weakness. Informative as it was, it was historical. It listed where tigers had been known to exist – even Ukraine was mentioned – but gave no indication of their present status, only that its range had diminished sharply, particularly during the nineteenth century. This prompted Chernikov to check the date of the book; 1892. Forty-six years ago; the world was much changed since then.

Chernikov left the library with mixed feelings. Although buoyed that he was now something of an expert on Caspian tigers – indeed, tigers in general - he was no nearer determining whether any still roamed Georgia. He could imagine his lengthy final report, peppered with innumerable facts regarding Caspian tigers. He could also imagine the General Secretary's response: 'Yes, but are there still tigers in Georgia?'

It was this lurking dread that decided Chernikov. He would have to travel to Georgia, a land infamous for thieves, banditry and insurrection, and find out for himself. Acutely aware such a decision would have been unthinkable only forty-eight hours before, it now seemed imperative. A visit would gain him time to draft a suitably ambivalent report, although stressing the success of the Party's policy on tigers, whatever that may be. The idea began to grow on Chernikov. He might be able to spin out the time away, blaming the Byzantine railway system for the delays. No-one who had ever travelled by Soviet railways could possibly doubt that. And being absent from the Directorate when its head, and possibly the Directorate itself, appeared to be under the scrutiny of the NKVD, might well provide some very useful distance from any responsibility. Despite the certainty of provincial discomfort, the more he thought about the idea, the more it made sense.

The train journey did not begin well. The train was a sleeper – it was a two-day journey – and Chernikov was allocated a spacious compartment commensurate with his status as a second secretary. But he also had to share it, there being two single bunk beds. He protested to the guard in the strongest possible terms, although it availed him nothing except the guard's silent animosity. Chernikov was not top of the list when tea was distributed.

His fellow-occupier proved to be a railwayman, a youngish fellow with a mop of dark, wavy hair surmounting an open, Slav face. He was on his way to a project in Daghestan. Only by careful, oblique questioning did Chernikov eventually learn Daghestan abutted the Caspian coast east of the Caucasus Mountains, and also shared a border with Georgia. Excellent; this was just the sort of background information he needed. In what passed for Chernikov's best jocular fashion, he asked the railwayman whether he ever saw any tigers there. The railwayman gave him a curious look, replying that, since this would be his first visit to Daghestan, the answer was no. But he would be pleased to keep an eye out and let Chernikov know if any showed up, provided he wasn't eaten first.

The train continued its way across a flat, monotonous landscape, although never at breakneck speed, or much speed at all. Indeed, there were times when it went so slowly, bolder passengers dismounted and stretched their legs by walking alongside. Occasionally the train stopped altogether, and not always at some small-town station. If it was stationary for a few minutes, passengers from the over-crowded third-class carriages dismounted en-masse and milled about in the vicinity of the train, tiny figures dwarfed by the vast emptiness of the Russian steppe. Never informed how long the halt might last, Chernikov suspected not even the driver knew. When signalled to move, the driver simply sounded his whistle, starting a mad scramble by the dismounted horde to regain the train. Chernikov, whose previous Soviet train experiences were not much different, wondered idly whether those in charge of the railways had yet been 'liquidated' and, if not, why not?

After the first hour or two, conversation with the railwayman began to flag. Even Chernikov realised there was a limit to the number of times he could press upon his fellow-traveller his, Chernikov's, second secretary status, his senior role within the Economics Ministry and the vital nature of his secret task. Silence descended until the railwayman produced a chess set and asked if Chernikov played. He did indeed, and was regarded as a moderately good player, not least by himself. Four games and four defeats later, Chernikov claimed a migraine and retired to his bed, stunned by the effrontery of the railwayman not just to win, but keep winning, self-evidently not inhibited by Chernikov's superior status.

The train reached Ordzhonikidze, gateway to the Caucasus, in the late afternoon of the second day, and here Chernikov alighted. He found a hotel close to the station. Although unimpressive, Chernikov was too tired to be choosey. It was a building of stark concrete construction and his room proved similarly bleak, although the walls had at least been plastered. Returning to the reception desk, Chernikov enquired how best to secure his passage to Tiflis, capital of the Soviet Socialist Republic of Georgia, and his eventual destination.

The receptionist, a sallow-faced man of distinctly foreign appearance, displayed cautious surprise. 'Do you mean to go by the Military Road?'

'Yes,' said Chernikov, who had carefully planned his journey from an atlas map. 'It is the most direct and quickest route from Moscow.'

'In summer, yes, that is certainly so. But this is April

and I haven't heard the road is open yet.'

'Not open. Why ever not?'

The receptionist squinted at Chernikov. 'You do realise the Military Road crosses the Caucasus mountains. The road through the Dariel Gap is thousands of metres high; it is snowed in for half the year.'

'Ah, the atlas did not explain that.'

'I expect it is a capitalist atlas.'

'Yes, it must be,' muttered Chernikov. Initiative suddenly absent, he found himself asking, 'What do you suggest I do?'

'Go to the town administration. They will put you right.' The receptionist smirked malevolently, pleased to see a Moscow apparatchik suitably humbled.

Early next morning Chernikov set out to find the town's administrative office, yet another utilitarian concrete structure. It was also very busy, crowded with a variety of humanity and overhung with a pervasive smell that Chernikov could only attribute to the presence of so many sheepskin coats. There were no orderly queues, merely a seething throng of people all trying to gain official attention for their particular cause. Opportunities for Chernikov to impress his favoured status upon any official remained frustratingly nil, his elbows and entreaties simply not sharp enough. In despair he made to leave the building.

Pushing his way through the door, he stood outside, recovering. While he did so, his glance fell upon a woman passing by. Something differentiated her from the average Ordzhonikidze female he had seen to date, somewhat smarter perhaps. And she had an intelligent face, accentuated by stylish spectacles. Normally, Chernikov would not have dreamed of speaking to a passing female, but his circumstances were far from normal.

'Excuse me, madam,' brought her to a questioning halt. 'I'm a stranger to this town and I need to get to Georgia, Tiflis in particular.' Chernikov hardly recognised his own voice, with its hint of supplication. 'I wonder if you are able to advise me? I've tried in there, without success.' He indicated the building behind.

She smiled, lighting up her face. 'I'm not surprised. This is not the best-run town.'

Facing him, Chernikov saw she was a little older than he first thought, perhaps similar to his own early forties. She was also attractive, reminding him sharply that his wife was not. Ludmilla Chernikova may have been attractive once, but twenty years of barren marriage had dulled his appreciation. Nor did this woman look shrewish, which Ludmilla had certainly become.

She was speaking again. 'Tiflis, you say?'

'Yes, I have business to attend to there.' To his own surprise, he forbore to mention his elevated status and the vital importance of his mission.

'Well, you can take the train to Baku and from there to Tiflis. It's a long, dog-leg of a journey but you appreciate the mountains are in the way. Much more direct is the Military Road, which I believe is now open. That would be quickest, but less comfortable than the train.'

'I see. I take it there is a bus service?'

'Yes, but there is no regular timetable. They wait until enough people turn up to warrant the journey, which is at least half-full.' She hesitated a moment. 'Do you have a heavier coat? It will be cold if you take the mountain route.'

Chernikov took this as a test of his manliness. 'This is actually a very warm coat, a tribute to its superior quality, I think. I'm sure it will look after me.' He could think of no excuse to extend their conversation other than to ask where the bus departed from.

'Go to the square, where the market is. You'll see the bus there. You need to hurry; they won't set off much after ten because no-one wants an overnight stop.'

'Then I had better go.' Chernikov managed a regretful smile, as if parting were such sweet sorrow. 'Thank you. You have been most kind, and helpful.' It was the closest he could come to gallantry.

'You are welcome. Good luck on your journey.'

An odd injunction, thought Chernikov, as he watched her walk away. What part could luck play on a bus journey? Abandoning this and any other thoughts provoked by the woman, he hurried back to the hotel, collected his case and set off for the square. There, he spotted not a bus as he knew them, but a somewhat dilapidated truck, surrounded by another crowd of restless humanity. Doubtful whether this was the right vehicle, he had to ask three different people before finding one who spoke Russian. He was assured it was going to Tiflis. Looking around, it was immediately clear to Chernikov there were considerably more prospective passengers than the so-called bus could accommodate. His first instinct was to accost the driver and advise that his status required preferential treatment but, viewing the unruly crowd, he decided against. Shortly after, when the driver began collecting fares, Chernikov used his elbows to new-found effect, obtained a ticket and scrambled aboard. He only just made it before any further entries were barred. Those shut out fell back with resignation rather than annoyance, which Chernikov thought remarkable.

The bus moved off before the passengers had settled down, causing more mayhem. Chernikov found himself holding a cloth bag out of which projected the head of a chicken, very much alive and eyeing him with malevolent intent. A young woman next to him had lost her baby, although optimistic it would eventually turn up. Twenty minutes later some sort of order prevailed, babies, chickens and sundry other goods restored to their rightful owners.

The truck soon began a slow, laboured ascent. When Chernikov cared to look, he was aware they were climbing into an ever-narrowing valley. He caught glimpses of a boulder-strewn river close to the road, rushing along in a foam-flecked torrent that put the truck's progress to shame. Little sunlight penetrated down to the road and Chernikov began to see patches of snow tucked in the more sheltered crevices. It grew noticeably colder, reminding him of the woman's comment about the suitability of his coat. He had already noticed some of the other passengers giving him curious looks. At first, he put it down to his smarter appearance but now he was not so sure.

After about two hours, the truck halted and, without any instruction, the passengers began to dismount. Chernikov followed, and discovered the road had been partially washed away. While the driver edged the truck around the crumbling edge, the passengers took the opportunity for a comfort break, Chernikov self-consciously following suit and glad to stretch his legs.

With everyone re-embarked, the truck resumed its journey and, being lunchtime, the passengers to eat. Various packages were produced and the contents attacked with what Chernikov soon observed was considerable relish. He had brought nothing. With growing discomfort, he watched segments of chicken, mutton, bread, fruit and other comestibles disappearing down receptive gullets, and pondered the foolishness of his own lack of foresight.

Eventually, the woman with the baby took pity and gave him an apple, while his other neighbour, a wrinkled veteran of a man, passed him a piece of meat. Looking at it closely, Chernikov saw it was flecked with unrecognisable detritus but, encouraged by sharpening hunger, decided it was worth the risk of food-poisoning. It proved tough, and nor could he determine its origin by flavour, but it went down surprisingly well.

Stops became more frequent as they neared the high point of the Dariel Gap. Sometimes, where melting snow had slid down on to the road, the passengers were obliged not just to dismount but help push the truck through the blockage. Chernikov's shoes became sodden and his coat, however superior, now lost much of its smartness. Since he had not only neglected to take food but also drink, he was obliged scoop up melt-water in his hands where it ran across the road, and the cold made his teeth hurt. Looking up at the sheer granite walls towering over the road, Chernikov thought it the most God-forsaken place on earth.

At last the truck began to descend but the landscape remained as wild as ever, barren and craggy, with the perpetually snow-capped Mount Kazbek dominating the western skyline. Beginning the descent seemed to put more heart into the passengers, even Chernikov, who was frozen to the marrow. Spirits rose even further when they reached the Pasanaur post-house where Chernikov, normally careful with money, was sufficiently moved to treat both his benefactors to a hot meal.

The truck arrived at Tiflis in the evening, the passengers going their separate ways without the slightest ceremony, even though Chernikov regarded their survival a major achievement. Cold, wet and weary, he made for the nearest hotel, the Grand Hotel d'Orient, a long, low stone building of some age. Here, in an attempt to coax life back into his battered body, Chernikov was able to secure a bath. Warm at last, its side-effect was the onset of extreme fatigue and he retired immediately to bed.

It was the following morning before he could summon the interest to consider his next move. Now wary of receptionists' advice, he used his improving initiative and found the office housing the Tiflis Municipal Soviet, the town's administrative centre. Here Chernikov found a dispiriting repeat of Ordzhonikidze's administration, a heaving mass of disparate humanity, each pursuing their own enquiry but with little sign of progress, let alone satisfaction. With dwindling hope, Chernikov looked into a number of offices without seeing anything that might offer help in his quest. There seemed to be no department title suggesting responsibility for tigers, and he was too embarrassed to ask.

Once again, he left the building and took stock outside. To his regret, no attractive woman presented herself to provide help and Chernikov was left to fall back once more on his initiative. He exercised this by sitting down on a low wall and contemplating. He studied the building opposite, large and elaborate, with an impressive six-pillared entrance overlooking a tree-lined square. It announced itself grandly as the Palace Hotel, and he wondered whether it might be better suited to someone of his status. Had he been better informed, he might have realised it was the former theological seminary where a young Joseph Stalin had been educated before opting for the life of a revolutionary. But in the pleasant April warmth, it was easier just to sit in the sun and do nothing.

Chernikov sat for some time, sunk in a curious mixture

of idleness and apathy. He might have sat a good deal longer but something caught his eye. Two smart uniformed men were walking past on the opposite side of the road. He recognised the uniform: NKVD. Normally, he would have shunned their presence, going to any lengths to avoid them. Now, he realised, he was desperate and the NKVD were acknowledged to be one of the few effective Soviet organisations. He got to his feet and, in an ironic reversal of roles, followed the NKVD men to their headquarters.

Not without a frisson of trepidation, Chernikov entered the building to find a cramped reception area, although no-one was present. A notice on the desk advised ringing the bell for attention, giving the impression few voluntary visitors were expected. Chernikov pushed a button, heard a faraway buzz and, very shortly, a man appeared. He wore civilian clothes rather than uniform and his young, anonymous face bore a puzzled expression, as if surprised to be summoned. Chernikov used his initiative to bolster his official status.

'I am First Secretary Chernikov of the Directorate of Soviet Economic Affairs in Moscow. I am on a very important mission on behalf of General Secretary Comrade Stalin himself.' Chernikov paused for effect, holding out his papers offering verification.

'It says here you are a second secretary.'

'There have been very recent changes of senior personnel at the Directorate. There was no time to update my papers.'

The man looked doubtful, as if any document error was an infraction meriting deep suspicion. 'It is not helpful to have incorrect paperwork. What do you want?'

Chernikov decided to go for broke. 'Some respect for a senior official, young man. I am in Georgia at the behest of the General Secretary and I shall be reporting to Comrade Stalin himself. I suggest you adopt a more helpful attitude if you care about your future career. Who is in charge here?' He was pleased with this outburst, the first he had delivered since leaving Moscow. He felt better for it. The NKVD man, on the other hand, was clearly shaken.

'Perhaps you need to speak to Captain Mykola.'

Hastened by Chernikov's forceful agreement, the man retreated from sight, reappearing a short time later to usher Chernikov along a corridor to Captain Mykola's office. Mykola himself was somewhat younger than Chernikov, and quite handsome enough to appear in films if he ever tired of the NKVD. He wore a suit similar to Chernikov's, although much smarter because it hadn't spent three days in uncongenial travel. On Chernikov's entrance, he rose from his seat and held out his hand.

'Welcome, comrade, welcome indeed to this humble outpost of the Soviet Union. We are honoured by your presence.' His voice possessed a warm, manly timbre that made it difficult to imagine him interrogating some desperate counter-revolutionary.

'Thank you, comrade, I appreciate you taking the time to see me.'

Mykola gave a wide, winsome smile that impressed upon Chernikov his own limitations in that department. 'We always have time for our Moscow comrades, and I am anxious to know how we can be of assistance.'

Here Chernikov faltered for a moment, although he had formulated a plan. 'It is a delicate problem, comrade. You should understand I am here on a highly confidential mission on behalf of the General Secretary himself. Sometimes a matter arises which requires a knowledgeable specialist view, and that is why I have been selected. For security reasons my task – which I regret I cannot reveal – requires a front, a subterfuge, under which I will proceed. However, these ostensible enquiries concern a subject with which I am not entirely familiar.'

Here Chernikov paused until Mykola filled the gap. 'And what might that subject be, comrade?'

There followed another, very long, pause before Chernikov could bring himself to utter, 'Tigers.'

'I'm sorry, I didn't quite...'

'Tigers, Captain Mykola; that is my cover story. For the uninitiated, I am here to determine whether tigers are still present in Georgia. In reality, I shall be undertaking my secret mission. Of course, to maintain my cover, I will also have to make enquiries about tigers, and that is where I have only limited expertise. Local knowledge would be invaluable and that is why I have sought your help.'

'I see.' Mykola frowned, although this hardly detracted from his good looks. 'May I ask who devised this cover story?'

'I really don't know. It was conveyed to me by a higher authority.'

'I see,' repeated Mykola thoughtfully. 'Perhaps cover stories are not their area of expertise, either. But that is beside the point. You need to find an expert on Georgian tigers, and I may be able to help you.'

'Really?' Chernikov's astonishment was palpable.

'Yes, I know just the man. He is well known to us, travelling as he does throughout Georgia, particularly in the mountains. I know he is in Tiflis at the moment because we spoke to him only the other day. About where he'd been, what he was doing, who he'd been speaking to, that sort of thing. He was very helpful and I'm sure he can be persuaded to help you.'

'That would be wonderful. And he would know about tigers?'

Mykola nodded sagely. 'He travels so far and so frequently he's bound to have run across one if they're still here. I can think of no-one more likely. He's from mountain stock; hunters, herdsmen, bandits. They know about these things.'

'He sounds the ideal fellow. And you think he would be willing to help?'

'I am certain of it, comrade. In fact, I guarantee it.'

'Excellent. And you know where I can contact this man?'

'No need to trouble yourself on that account, comrade. I will arrange for you to meet him here. If you care to present yourself at nine tomorrow morning, I'll introduce you.' Captain Mykola's smile became quizzical. 'Do you have a change of clothing by any chance? After all, you have a cover story to maintain. If, as I suspect, you have to travel into the mountains, to put it diplomatically, you will stick out like a sore thumb dressed in a suit.'

Chernikov's face registered acute concern. 'No, I'm afraid I haven't. I may have been remiss, but I didn't realise I would need to travel into the mountains...' His voice petered out.

Mykola's bonhomie was restored. 'Not to worry. I will arrange a change of clothing for you. And suitable boots. And a hat. They will be waiting for you tomorrow, along with your guide.'

Chernikov, astounded by this demonstration of goodwill, was effusive in his thanks. Captain Mykola, rising star of the Soviet NKVD, personally saw Chernikov from the building before returning to his office to begin new, urgent, enquiries.

The following morning saw Chernikov arrive promptly at the NKVD headquarters. He was shown into a side room furnished only with two chairs and a small table, on which rested a pile of clothing. A minute or so later Mykola entered the room, followed by a stony-faced man who looked as though he had suffered a poor night's sleep. In contrast, Mykola had clearly enjoyed a thoroughly restful night, smiling happily as he announced, 'Comrade Chernikov, let me introduce you to Tamaz, who has volunteered to be your guide. He is just the man to lead you to those elusive tigers.' Chernikov and Tamaz shook hands, the latter without enthusiasm. Mykola pointed to the table. 'And here are the clothes I promised. With these, you will really look the part of a tiger hunter. But be careful; it's a sheepskin coat, so mind you don't get eaten.' While Mykola laughed handsomely at this witty aside, Chernikov managed only a smile and Tamaz remained stony-faced.

'I must go,' announced Mykola, 'the work of securing our benevolent State is never done.' He turned to Chernikov. 'If you leave your clothes on the table, we will put them somewhere safe. Your replacements should fit well enough but I do ask that you try to return them within seven days. Any longer and we really ought to charge the lender with something, and that means irritating paperwork. I'm sure you understand.' He held out his hand. 'Good luck, comrade. Find those tigers and surprise us all.'

With the departure of Mykola, Tamaz turned his back as Chernikov began undressing. He was grateful for this courtesy, aware he cut an unimpressive figure. Tamaz, on the other hand, looked sufficiently sturdy to suggest it would be an even match if required to fight a tiger. Not as handsome as Mykola, he was nonetheless another fine-looking man with European features rather than Slav or Mongoloid. Chernikov struggled to determine his age, which seemed to change between his glances. In the end he settled for late forties.

His new clothes were not new. In fact, they bore a distinctive smell, the odour he now associated with any close-packed Georgian crowd. They proved a reasonable fit, except the boots, which were a shade large for Chernikov's more dainty feet. There was no mirror, so he was obliged to ask Tamaz how he looked, receiving a terse, 'It will do.'

It was only after they left the NKVD headquarters that Chernikov sensed Tamaz becoming less tense. He tried to initiate a conversation, not least because he hadn't the faintest idea of any plan. 'Well, Tamaz, what do think we should do now?'

'We'll pick up a truck that's heading for the mountains.'

As good as his word, Tamaz led the way to an industrial area where they soon found a truck due to head east, although they were obliged to sit with the load because a pregnant woman occupied the other cab seat. Climbing aboard, they settled down among sacks, boxes and a piece of machinery which defied identification. There was no tarpaulin cover; if it rained, they would get wet. But it was a fine April day and, as they cleared the outskirts of Tiflis, Tamaz's spirits seemed to rise. He made the effort to address Chernikov.

'I understand you are looking for tigers.'

'Yes. Well, more to ascertain whether any are still present in Georgia. That is my task.'

'Are you aware none have been seen here for years? The last one was shot near Tiflis in '22, and that was a rarity. It probably followed the Kura valley up from the south, where they are more known. A young male, looking for a territory and a mate. It killed some livestock, which ensured its own death.'

'I see,' said Chernikov, sucking his teeth. 'Sixteen years; that long ago? And no sign since?'

'Not that I know of. It's possible one may have slipped in, but I can't believe it stayed or someone would have noticed and spread the word.'

It was now Chernikov who went quiet, wondering why he was embarking on this journey if there was virtually no prospect of finding the animal. With the information gleaned so far, he could already write a suitably ambivalent report. He roused himself to ask, 'Where are we going, exactly?'

'There is a man you should see. He is old now, but his memory is good. He has lived in the mountains all his life, the southern mountains near the Caspian Sea, more traditionally where tigers occurred. His ancestors also lived there, and their knowledge passed down.'

'Is it far?'

'Yes,' said Tamaz, in a tone of finality. Dispirited further by this answer, Chernikov lapsed into silence, settling as best he could among the sacks. The expression 'wild goose chase' loomed large in his mind, with 'goose' and 'tiger' all too easily interchangeable.

There were other travellers on the road, more usually horse-drawn carts than engined vehicles. Mounted men were also present, sitting comfortably astride their small, shaggy horses as to the manner born. Having left Tiflis behind, Chernikov was surprised to see pedestrians, including women, often carrying substantial loads or pulling small, overloaded carts. He wondered whether they were walking to Tiflis, in which case he respected their hardiness. At a couple of villages, their truck stopped and unloaded stores, at which Tamaz helped and Chernikov felt obliged to follow his lead. The heavy sacks made his arms ache.

As the truck began to climb into the foothills, villages became sparser and smaller, the forest more prevalent. Despite the uncomfortable ride, Chernikov dozed for a while. When he woke, they were in the mountains, the truck's engine labouring on the inclines. It was noticeably colder. Chernikov could see snow on the peaks but, mercifully in his view, none on the lower slopes. Tamaz was awake but still uncommunicative.

In mid-afternoon they reached a village where they parted company with the truck. 'The road turns south here,' explained Tamaz, 'and begins the descent. We are going further into the mountains. Can you ride?'

Chernikov had not ridden since he was a boy, but would not admit it. 'Yes, although the opportunities are few in Moscow.'

It was a typical mountain village, each property adjacent to a low barn or store. Sheep and goats were enclosed in paddocks while chickens, dogs and occasional small children seemed to wander about at will. Tamaz led the way to a single storey log dwelling, its roof sharply pitched to throw off the snow. It was more substantial than its neighbours, the owner presumably more successful, or important. Chernikov was left waiting while Tamaz disappeared inside, nearly half an hour elapsing before he emerged to announce, 'Everything is arranged.'

Shortly after, a young boy appeared from behind the house leading two horses. They were saddled after a fashion, little more than leather and sheepskin coverings. Panniers hung from the withers of one horse, a rifle in a scabbard from the other. Tamaz spoke to the boy in a language that was not Russian, but the boy looked pleased before running back into the house. 'Let's get going,' said Tamaz, swinging easily on to the horse bearing the rifle. Chernikov, mounting less adeptly, was pleased to feel reasonably comfortable, reminding him of his youth. Leading off, Tamaz spoke over his shoulder. 'It's late to start this journey but I want to get on. It will mean spending the night at a post-house.'

The light was fading before they reached their overnight stop. The 'post-house' proved something of a joke on Tamaz's part, for it was merely a hut set back off the track. Chernikov said nothing but was glad to find the hut contained a small stove and a supply of firewood laid in. He was already chilly, and it would get much colder overnight. They ate cold provisions supplied in the saddlebags, and made hot drinks thanks to a pot left by the stove. Chernikov was no outdoors man, but even he appreciated the survivalist nature of the hut.

Once they had eaten – and there being nothing else to do – Tamaz unbent sufficiently to ask Chernikov about his job in Moscow. To Chernikov's surprise, he found himself reluctant to stress the vital importance of his work and position. Here, deep in the Caucasus mountains, he was acutely aware production targets for the current five-year plan seemed utterly irrelevant. On the other hand, searching for tigers suddenly made much more sense. In fact, it made sufficient sense that Chernikov was moved to ask Tamaz whether he believed tigers were still present.

'I'm very doubtful. Everything is against them. In the past, yes; more wild places, fewer people, less livestock, they stood a chance. But it was always easier for a tiger to kill a sheep than a deer, and when they did that, they were doomed. Guns, traps, poison; there was no escape. Did you know tigers were classed as vermin by the authorities, something to be eradicated, even recently?'

'No, I didn't.'

'Yes, there was a bounty if one was killed. Even the army was involved, tiger hunting being part of their duties. It only stopped about ten years ago.' Tamaz gave Chernikov a rueful look. 'That's why I'm so doubtful. But, tomorrow, we shall see a man who knows better than anyone.'

Chernikov did not sleep well, finding the hard wooden bunk a habit not yet acquired. Cold and uncomfortable, he woke early to find Tamaz re-lighting the stove. They left after a minimal breakfast but not before extinguishing the fire, cleaning out the stove and replenishing the firewood, Chernikov using a small axe to split kindling, another reminder of his childhood.

Back in the saddle, their track was by no means all uphill. It rose and fell, sometimes steep, occasionally surprisingly level, but always deeper into the mountains. The forest dominated, largely conifers at these altitudes, although sometimes the trees thinned inexplicably, giving way to small meadows alive with butterflies. Chernikov heard the mewing cry of an eagle and spotted it high above, a distant silhouette effortlessly riding the wind. They passed another hut but Tamaz did not stop, preferring to eat on the move.

Early in the afternoon Tamaz veered away from the track and dismounted. 'This is a short-cut but we'll have to lead the horses for a while, it's very steep.' He was as good as his word, Chernikov struggling to keep his feet as they climbed. Even the sure-footed horses became nervous, reflected in their rolling eyes and occasional whinnies. But they did not climb far before the incline began to lessen. Tamaz remounted and led the way up what proved to be a col between two outcrops. As they breasted the col Chernikov stopped, dazzled by the sight of the sun flickering on the ripples of a long, reed-fringed lake. Flanking the lake, thinly wooded slopes rose high above and, beyond the valley, Chernikov could see distant mountain peaks capped with snow, all illuminated by sunlight as if better to emphasise their beauty. Except in picture books, he had never witnessed such a sight, and it took his breath away.

It was mid-afternoon when they reached a group of five low buildings, hardly enough to be called a hamlet. Smoke rose from two of the chimneys but this failed to dispel the sense of isolation. It was only occupied during the summer, Tamaz explained. More people would arrive soon, but not many more. Tamaz did not stop in the hamlet but pushed on a short distance until a single cabin came into view, tucked away in a natural amphitheatre largely clear of trees. A small paddock accommodated a horse and a handful of sheep, while a few chickens scratched a living among the rough vegetation.

Tamaz dismounted and tethered the horses, leading Chernikov to conclude they had reached their destination. Tamaz entered the cabin, reappearing a few minutes later to beckon Chernikov inside. The interior was gloomy and spartan, it seeming to Chernikov little better furnished than their over-night hut. The dominant item of furniture was a single bunk bed covered with an animal skin which Chernikov did not recognise. Beyond the bed, a long-muzzled rifle occupied prime position on the wall. A short, elderly man stood beside a lit stove, watching Chernikov advance hesitantly into the room.

Tamaz introduced them, although Chernikov barely caught the name, which sounded like Gimlek. 'He doesn't speak Russian,' explained Tamaz, 'so everything will have to go through me. I have told him you are interested in tigers, which pleased him. He is willing to help.'

Chernikov smiled gratefully at Gimlek, whose grey eyes studied him from deep within twin clusters of fine wrinkles. 'Has he always lived here?' Tamaz did not relay this to Gimlek, immediately replying on his behalf. Yes, he has lived his entire life in the mountains, not always in this place but always in this region. He is a herdsman but also a great hunter, living on the wild creatures found in the mountains. On the bed is a bearskin, for example. They are good to eat and also provide much excellent grease. Years ago, Gimlek acted as a guide for hunting parties, usually Czarist officers who paid well if they obtained trophies. The revolution put a stop to that, although Soviet officers continue to hunt but not to the same degree.

'And tigers were here? Were they hunted?'

Tamaz translated and Gimlek gave a long, detailed reply which Tamaz relayed. Tigers were more known in Gimlek's younger days, although scarce in the mountains. If they stayed, it soon became known and they were always killed. People were afraid for their livestock but it was also manly to kill a tiger. There were more tigers in his grandfather's day, but hunting gradually depleted their main food source, the deer and wild pigs. When they became scarce, everything suffered; lynx, leopards, bears and, of course, tigers. The Caspian marshes were drained for agriculture, oil was discovered, bringing many more people. Much has changed for the worse, to the detriment of the wild animals.

Chernikov nodded his acknowledgment. 'Can Gimlek

remember when he last saw a tiger, or signs of one?'

When Tamaz translated this, the old man's brow furrowed, and Chernikov thought he detected a trace of sadness. It is many years now, relayed Tamaz, possibly more than ten. Gimlek did not see the tiger, only its pug-marks. They were not large, probably a young male. He saw pug-marks on three occasions over perhaps a month, then nothing. He thought it must have moved on, looking for a mate. He told no-one and was glad it wasn't killed. That was the last time.

Chernikov was surprised to see how obviously the old man was affected by these recollections. As a hunter, he had undoubtedly played a part in diminishing the mountains' wildlife and now, late in life, perhaps he had come to regret it. Chernikov had only one more question. 'Does Gimlek think there could be tigers anywhere else in Georgia?'

When translated by Tamaz, Gimlek hesitated. Not in Georgia but possibly further south, around Lenkoran and the Persian border. They preferred those drier areas, although they also liked the Caspian reedbeds when the wild pigs lived there. Gimlek did not know how many tigers were left but they must be scarce, otherwise young males would still travel north to the Caucasus.

Chernikov's mission seemed complete. There seemed little point in questioning Gimlek further and he told Tamaz so. They took their leave of the old man who, Chernikov noticed, was still subdued. He could think of nothing to say that might lift Gimlek's spirits except to offer profound thanks for his help in this very important mission, which produced no discernible response. Perhaps it lost something in translation.

It was too late to begin the return journey, Tamaz

advised, so they rode back to the hamlet, turned the horses into a paddock and made use of one of the empty cabins after Tamaz spoke with a neighbour. Chernikov slept well, although whether this was due to becoming hardened to beds without mattresses or because he was simply very tired was difficult to say. They left in the morning only after Tamaz had completed a detailed inspection of the cabin that left it tidier than they found it.

As they began their return journey, Chernikov began to consider what he had achieved. It hardly helped that the sheer pointlessness of it all was obvious even to him, the unquestioning bureaucrat. How was it possible for a single, off-the-cuff remark by one man to result in a minor, faceless apparatchik having to travel hundreds of kilometres in search of some almost mythical creature? Back in Moscow he had hardly considered that absurdity for a moment, but out here... Chernikov looked around at the forested mountains. Here, even he had seen eagles, heard the drumming of a woodpecker and glimpsed the white, bobbing rump of a departing roe deer. It was an utterly different world.

More than that, the people seemed completely engaged with their own lives, apparently oblivious of any ongoing purge. Perhaps the concept was beyond their understanding, the constant, lurking dread that one night there could be a knock at the door. But it was only too real to Chernikov, and many others far braver than him. At least here in the mountains his fear had dwindled almost to nothing, although he did not doubt it would resume on the train back to Moscow. In a flight of fancy, he began to ponder what it would be like to obtain a transfer to Tiflis, as chief commissar for sheep, say, or inspector of Georgian chickens. Even better, he could be Director of the Tiger Census, a post for which he was now eminently qualified. He wanted no staff – they were a nuisance – except for a pretty young secretary with whom he would become romantically attached.

It was all nonsense, of course. He could not imagine there were any roles in Georgia for which he might be qualified, let alone appointed. Perhaps he could just disappear, last seen boldly heading into the mountains, never to return. A supposed victim of banditry or, even better, eaten by a tiger. Yes, that was it: presumed killed and eaten by a tiger even as he tried to discover whether any still existed. That would be the perfect. Then he could adopt the life of a blameless peasant, free at last from the tyranny of the dreaded night-time knock on the door. There was just one snag; he didn't speak a word of the language, of which Tamaz said there were more than forty different dialects, one for each valley. Chernikov sighed and shifted his saddle-sore seat.

They reached the village too late to catch a truck but Tamaz had sufficient contacts to ensure they slept in reasonable comfort as guests. In the morning, they secured a lift in a truck bound for Tiflis, even managing to obtain a cushioned seat in the cab, albeit a tight squeeze. Arriving in Tiflis in the early afternoon, Chernikov thanked the driver and climbed down from the cab, assuming he and Tamaz would now part company. To his surprise, Tamaz said he would accompany Chernikov to the NKVD headquarters, saying he was required to report their safe return. Although mildly puzzled by this, Chernikov gave it little thought. His association with Tamaz had remained minimal throughout, the man proving vital where necessary but otherwise an enigma. Even having shared a great adventure – at least, in Chernikov's eyes – and now walking together to the NKVD building, Tamaz had little to say. But Chernikov dismissed these thoughts, more interested in reclaiming his own clothes and returning to the hotel for a bath and a good meal.

No-one was in NKVD reception, so Chernikov again resorted to the bell-push. A different young man appeared this time, although bearing a disquieting resemblance to the original, suggesting they might be twins, or clones. But they were evidently expected, because he immediately declared that Captain Mykola would be pleased to see Chernikov. Tamaz apparently not required, Chernikov glanced uncertainly at his guide, unsure whether to say thanks and goodbye. Tamaz's expression was unreadable.

On entering Mykola's office, his greeting was effusive. 'Comrade Chernikov, you are safely returned. That is excellent news. And not a single limb lost to a tiger.' A flash of immaculate white teeth accompanied a wide smile. 'And were you successful? Did you find any tigers?'

'No, I'm afraid not. It's really rather sad; plenty of mountains and forests but no longer any tigers. And we are to blame it seems, Captain Mykola. Well, not us personally but humankind in general. It seems the last sighting was more than ten years ago, and little likelihood of a repeat.'

'Ah, a terrible shame, as you say.' Mykola leaned back in his chair. 'However, do not be too disheartened. I have good news for you, which deserve my heartiest congratulations. In your absence I have heard from your Directorate: you have been appointed First Secretary!'

Chernikov sat silent, momentarily stunned. 'But, how...?'

'I can see you are overwhelmed, comrade, and no wonder. You come back from a daunting excursion into the wilderness to find, not tigers, but that you have been promoted. The world moves in mysterious ways, comrade, very mysterious indeed. But you appear a little disconcerted by this news, if I may say so.'

Chernikov was less disconcerted than deeply troubled. A promotion to First Secretary moved him dangerously up the ladder; more visible, more accountable, more exposed. If only it had come when the purge was definitely over... Before he could speak, Mykola resumed, a faint frown creasing his immaculate brow.

'I'm a little concerned, comrade. Is this promotion not what you expected, or perhaps even wanted?'

Chernikov searched for some, or any, suitable words. 'You may not be aware, Captain Mykola, but, back in Moscow, things are a little... difficult.'

'Ah, I see. Well, that explains it,' said Mykola, although stopping short of an explanation, which prompted Chernikov to mutter, 'I'm not sure I understand.'

'Let me help you, comrade. You see, I was a little concerned when you arrived here at Tiflis NKVD headquarters completely out of the blue. In fact, I was so taken aback I contacted my colleagues in Moscow. They referred me to your Directorate and I spoke to Comrade Kirin. It was he who mentioned your promotion. But he also asked where you were and what you were doing. Of course, I told him you were on an important mission, ostensibly searching for tigers but this was a cover story for another more secret mission, on behalf of the General Secretary himself.'

Seeing Chernikov still baffled, Mykola continued, 'I must say I was somewhat surprised to discover Comrade Kirin knew practically nothing about your mission, only that you had told your deputy you needed to go to Georgia on an unspecified but very secret task. Kirin was astonished to learn it concerned tigers, and dumbfounded when I told him this was merely a cover story for your real mission on behalf of the General Secretary.'

Chernikov's bafflement descended into alarm. 'But surely Acting Director Orlov has explained everything to Kirin?'

'Ah, I can see you are out of touch. Things have changed while you were in the mountains. I understand Acting Director Orlov is presently indisposed and Comrade Kirin is now Acting Director.' Mykola smiled, although humour was patently lacking. 'Kirin's appointment has moved you up a rung but, understandably, he needs you to account for your absence. You have to admit, comrade, that your alleged mission looks a little – how shall I say? – unlikely from where both Kirin and I are sitting. Comrade Kirin knows only what your deputy has told him – practically nothing – and I am unclear as to the true nature of your visit to Georgia.'

Chernikov's face reddened. 'I don't understand about Comrade Orlov; he was only just appointed. Surely he can still be contacted to verify my mission?'

'I cannot help you there, comrade. I am not informed about the machinations of the Economics Ministry in Moscow, I'm glad to say. However, your mission to Georgia is of interest to me, particularly the second, ultra-secret mission, which seems to be a mystery to all but yourself and Comrade Stalin.'

Chernikov grimaced, his complexion suddenly drained of colour. He spent some moments studying the cluttered desk-top before lifting his eyes to look at Mykola. 'There is no second mission, comrade. I made it up because the real mission about tigers was so embarrassing. I thought I would be a laughing stock if people knew the truth so, after

I was tasked by Acting Director Orlov, I told my deputy my role was secret. It seemed to work; he looked surprised but impressed, so I thought I would keep to that line. It seemed a good idea at the time.'

'Our little human vanities, eh, comrade; where would we be without them?' With one elbow resting on the desk, Mykola raised a hand to his clean-cut jaw in a gesture suggesting deep, even caring, thought. 'It's quite fascinating; your story reminds me of a snowball. Your little deception is the snowball, small and seemingly harmless, but as it rolls downhill, it becomes larger and larger until it becomes a giant boulder of snow careering out of control, a danger to anyone who gets in the way.'

Chernikov leaned forward in his chair. 'I'm not sure I grasp...'

'Your story,' continued Mykola, 'started small but grew to involve other people, not least myself. You see, I am going to have to account for your activities here in Georgia and the fact that you have been consorting with a known subversive, Tamaz Agiashvili.'

'A known subversive? Tamaz? But you found him for me.'

Mykola was sympathetic. 'I did indeed, comrade, because I thought he was just the man to help you. Knows the country like the back of his hand as well as lots of people. Very interested in tigers. And it all made perfect sense until your snowball crashed into this very building, bringing a problem for me. Imagine how will it look to my superiors if my report says I arranged for a known subversive to accompany you on an unknown secret mission somewhere in the restive mountains. You see my difficulty.'

Deeply alarmed, Chernikov could only blurt, 'But I am

blameless, comrade. I understand what you are saying but I am blameless. Tamaz hardly spoke, let alone anything subversive. And if he is a menace, why is he still free?'

'I understand it must seem confusing, but it's all due to recent history here in Georgia. Tamaz's father was part of the movement that declared Georgia a breakaway state after the revolution. It didn't last long, of course, because Georgians are always quarrelling and are utterly incapable of governing themselves. After a couple of years of chaos our Soviet forces took back control. There was another uprising in '24 which failed again, but you can see why we keep an ear to the ground. I'm afraid Tamaz is tainted with the sins of his executed father, but it's useful for us to keep him in play.'

Chernikov's shoulders slumped. 'No-one told me any of this. I know Georgia has an unruly reputation but I thought it was just straightforward banditry.'

Mykola shook his head sadly. 'If only it were that simple. The trouble is, thieving, feuding, banditry, murder, anarchy – it's in their blood, comrade, and they are never happier than if all five can be indulged at the same time. I'm not Georgian myself, thank God – could you possibly have guessed? – but my role here is to help save them from themselves. Only now this complicating factor has intruded onto my work, which can't be lightly dismissed.'

'But what can we do,' pleaded Chernikov, 'to extricate ourselves from this difficult situation? What do you advise?'

'Hmm, a difficult situation indeed,' murmured Mykola, apparently deep in thought. Chernikov fiddled nervously in his seat until the NKVD captain suddenly gazed at him intently. 'I can think of a solution, if you are willing to hear it?'

'Yes, anything.'

'Well, it seems to me your misdemeanour is so comparatively minor, it would be best to ascribe it to some sort of breakdown, overwork being an excellent example. You have been too conscientious in pursuing the current five-year plan; surely that would ring true. Cracking under the strain, you desperately need to get away but, such is your mental state, you can only dream up a hopeless tale about counting tigers in Georgia, a story so patently ludicrous it will be compelling evidence of the depth of your breakdown. That, I'm sure, will strike a sympathetic chord with anyone looking at your confession, even within my own organisation. After a few weeks in hospital, you'll be as right as rain.'

Chernikov shifted uneasily in his seat. 'Did you say 'confession', comrade? I'm not sure...'

'Did I say confession? I thought I said 'explanation' but 'confession' may have slipped out inadvertently. It's a hazard of this job, I'm afraid.' Mykola laughed, although hardly apologetically. 'Now, we need to tie up the administrative ends. Foreseeing our difficulties, I prepared your written explanation earlier, which you should read and then sign. I think you will find it follows our conversation very closely.' He passed two sheets of typewritten paper across the desk. As Chernikov began to read, Mykola continued, 'Of course, I will write my own report supporting your explanation in every detail. That should be the clincher, ensuring you a comfortable stay in hospital somewhere, possibly even here in Tiflis, with its beneficial climate.'

Chernikov finished reading the statement and looked up, overwhelmed at the speed and perplexity of events. 'Isn't there an alternative, if I prefer not to...'

Mykola's bonhomie suddenly scaled back to a half-smile. 'Yes, there certainly is, comrade. You will be escorted back to Moscow and my colleagues there will carry out their own investigations.'

'But my report to the General Secretary? I see my explanation makes no mention of it. Won't Comrade Stalin be enquiring where it is?'

'I must be honest with you, comrade. Rather than a comfortable few weeks in hospital, pursuing this alleged link with the General Secretary will ensure you spend the rest of your life in a secure institution. But, of course, it's your choice, Comrade Chernikov.' Mykola picked up a pen and held it out.

Chernikov signed both sheets of paper.

'Excellent,' beamed Mykola, 'now we can get you changed back into your own clothes again. We'll be looking after you until alternative accommodation is arranged. We've picked up your things from the hotel, which should make your stay here more comfortable. It only remains to thank you for your co-operation, comrade. I must say I've never come across such a strange case as this, very challenging, but I'm glad we've been able to resolve what could have developed into a very tricky situation for both of us. As you say, these are difficult times, and we are left to make of them what we can.'

A knock on the door was followed by the entry of the man from reception, who immediately announced, 'Follow me, please.' Startled, Chernikov glanced at Mykola, only to find his attention had reverted to the paperwork on his desk. Chernikov stood up and walked uncertainly towards the door. As he was about to pass through, he heard Mykola say, 'Oh, when you've changed, just hand the borrowed clothes back to the man in the next cell – he's been a bit chilly without them.'

With the departure of Chernikov, Mykola leaned back

in his chair, well satisfied with his handling of this unusual case. His instinct to send Chernikov far into the mountains while he made judicious enquiries had proved a masterstroke. Another counter-revolutionary safely neutralised and yet another confession obtained without recourse to a single blow. Of course, Chernikov's confession would have to be corrected here and there, but he had access to an excellent forger. He wondered when his promotion might be expected. Major Maxim Mykola, fast-rising star of the secret police; it had a satisfying ring to it. And when it came to the NKVD New Year party, his story about Chernikov searching for tigers was certain to be an absolute hoot.

Milton Keynes UK
Ingram Content Group UK Ltd.
UKHW010613250624
444652UK00001B/5